Phoebe

&

the Rock of Ages

The Gustafson Girls #3

BECKY DOUGHTY

BraveHearts
Press

10 9 8 7 6 5 4 3 2

♥ ♥ ♥

Where can I go from Your Spirit?
Or where can I flee from Your presence?
If I ascend to heaven, You are there;
If I make my bed in Sheol, behold, You are there.
If I take the wings of the dawn,
If I dwell in the remotest part of the sea,
Even there Your hand will lead me,
And Your right hand will lay hold of me.
If I say, "Surely the darkness will overwhelm me,
And the light around me will be night,"
Even the darkness is not dark to You,
And the night is as bright as the day

♥ ♥ ♥

ONE

"Put your clothes on, Brandon," Phoebe ordered. "We're done here."

The man strutted across the room—yes, *strutted*—and scooped up the white bathrobe he'd draped over the back of one of the throne-like chairs they'd used as a prop earlier. He didn't bother slipping into the robe, just hooked it on a finger, flung it over his shoulder, and headed toward the dressing room.

If Phoebe was a betting woman, she'd put money on his clothes being neatly folded and stacked in his designer man-purse, Italian leather shoes on the bottom, wallet, watch, and jewelry tucked inside one of them, then his pants, shirt, socks. He wore his underwear during each shoot, but only at her insistence.

Phoebe grimaced. Why did men feel so at home in their own skin? She knew times were changing, that around the globe, men were becoming increasingly body-conscious, investing in beauty products and cosmetic surgery almost on par with women. But as a whole, they just seemed to be less inhibited than her female clients.

It was jobs like this that made Phoebe question her sanity. It was jobs like this one that tainted every other aspect of her career choice. It was jobs like this that made her want to throw in the towel and go back to work for Maurice "Creepo" Salazar at *Gossamer Magazine*. He kept calling, kept offering her more bait in the form of money, convenient hours, and a clientele list that made her bank account sit up and beg, but she was holding her ground. She wasn't interested in working on any more adult-themed photo shoots, no matter how good the pay.

"Because I'm following my dream," she muttered, her voice flattened by sarcasm as she considered the fact that she'd just spent an hour photographing a nearly naked man in her home studio.

Glamour photo shoots and professional portfolios were an easy way for her to pay the bills, thanks to digital photography and her natural talent for capturing her models' best poses. But bodice ripper covers? It was her shameful little secret... she hoped. She'd seen a few of her covers on books in Renata's collection, and even though her sister was most likely more interested in the words between the covers than in the covers themselves, there was always the possibility she would read the credits one day and discover the truth.

Phoebe shuddered involuntarily.

She glanced around the large studio, her eyes landing first on her easel, then pausing on the potter's wheel. She waited for the familiar tug, for the tingle in her fingertips, the racing pulse. But it didn't come. In fact, there were many days when the urge to pick up a lump of clay no longer consumed her. She sighed deeply, then turned her attention back to the images of the nearly naked man on her monitor.

Brandon really was exceptionally handsome. There wasn't a bad pose in the whole series. Even the shots with his eyes closed worked for the dreamy time-travel feel she was trying to capture. She'd have three cover options ready before the end of the week.

And honestly, she'd much rather take trashy pictures in secret for Rosemary Ramsey at Vineland Publishing than do Creepo's dirty work for him over at *Gossamer*.

• • • • • • • • •

By the time Phoebe closed down her design program, she was running late.

As usual.

She touched up her scarlet lipstick, tied a colorful scarf around her head, braided her long curls so they wouldn't get any more tangled than they already were, and snatched up her huge shoulder bag. Scrambling up into Xena, her Jeep Wrangler, she tucked her floor-length skirt under her thighs so she wouldn't accidentally flash anyone driving beside her. She grimaced at the way the strap of the seat belt rubbed at her neck; she lifted the chunky chains she wore out of the way. Then she slipped on her blue-tinted, frameless sunglasses, the ones that highlighted the blue-black sheen of her hair.

After backing out of her driveway, she floored it, anxious to be on her way. It wouldn't be dark for hours still, and the afternoon sun felt good on her skin after sitting still for so long in the air-conditioning. One of her favorite things about living in Southern California was how much of the year she got to drive without the cover on her Jeep.

Xena was an older model, her compact shape and big wheels more to Phoebe's liking than the sleeker, larger design Wrangler was putting out these days. The Jeep's age, however, meant more trips to the auto shop, but Phoebe had a friend in the business, Stan Jacobson, who gladly traded mechanical repairs for any cover shoots she could land him. He was one of her favorite male models because he somehow made hard work and grunge look really sexy, and the authors and publishing houses she worked with were beginning to specifically request him. Besides, he was a really decent guy, too. Keeping him clothed was never an issue, and Phoebe didn't believe she'd ever seen him swagger or strut.

She'd made it about halfway to Juliette's place when she felt the slight hiccup beneath her. Then Xena let out a polite cough. Phoebe's eyes landed on the fuel gauge, but she already knew what she'd see.

Below empty.

She'd meant to get gas on her way home yesterday, but there always seemed to be some pressing reason for her to get to the next place she was going. Case in point: right now, she was running late and had hoped she could hit the gas station *after* the G-FOURce today. But she'd been driving on fumes for two days now, and her luck appeared to be running out.

"No! No, no, no, no!" she growled, her be-ringed hand smacking the steering wheel in frustration as the Jeep spluttered again, this time a little more vehemently. "Come on, Xena! Just a little farther. Come on, baby!" There was a gas station around the corner and Juliette's was only a few blocks beyond that. So close....

Another cough, wheeze, and a shudder, and then the warrior princess moaned and passed out beneath her.

Phoebe coasted to the side of the road, grateful she'd opted not to take the cross-town freeway. There was nothing worse than being stranded on the side of the freeway in a billowy skirt and a topless vehicle in rush hour traffic.

"Been there, done that," she muttered, rolling her eyes.

She sat there for a few moments, weighing out her options. She could call Juliette and tell her she'd be later than usual, and then ring up Grandpa and have him bring her a can of gas.

For the second time this month.

She'd have to endure his lecture, along with the look in his eyes that told her he knew she knew better.

She could call Stan, whose shop was only about a mile away. Let him tease her mercilessly, listen to him remind her that her negligence would be the death of Xena, and then bribe him with dinner, maybe. She'd have to bail on the G-FOURce meeting altogether, though, and that wouldn't go over well with her sisters. Her being late again was already going to be a problem.

She'd just suck it up and walk to the gas station and back. She was a big girl. She didn't need a man to rescue her. And she did have three gas cans in the back of the Jeep already, courtesy of Grandpa, Renata, and, well, she couldn't remember where she got the third one. Maybe she'd bought it herself.

Frustrated at her own ineptitude, Phoebe bolted from the vehicle and slung the long strap of her purse up on her shoulder. She reached for one of the gas cans lined up neatly behind the jump seat and gave it a hopeful shake. No luck. It was empty. With a sigh, she set off, thankful she'd worn her Gladiator sandals today, and not the macramé platforms she'd been considering. They would have complimented her Boho flower child look better, but they were far more decorative than functional. The walk to the gas station and back would not have been fun.

All six fuel pumps were in use. Of course. Phoebe couldn't remember the last time she'd seen the place so busy.

She tried to appear nonchalant as she stood behind a car, waiting for the line to move forward. She dug her phone from her shoulder bag and sent off a text to Juliette.

Be there soon. She started to key in an explanation but ended up just erasing the excuses and sent it with only those three words. She didn't even bother apologizing.

Renata would roll her eyes, Gia would enjoy the extra minutes she could spend playing with Juliette's dog, Bob, and Juliette would make excuses for Phoebe, anyway.

It was the first G-FOURce meeting they'd had since Renata had returned from her honeymoon last month, and truth be told, Phoebe knew there was more to her tardiness than just bad habits. The larger Renata's belly grew, the less Phoebe wanted to be around her. For some reason, this pregnancy jabbed at places in her heart that none of Renata's other ones had.

In fact, it was Phoebe's fault they hadn't met two weeks ago. She had canceled at the last minute, hoping to get out of it completely. They'd simply gone and rescheduled, though, and she wasn't about to bail again. It was just putting off the inevitable. The G-FOURce would go on, come hell or high water.

Her phone beeped.

That's fine. Victor is still here anyway. He picked up some of Mona's pastries for us—I'll make sure no one licks your scone before you get here.

Juliette had an uncharacteristically perverse thing about licking stuff to mark her territory. Phoebe had a sudden—and slightly unsettling—visual of her oldest sister licking Victor, claiming him the same way. The idea made her laugh out loud, partly because she could almost see Juliette going for it and then bursting into tears over how inappropriate it was. And poor, ultra-conservative Officer Vic Jarrett, with his bullet-proof vest and freshly pressed uniform all tucked in and battened down, his storm cloud eyes, naturally bronzed forearms, and long-fingered hands....

She noticed that kind of thing. It was her job to notice people's assets.

Would he blush? Let fly that slow misty morning smile of his?

"I wouldn't mind licking you myself, big guy," she murmured with due appreciation, stepping up and slipping her credit card into the payment center on the pump.

A low chuckle emanated from the backside of the dock, bringing her up short, the gas can still clutched in one hand. She whispered a word she never said around her sisters.

Moving ever so slowly, she leaned slightly to the left and peered around the pump, her eyes widening at the shiny black Harley propped up on its double kickstand, its rider standing with his back to her, one hand cupping his neck just below his damp hairline. A denim jacket was draped over the wide bike seat, a black helmet resting on top of it, and he wore faded black Levis and a casual gray T-shirt. He turned slightly, and she froze, afraid to make any sudden moves lest he notice her.

Angular profile, no scraggly gray beard, not even one of those three-day scruffs she really did not like. They were fine to look at from a distance, but not up close and personal. Not with porcelain skin like hers. No potbelly, no tattered shirt with the sleeves ripped off, tucked into dirty jeans held up with a big-buckled belt. No faded tattoos of naked women up and down his arms.

Phoebe knew she was stereotyping, but this part of California was home to a huge community of bikers who made their two-wheeled vehicles a lifestyle. With summers that lasted more than nine months of the year, it was ideal for motorcycles. And many of the clubs were still made up of old schoolers, fitting the stereotype to a T.

But this guy?

His tousled hair looked like he'd run his fingers through it after removing his helmet, and his full mouth was set in a wide grin as he studied the phone in his hand. Phoebe let out a quiet sound of relief. He must have been laughing over something on his phone, not at her comment about licking Victor.

She lifted the gas nozzle from its slot on her side of the pump and began to fill her gas can, making as little noise as possible. She really didn't want to be caught in this predicament by anyone, no less by the handsome biker only a few feet away.

Phoebe breathed through her nose as she watched the two-gallon can fill quickly. She loved the smell of gasoline fumes; they always triggered memories of her father standing in the open door of their family van, talking to his girls while he filled the tank. It was one of the few vivid images she could conjure up of him after all these years, without the help of a photo, anyway.

She returned the nozzle, grabbed the receipt that the machine spat out in exchange, and crouched down to screw the cap on the can before picking it up. She took a step away from the pump, careful not to let the flat soles of her sandals slap loudly on the concrete under her feet.

"You need help with that?"

TWO

It's okay, Phebes. Just put on your big girl panties and play nice. She turned to glance over her shoulder at the man who moved around the pump to her side of the dock. The grin still decorated his face, making her smile back in response as she assured him, "I'm fine. But thank you."

"You run out of gas?" he asked, his gaze darting around, presumably in search of her car.

Phoebe took a deep breath and let it out slowly. Talk about a dilemma. The guy clearly wanted to visit a bit, to help out a damsel in distress, and she usually didn't pass up an opportunity like this. Especially since she didn't pick up on any pervy vibes, but a seemingly genuine intent to play Prince Charming. And a rather delicious Prince Charming at that, if a girl liked the rough-and-tumble biker look. Which, surprisingly, she found she did today. At least on this guy. *Wouldn't mind licking—shut up, Phebes!* Good grief. Too much sun or something.

She was a little embarrassed, however, at the circumstances surrounding her dilemma. She didn't have a problem using her feminine wiles when it served her purposes, but she was not needy and hated being misconstrued that way. Besides, she reminded herself again, she was late, and she didn't want to give Renata any more reasons to judge her beyond what she already had in her arsenal.

On the other hand, nor did she want to hear about Renata's honeymoon, or her pregnancy, or her happily ever after rocket-speed romance with Tim Larsen, the beefcake who was now her husband. What Phoebe wouldn't give to photograph or paint *that* man at least once. Or lick him. Not that she'd ever do either. She wasn't interested in other women's men, especially not her sisters' men. That said, she would be the first to admit that her two older sisters had landed themselves some fine specimens, no doubt about it. And the guy standing in front of her—

He cleared his throat, and she started, nearly dropping the gas can that was quickly growing heavy in her hand. "Oh. I—um, yes. I ran out of gas. But I'm just around the corner." With a flash of what she knew was her most beguiling smile, Phoebe made to leave again. "Thank you, anyway."

The man was not so easily dissuaded. He fell into step beside her and gestured toward the gas can. "Let me help."

Phoebe hoisted it out of his reach, the weight of it pulling painfully on her wrist. "I'm fine. Really."

"I'm not arguing that, ma'am." He grinned, one side of his mouth quirking up in humor. "I'm only offering my help."

"Demanding is more like it. Besides, maybe you're just trying to steal my gas can now that I spent my hard-earned cash to fill it." She teased him back, enjoying the banter a little more than she should, knowing her sisters were waiting for her to get there so they could start the meeting.

He laughed openly, genuinely. "Scout's honor. I won't steal your gas can. I'm Trevor, by the way." He thrust his hand toward her and after only the briefest pause, she shook it.

"Phoebe." But when she withdrew her hand, he didn't lower his. She cocked her right eyebrow at him, her head at a slight angle. "What? Was that handshake not good enough?"

"Your gas can. Please. Let me carry it for you."

"But your bike. You can't just leave it here while you go for a walk with me."

"Sure, I can," he insisted. "If you'll give me five minutes, I'll park it in front of the shop to free up the pump." He noticed her hesitation. "Okay, fine. Three minutes. Just give me three minutes." When she still hedged, he added, "I guarantee we'll make up those three minutes if I'm carrying that can instead of you. It's going to get heavy if you have very far to go."

Phoebe laughed resignedly. "You win. I'll wait. But I'll hang on to this while you move your bike." She patted the side of the plastic can. "If you're not back in three minutes, I'm heading out, because I'm running very late as it is. You'll have to catch up to me if you still want to help."

Trevor saluted her and circled back around the pump. He scooped up his gear and threw a leg over the bike, shoving his jacket into the helmet and propping it on the seat between his thighs. A moment later, the Harley cleared its throat and rumbled to life. Phoebe closed her eyes briefly, wondering what on earth she'd just gotten herself into.

"Two minutes, fourteen seconds," Trevor announced, jogging up beside her. "I timed it, did you?"

"Where's your helmet? And your jacket?" His gloves were gone, too.

"Locked the helmet on the bike. And if someone needs a jacket so badly that they need to steal my rag, they're welcome to it." Trevor grinned and picked up the gas can she'd set on the ground at her feet. "Lead the way, fair lady."

They more than made up the two minutes and fourteen seconds she'd waited for him. Trevor wasn't tall, and he didn't have extraordinarily long legs, but he moved with great exuberance, and she could barely keep up. "You're practically walking in circles around me," she chided. "Do you need to use the restroom? Or are you just anxious to get this over with?" She was only teasing him, but she'd never met a guy who had this much energy before.

"Nah, it's all good. I'm just easy to please, that's all." He turned and walked backwards so he was facing her, swinging the red can at his side as if it was empty. "I mean, come on, Phoebe. A beautiful day, a beautiful woman, and a chance to help someone out of a bind. What's there not to be pleased about, hm?" He dipped his head to one side, watching her, that cock-eyed smile never leaving his face.

"I think you might be certifiably crazy." She shook her head as he barely missed backing into a postal box on the sidewalk. "I should probably take that thing and run in the opposite direction." She pointed beyond him. "Except my Jeep is right there."

In minutes, Trevor had emptied the contents of the can into the tank, capped it, stowed it in the back of the Jeep, and was holding out his hand for her keys.

She hesitated, wondering briefly if he was going to start Xena up and take off with her, but then remembered his bike parked in front of the gas station. He couldn't very well steal her car and rescue his bike, too. The look in his eyes told her he knew exactly what she was thinking, and his words all but confirmed it.

"Just want to make sure it starts up for you before I send you on your way. Here." He dug in his back pocket for his own set of keys and offered them to her. "Collateral. If I steal your ride, you can have mine."

She exchanged keys with him just to play along and eyed him appreciatively as he swung up into her front seat.

He turned the key in the ignition, but didn't start the car. He simply sat for a few minutes, listening for something. "Making sure the fuel pump kicks on," he explained when he saw her curious look. "These older Jeeps don't like to run out of gas. The fuel pump pulls from the bottom of the tank, and when the tank runs dry, the pump will suck up whatever is left. With an older vehicle like this one, the debris from the bottom of the tank could wreck your pump. Believe me, you don't want to have to replace a fuel pump if you don't have to."

He said it so nonchalantly that it didn't even feel like a reprimand. She scrunched her nose at him, anyway. "You sound like my grandfather," she retorted.

Trevor gave the gas pedal a few pumps, rotated the key the rest of the way in the ignition, and the trusty little Jeep coughed, spluttered, and started up without any further ado. He left it running and hopped out, holding out a hand to help her up into the driver's seat. "Your carriage awaits," he murmured, and bowed over her hand before releasing it.

And with that, he circled the hood of her car and stepped up onto the sidewalk. Saluting her, he said, "You're good to go. I know you said you were running late already, but you should probably fill that tank soon. Two gallons won't get you far."

"Wait," Phoebe said, stopping him before he walked away. "I'm heading right to the gas station. Get in. I'll give you a ride."

This time, he was the one who hesitated.

She laughed out loud, letting her head fall back against the seat. "Are you serious? Do you think I'll kidnap you or something?"

He made a pretense of hemming and hawing, shuffling his feet and cupping his chin, his eyes shining with humor. "The thought had crossed my mind, you know."

Phoebe mimicked his words from earlier. "Scout's honor. I won't steal your virtue. Come on. Before I run out of gas waiting for you to make up your mind." She held up the small ring of keys he'd given her. "Besides, I don't think you'll get very far without these."

He climbed in and buckled his seat belt, taking his keys from her. His fingers brushed the palm of her hand, and a pleasant tingle raced up her arm. "You drive a hard bargain, lady. But thanks. I'm actually running late, too. I was on my way to meet a friend, but for some reason, I felt compelled to pull into the gas station to top off my tank."

The way he said it made Phoebe sit up a little straighter. "For some reason?" she asked, wondering too late if she really wanted clarification.

"Yeah. Just had an inclination that I needed to stop. So, I did, and there you were, needing my help." He tapped the side of his face just in front of his ear. "Pays to listen."

Before Phoebe could come up with a suitable response—and quite honestly, she didn't have any clue *how* to respond to that—they were pulling up to the same pump where they'd first crossed paths. Trevor leaped out, waited while Phoebe paid, but refused to let her pump her own gas. The conversation stuttered a little, Phoebe waiting for the guy to make his move; ask her out, ask for her number, *anything.*

But he didn't. He just kept smiling in a pleasant way, obviously completely at ease with silence.

Phoebe, on the other hand, resisted the urge to fill the void with invitation-laden small talk. If he wasn't interested, she wasn't going to twist his arm. There was nothing more pitiful than a woman who couldn't take a hint.

When he was through filling the tank, she thanked him again, but took extra care not to overdo it. Just because she *felt* like she owed him more, he didn't need to know that.

Once again, he stood back and saluted her, then watched until she'd pulled out onto the street.

She glanced over her shoulder to see him climbing on his bike, helmet on, no jacket. He had a rather lovely back—she couldn't help but wonder what it would look like on the cover of a romance novel. The sound of his motorcycle roaring to life made her smile; it was so loud, so in-your-face. She kinda liked it.

The rumble didn't fade the farther she got from the gas station. She peered up into her rear-view mirror and was both startled and pleased to see him following her.

THREE

Trevor could feel the grin on his face. It was making his cheeks ache, but for the life of him, he couldn't stop. He'd been smiling like a buffoon since he'd heard the husky voice curl its way around the pump, saying she wouldn't mind licking him.

Okay. So, he knew she hadn't meant him. The way she'd said it, though, made him laugh out loud, and hey; a guy could dream, right? *Right. Dream on, big guy.* He used her words to mock himself.

But when he'd peered around the pump, it was only her. No big guy anywhere. And oh, what a woman she was.

Drop. Dead. Gorgeous.

A woman alone. Without a car.

He took in the gas can thumping against her leg as she stepped away from the dock. From there, his gaze traveled up the length of her, his curiosity piqued. She wore a long, colorful skirt that skimmed the top of her feet which were encased in some kind of strappy sandals. A see-through cream top did nothing to hide a turquoise bra with what appeared to be little red hearts or flowers all over it, and even though he didn't allow himself to look too closely, Trevor got the feeling she'd intended the bra to be visible. Her neck was draped with an assorted collection of chains and pendants, and the chunky jewelry on the fingers of both hands echoed the look.

Around her head she'd tied a scarf, Gypsy-style, and her sunglasses perched low on her nose. A thick rope of a black braid hung beneath the fluttering ends of the scarf, the tip of it, like a paintbrush, sweeping back and forth across the curve of her back.

Her voice, full and throaty, flowed out from between lips painted scarlet, and he caught himself watching her mouth move, mesmerized. He couldn't remember what color her eyes were, but he didn't care. All that had mattered was the way she'd watched him, challenging him, analyzing him, judging him.

And trusting him.

He'd seen the moment things had shifted. As though the shutters opened, and the welcome mat came out. He wouldn't exactly call it seduction—they were, after all, at a gas station—but he was pretty sure he'd seen anticipation in her bold gaze.

It made him want to straighten his shoulders, throw back his head, and pound his chest while he bellowed like a jungle man. "Me Trevor. You Phoebe," he muttered, mocking himself as he took off down the road, the wind whipping away his words as he picked up speed.

Her Jeep was just ahead of him. He pulled up behind her close enough that he could see her watching him in her rear-view mirror. He didn't bother pretending he hadn't noticed, but smiled even broader, his jaw now threatening to seize up on him.

When they reached the next intersection, he pulled up beside the driver's side of the Jeep.

"You following me?" she hollered over the rumble of his bike. There it was again, that anticipation, an invitation in her slanted eyes.

"Maybe," he shrugged, glad for his dark glasses so he could openly study her without feeling like a pervert. Yeah, she was sexy. Petite and lean, but not waifish, with some very feminine curves in all the right places. Her skirt had risen high on her thighs from the breeze billowing around the open-topped vehicle, but it was her face that kept drawing his gaze. The way her mouth moved when she spoke, the slow, intentional way she blinked—not those fluttering fangirl eyes he got before, during, and after every show—the tilt of her head, as though angling her face for a kiss she knew was coming.

Her eyebrows rose above the top of her sunglasses, and she casually smoothed her skirt down over her knees, tucking it carefully beneath her thighs.

"Or maybe I'm just heading in the same direction you are." He shifted into first gear as the light turned green.

Phoebe nodded noncommittally and turned right without switching on her blinker. He wondered how she would react when she realized he was turning right as well. He could see she was still watching him in the mirror, but her expression now showed signs of wariness.

"Good girl," he muttered, glad to see her mounting caution. "You don't know me from Adam."

When she slowed ever so slightly in front of Juliette Gustafson's condo, Trevor found he was holding his breath in disbelief. *No way.*

The wave of disappointment that crashed over him as she kept going surprised him. Had he really thought she'd be stopping the same place he was?

"Well, Lord," he chuckled, swinging the bike in a wide U-turn so he could park right in front of the house. "That was the most amazing encounter. Thank you for making me smile today. And for making my pulse race like that. For reminding me how awesome it is that you made man *and* woman." He rubbed the heel of his palm over his heart. He unbuckled his helmet, slipped off his gloves and shoved them into it, then swung his leg over the bike and stepped up onto the parkway... just as Phoebe came tearing back down the street toward him. His heart thudded to an abrupt halt, and then leapt into action again, as though playing some high school marching band number at high speed.

He took one step toward her car, and then waited while she swung her legs out and dropped agilely to the street, circled the front end, and stepped up onto the grass in front of him. She was obviously on a mission, and he thought it might behoove him to stand still and brace himself for whatever was coming.

Didn't mean he had to stand still in silence.

"So maybe you're following me," he said, his head cocked a little to one side. He ran a hand through his hair, the action making it flop messily across his forehead.

"What are you doing here?" Phoebe asked, pausing several feet away, hands on her slim hips. "Do you know the people who live here?"

For some reason, her abrasiveness only made him want to pet her, to soothe her ruffled feathers. *Get your head in the game, man.* "I do, in fact,"

Trevor said, his eyes glued to her face. "My sister lives here." He glanced over his shoulder at the front door expectantly.

Phoebe frowned and crossed her arms, her brows shooting up derisively. She had rather expressive eyebrows. "Really. *Your* sister?"

"Absolutely." Should he expound on the whole 'sister in Christ' thing?

"You're lying," Phoebe declared, her jaw tight, her eyes flashing. She wasn't playing games anymore. "In fact, the woman who lives here is engaged to a police officer. One who happens to be here right now." Her tone turned the statement into a warning.

Trevor held up his hands in surrender, the helmet still clutched in one, but he didn't give in to the urge to step back. Clearly, this woman knew Juliette. "Right, right," he said quickly, keeping his voice calm. "A police officer who happens to be like a brother to me. So when they get married, Juliette will be like my sister...." He trailed off, lowering his hands slowly.

Phoebe's face relaxed, her chin lowering as she considered what he'd just said.

And then he saw it. When she lifted her eyes to meet his in that slow, guarded way he'd seen Juliette do a dozen or more times since the first night he'd met her, recognition washed over him like a rushing wind. He laughed out loud.

"And you must be one of the Gustafson Girls." He held out his hand. "Let me start over. I'm Trevor Zander. Friend to Vic Jarrett who is, as you say, engaged to the delightful Juliette Gustafson. The same Vic Jarrett I was supposed to meet over here about half an hour ago to rescue him from some sister club, or a secret 'girls-only' thing, or something equally terrifying."

"But you got waylaid by a damsel in distress," Phoebe concluded for him, a hint of a smile tugging at her full lips.

"An honor and a privilege, both," he replied, dipping forward slightly in a quick bow.

Phoebe made a small snorting laugh, an odd, unladylike sound coming from the beautiful woman, and then held out her hand to him, shaking his for the second time that day. "And yes, I'm one of the Gustafson Girls. Phoebe Gustafson. And Juliette is my for real sister. By birth. Not by marriage."

Trevor narrowed his eyes and studied her, pretending to search her face for some familiarity. "You know, in the right light, at the right angle..." he pursed his lips and furrowed his brow. "I don't know. I still think I might have to go with stalker."

Phoebe snatched her hand from his and gently poked him in the shoulder. "As far as I'm concerned, the verdict is still out on you, too, mister. And relax. Your face might freeze that way. You haven't stopped grinning like a creepy creeper this whole time and it's creeping me out."

He laughed out loud. "Really? The ladies usually dig the piano key smile. I could have sworn it was working on you, the way you just about tore my head off there a minute ago."

She rolled her eyes and turned away, then surprised him by slipping a hand into the crook of his arm and gesturing toward the front door of Juliette's condo. "Come on," she said, giving him a little extra tug. "We're both late, and now I don't have to face the wrath alone. You can be my protector."

Trevor moved into step beside her, and they crossed the lawn together. He liked the way that sounded, the idea of looking out for Phoebe Gustafson, of standing between her and danger, even if the danger was only in her mind. He knew Juliette and Gia, and he didn't imagine the fourth sister, Renata, was anything to worry about.

He liked the way it felt to walk beside this effervescent woman, her fingers light and cool wrapped around his forearm. And he liked the way the smile on her face—not creepy at all—seemed to reflect the one he knew he still wore.

FOUR

Of all the people in the world to have rescued her on the side of the road, who would ever have imagined that it would be Juliette's Jesus freak friend. The guy who had taken her tightly wound sister for a motorcycle ride that had rocked her world and turned her life inside out.

But Phoebe had imagined him to be one of those starving musician types with smooth faces and soulful eyes. Not this rough and tumble, hint of a five o'clock-shadowed, gentleman-in-jeans kind of guy. He dressed like a rocker right out of the 90s with his shaggy hair badly in need of a trim, his worn black denim, and scuffed boots. But his face was bright and open, his eyes clear. This guy oozed... *happiness?* No, that wasn't quite it. But he practically vibrated, like he was plugged into an alternate source of energy, lit up from the inside out.

Or maybe he'd just had some good coffee before they crossed paths at the gas station.

They reached the door, and Trevor lifted his fist to knock. Phoebe rolled her eyes and unceremoniously pushed open the door and pulled him inside. "We're here!" she called out.

Bob, Juliette's scruffy rescue dog, came bounding into the tiny foyer, his toenails scrabbling on the tile. Close on his heels was a frantic Mr. Bobo, the next-door neighbor's miniature terrier who was likely over for some playtime. Both dogs pulled up short at the sight of Trevor, but Phoebe crouched down to greet them, and after some serious sniffing and circling, the animals granted their approval of both the new arrivals.

Through the arched opening, Juliette, Renata, Gia, and Victor all watched the exchanged greetings with varying expressions. Victor's observant gaze darted back and forth between Trevor and Phoebe, his slashing eyebrows raised in question, but his mouth was already curling up in welcome. Juliette, who sat beside him, one hand in his, smiled brightly, looking suspiciously tickled to see them standing there together. In fact, Gia wore the same look, only amped up about five notches. She was bouncing just the slightest bit on a big cushion on the floor. Gia already knew Trevor through her best friend, Ricky; he was Ricky's cousin, if Phoebe remembered right. It was Gia who had added Trevor to the list of Monday ManDates, the blind date intervention the sisters had concocted to get Juliette out of her post-breakup slump just over a year ago.

Renata, bless her stiff upper lip, simply stared at them, her arms crossed over her bulging belly, apparently expecting an explanation for the holdup. Her distant expression told Phoebe it wouldn't matter what she had to say in her own defense. She'd already been weighed, measured, and found wanting. Nothing new there.

"Officer Jarrett," Phoebe purred as she rose to stand, loathing the way she automatically slipped into her sleaze-girl persona in reaction to Renata's judgment. But for as long as she could remember, this was the *modus operandi* with the two of them; Renata judged Phoebe, and Phoebe did her best to live up to that criticism. At least in front of Renata.

Slipping her arm back through Trevor's, Phoebe continued in her overly honeyed voice. "Look who the cat dragged in!"

"I take it you're the cat," Renata murmured, loud enough for the whole room to hear. But the tone of her voice made Phoebe pause. She didn't *sound* angry. In fact, she sounded like she was teasing her. Not taunting her. Not challenging her. Just ribbing her.

"Mrreowrr," Phoebe purred, and Renata actually grinned. But Phoebe felt Trevor tense beside her, felt the muscles of his arm bunch beneath her fingers. He didn't move otherwise, but she sensed his withdrawal. He probably wasn't interested in being the toy she batted around in front of her family. She couldn't blame him. So, she pulled away first, making it her move rather than his, and stepped back a little, indicating with a sweep of her hand that he should go ahead of her into the living room.

From the corner of her eye, she studied Trevor as he crossed to where Victor and Juliette stood, the two of them having risen to welcome the late arrivals.

Sometimes it still surprised Phoebe to see Victor in her sister's corner of the couch, his arm draped territorially around Juliette's shoulders. Everyone knew that was Jules' spot, and the fact that she'd surrendered it to Victor spoke volumes about his place in her heart; maybe even more than the pretty new engagement ring she wore on her finger.

Trevor and Victor exchanged one of those handshake-hug combos guys do, complete with some back-thumping, and maybe even a grunt or two. He gave Jules a quick side-hug, and then Gia, who had leapt up, too. Side hugs? Was he afraid of breasts?

As comfortable as the guy seemed in his own skin, she found the notion oddly incongruous. Besides, hadn't he taken Jules for long rides on his motorcycle, with her pressed like a spider monkey to his back, her legs wrapped around his thighs? No avoiding full body contact there.

Then again, this was the same guy who'd told Jules he had a rule about not being alone with a woman inside her home. Good grief. Being alone with men in her home was how Phoebe made her living. *I guess I won't be snapping any pictures of Trevor Zander*, she mused. A tiny plume of disappointment swirled around inside her before she caught herself and almost snorted out loud over the direction of her thoughts. *Aidez-moi! What are you thinking?*

Victor introduced Trevor to Renata, who apologized for staying seated. "I just got comfortable, which is quite a feat for me right now. I don't mean to be rude—I hope you don't mind." Trevor assured her he was not offended at all.

Phoebe crouched down to give Bob and Mr. Bobo a little more attention. The dogs kept her focus off the man who was explaining to everyone the circumstances of how they'd met. She didn't want to see Renata roll her eyes, or Jules with that 'you know I love you anyway' look on her face.

"I honestly don't know why I stopped at the gas station today. I was already running late—"

"Nothing new there," Victor cut in, clapping Trevor on the shoulder. "You'll be late to your own funeral, my friend."

"Dude. Seriously, right?" Trevor gave a good-humored chuckle, obviously unaffected by the teasing. "But I got that nudge—you know, the one in your gut that makes you sit up straight?—and I pulled in and topped off my tank. All two gallons worth of fuel. So, I sat there, waiting, wondering who or what I was there for." Trevor nodded toward Victor. "That's when I texted you that I was on a mission, so you had to give me extra time."

"My sister was your mission?" Renata asked skeptically.

"Actually, she was." Trevor spoke with complete confidence.

Phoebe still wasn't watching him, but she listened carefully, wondering how he'd make her sound. If he said anything along the lines of "little lady" or made fun of her vehicular negligence, she'd be ticked. At him for shaming her in front of her sisters, but more so at herself because it was her own carelessness that had gotten her into the situation in the first place.

"As soon as I heard the pump speak to me, I knew I was at the right place at the right time."

Phoebe frowned. Her lewd comment had been a sign to him? This was new to her, too. And she thought she'd heard them all before, every pick-up line in the book.

"The pump spoke to you?" Gia wasn't really that gullible, but she often bit first when the opportunity arose. It sometimes made her come across as empty-headed, but Phoebe knew it was because her little sister was guileless, and she thrived on getting glimpses into other peoples' lives. If there was a story to tell, Gia was all ears, responding readily to every cue.

"Actually, your sister spoke to—well, to someone—" Trevor broke off, and she could hear the smile in his voice and hoped he'd keep her comment to himself. She steeled herself for it anyway, accustomed to men taking her words and twisting them for their benefit. "But because she didn't have a car, she was standing directly behind the pump, and I didn't see her. So, for a moment, it did appear that the pump was, um... paying me a compliment."

Renata laughed out loud. "Oh no. What did she say? What did you say, Phoebe?"

Phoebe plastered a saucy smile on her lips and angled her gaze so she was looking at her sister sideways. Then in dulcet tones, she murmured, "I said 'I wouldn't mind licking you myself, big guy.'"

"Phoebe Gustafson!" Jules gasped from across the room and then covered her mouth with her hand. The sound of stifled giggles was unmistakable. Renata's eyes just widened, but she said nothing.

"I didn't mean Trevor," Phoebe assured them. "I didn't even know he was there." But then she remembered who she'd been thinking of when she'd said it, so she averted any questions by adding, "Not to say that you're not lickable, Trevor Zander."

"Phoebe!" That got the expected response out of Renata.

"Who did you mean, then?" Gia asked, her wide smile lighting up her whole face.

So much for averting. But before she had to pull an answer out of her hat, Victor saved the day.

"You sound like Juliette," he laughed, his arm around his fiancée's waist. They were still standing, Trevor nearby. And Trevor still wore that crazy grin. Did he ever *not* smile? "She's always licking things to mark her territory."

Phoebe pointed at the couple. "Exactly! Jules had just texted that she wouldn't let anyone lick my scone before I got here." She wasn't going to outright lie about who her intended victim was, but she had no problem alluding to the idea that she'd meant her pumpkin scone. That was all Renata needed; to know that Phoebe had entertained the notion of licking Victor or Tim. She'd never hear the end of it.

"Honestly," Trevor interjected, "I don't think I've ever been propositioned that way before, and there was no way on earth I was going to let that one slide. So, I rounded the pump and got even more validation."

Phoebe's body tensed, waiting to hear condescension settle into his tone.

"A beautiful woman on a beautiful day getting ready to walk a block to her car with a heavy gas can in hand. I mean, come on. If that wasn't a 'stop and enjoy the wonders I've created' nudge, I don't know what is."

Phoebe did look at him now. She honestly couldn't tell if he was serious or not, if he was patronizing her or complimenting her. In fact, he almost made it sound as though *she'd* been the answer to *his* dilemma, not the other way around.

"Well, thank you for getting her here safely," Renata spoke up, apparently ready to send the guys on their way and get the G-FOURce meeting started. She glanced down at her watch, a chunky gold thing Phoebe remembered their mother wearing. "Shall we?"

And that was that. Victor, in his customary reserved way, leaned down and kissed Juliette on the temple in farewell. He murmured something in her ear that made her smile and dip her chin to hide her blush, and then the two men headed toward the door, promising to be back in a couple hours.

"I'm taking Juliette out to dinner tonight, so I'm laying down the law here, ladies," Victor warned from where he stood just inside the foyer, legs braced wide beneath him in a posture that said he was brooking no arguments. "No crying after I leave, got it?" He pointed at each one of the sisters. "This G-FOURce needs to be a tear-free zone today."

Trevor, passing close to Phoebe, who had stood to say goodbye, offered her his hand once again, and said, "For all the right reasons, I'm glad you ran out of gas today. It was good to finally meet you, Phoebe Gustafson." Then he nodded, slipped past her, and followed Victor out.

FIVE

PHOEBE GUSTAFSON. PHOEBE GUSTAFSON. Why did she look so familiar to him? He toyed with the sound of her name again, wracking his brain for clues, for memories, for anything that would give him a hint as to who she was. Other than the fact that her genetics clearly marked her as Juliette's sister, however, he could think of nothing else.

But those eyes. That mouth. Even her hair stirred something long ago forgotten—

"Earth to Taz." Vic rapped his knuckles on the tabletop, his tone cajoling. "Where are you, man?"

Trevor lifted his gaze from the basket of Buffalo wings he was absentmindedly prodding at and grinned. "Taz back to earth. I'm here now. Sorry. What did you say?"

"I just asked how long you're planning on being in town this time." Vic sat upright in his bench seat, his military bearing almost comedic in contrast to Trevor's casual slouch. "Particularly if you'll be here in the spring. Early April, to be specific."

Trevor picked up a sauce-drenched wing and shook it at Vic. "Why? You need a wingman for some special occasion?"

Vic just stared at him across the table, not saying a word, not cracking a smile, but Trevor knew he'd caught the terrible pun by the way his friend's jaw clenched, as though he were trying to bite back a response.

"I'm actually here for at least six months." Trevor dropped the wing back into the basket in front of him and wiped his fingers clean on his napkin before continuing. "After the surprising success of the last album, I'm taking some time just to write and record. I'll do some local gigs, but nothing that will take me away from home for more than a day or two." He leaned forward, unable to contain the excitement he felt over the project brewing inside him. "Dude. I have these songs that keep going through my mind, songs that all tie together into a story line; a concept album, you know? My agent isn't feeling it, though, and he says he doesn't think he can sell it. He basically told me that my mainstream audience won't listen to it."

"Why not?" Vic asked, taking the napkin from his lap and laying it neatly beside his empty plate. Big Mike's had the best Happy Hour appetizer menu in town, which made it a great pit stop for the two men. Rather than the dollar drinks, they came for the all-you-can-eat wings, the overstuffed potato skins, and the bottomless chips and salsa with a side or two of fresh guacamole. And the huge monitors that offered a smorgasbord of sports to choose from, of course. Although today, they weren't really paying attention to who was playing.

Trevor shrugged. "Doesn't matter. I know it's what I'm supposed to do. It's like there's this—" He brought both hands up in front of his chest as though holding a ball. "Like there's something *alive* inside my chest just hammering to get out." He took a sip of his iced tea. "And even though he doesn't necessarily agree with me on this, Phil trusts me. We made a lot of money off the tour, which, from what I hear, isn't always the case. So I'm set to take some time to work on this side project, and Phil will wait to start pushing for the next album until I'm finished with this one. I told him six months."

"Perfect. Because Juliette and I have set the date for the first Saturday in April. And yes, I'd like you to be my wingman." Now Vic was grinning, but Trevor thought it probably had more to do with the thought of finally being married to Juliette than the bad wing joke.

"I'd be honored." He raised his iced tea glass between them, and Vic lifted his coffee cup in response. "Any chance you might want a song?"

"Juliette wouldn't have it any other way."

Trevor nodded, the memory of his evening spent with Juliette Gustafson almost a whole year ago now, when he sat beside her as she discovered what it meant to surrender, to forgive, and to accept the truest of all love. He couldn't have asked God for a better wife for his best friend.

"Excellent." Vic nodded, then angled a quizzical look at Trevor. "One more question."

"Shoot."

"Where did you go just now?"

A loud group of women swept past, the aroma of flowers and vanilla and something else purely female swirling around them. Trevor glanced up, catching the eye of a brunette who flashed him a glossy smile and a bold gaze. He nodded politely and looked back at Vic, but before he could speak, the woman paused at their table and cocked her head at him.

"Do we know each other?" she asked, her childlike voice a bit of a surprise. She wore a dress that made Trevor embarrassed for her, and when she placed both palms on the edge of the table and leaned forward a little, he felt embarrassed for Vic and himself, too. That much cleavage should have a rating stamped on it, or at least require one of those black censor strips when in public. He had to bite on his bottom lip to keep from grinning at the thought, lest she think he appreciated the view for the wrong reason.

Not that he didn't appreciate the show. He did. A woman's breasts were incredibly alluring to him, and when they were so freely displayed, it was tempting to indulge in the eye candy.

Trevor shook his head, forcing his gaze to stay focused on her face. "I don't think so," he said, keeping his smile polite, but his tone reserved. The three other women in her party now circled around the end of the booth.

"Well..." She drew the word out and then lifted one long-fingered hand and held it toward him. "My name is Carrie. And you are?"

"Trevor." He held up both hands, even though they were clean. "You don't want to shake my hand. I've been eating wings." He didn't bother extending the introduction to include Vic. He didn't want to open up a conversation with the woman, and he knew Vic wouldn't be interested in doing so either.

Carrie lowered her hand back to the table and shrugged. "Trevor. I've been over there sitting at our table trying to guess your name for the last half hour. I thought maybe Adam or David. But I like Trevor. It suits you. You don't mind if we join you for a bit, do you?" In a swift and practiced move, she pivoted on her heel and slid into the bench seat, bumping up against him to get him to scoot over to make more room. "Are you going to tell us your friend's name?"

"Excuse me," Vic interjected. "Carrie, right?"

She nodded, leaning forward expectantly, and shot an encouraging look at one of the other girls who made a move toward Vic's side of the table.

"We were in the middle of a private conversation." His tone was kind, patient, but firm, nonetheless. The group fell silent for a breath of a second, and then Carrie slowly slid back out of the bench and stood.

"Well," she said, her eyes bright, her odd, girlish voice rubbing Trevor the wrong way. "At least you can't say we don't know each other anymore, right, Trevor?" She winked at him, and then pushed through the circle of women and led them away.

"Wow," Trevor muttered, glad that Vic had been there to run interference. "Thanks. Kinda caught me off guard." He took another sip of his tea.

"So, my friend," Vic said after a few moments of silence. "How are you doing with all that?"

Trevor knew he was being vague because they were in public—in the privacy of either of their homes, he would have been much more straightforward. Trevor would be thirty-five in a month, and being a single, red-blooded, healthy human being wasn't always very easy for him.

"Honestly? I need to get married, man. I need a wife. I feel like Paul was talking straight at me when he said, 'It is better to marry than to burn with passion.' Dude." Trevor shook his head and smiled openly. "I'm doing really well, though, all things considered. As long as I keep busy and focused on what God's got me doing, I'm good."

"Sounds exhausting," Vic replied. "I mean, a man has to rest, you know."

"Yeah, but when I rest, my guard comes down. It's a battle, Vic, even after all these years. I just keep praying, asking, begging God to send the right woman to me, but...." His voice trailed off. It didn't sit well with him that everyone else seemed to have someone special in their lives. Sure, Vic was only now getting married, and he was even older than Trevor, but Vic had been in a couple of comfortable, if not passionate, relationships over the years. Trevor, on the other hand, had always seemed to be in the wrong place at the wrong time. Or with the wrong person.

That was how he'd felt about Juliette Gustafson, the girl who'd be marrying Vic next April. Even though he didn't date casually, he'd agreed to go on a blind date with her at Gia's request, for no other reason than that he'd felt the Lord compelling him to do so. All evening long, he'd prayed about her, asking God if she might be the one for him. But the whole time he was with her, as much as he enjoyed her company, the way she felt pressed against his back when she rode behind him on his bike, even after she'd invited Christ into her life, removing that last barrier between them, he'd known the answer was *no*. Not because she wasn't beautiful. Not because he didn't think she'd be a wonderful wife. Not because he could find anything *wrong* with her at all. But because he'd known she wasn't the *right* one.

Just like all the other women who'd come and gone in his life.

Not that they were *in* his life. And that was the problem. They lived alongside his life, but none of them were really a part of his life.

And he was weary of being alone.

"I won't settle, though. So, I just keep praying. Keep asking." He shook his head and finally lowered his gaze, his stomach clenching a little at having to admit his weakness, even to this friend who'd walked him through some difficult times. "It's tough, man. Women like Carrie? They're everywhere, especially on tour. It doesn't matter that I'm a Christian, that I'm singing songs about Jesus and surrender and obedience and grace. I can't tell you how many times I've had the opportunity to have my fill of some pretty Christian girl offering me a lot more than Carrie just did." He dipped his head in the direction the group of women had gone. "Holding out for marriage when sex is almost standard protocol as part of getting to know someone these days is like hanging onto a tiger by the tail. Not only do I come across as aloof and prudish to people, but I can't, even for one moment, relax my grip, or I'll fall, Vic. Crash and burn, you know?"

"That might be obedience, but there doesn't seem to be any peace in it."

Trevor lifted his head and met his friend's eyes. He chuckled, but there was no humor in the sound. "No. There's no peace in it. It's hell right now. I need a woman, Vic. But I know I don't just *need a woman*," he said, using his fingers to make air quotations around the phrase. "It's not just sex, although that would be fantastic, too." He touched a drop of condensation on his glass with the tip of his finger. "I need a woman who belongs to me, one I belong to." He wasn't jealous of Vic, but at that moment, he wanted to trade places with him more than anything. "These days, I actually wake up already feeling defeated, struggling before I even get out of bed. This isn't right, living like this."

"How's your thought life?" Vic asked, his voice low, gentle, understanding. "What are you doing with your alone time?"

Trevor released a quick snort. "It's a twenty-four-seven struggle, man. Twenty-four-seven." He paused just for a moment, but then continued, knowing he could trust Vic implicitly. "Today at the gas station, Phoebe's licking comment? In that lounge singer voice of hers? I think I might have lost consciousness for a second or two."

Vic laughed out loud, but nodded. "I can imagine."

"So, I thank God in all sincerity for creating beautiful women like Phoebe Gustafson and her sisters. I thank him for putting her in my path, for letting me feel that rush of adrenaline and desire, because it means that at least everything is working the way it should, even if I'm not supposed to act on it. I try to be positive about every aspect of it, you know? I mean, he made women with all those curves and dimples, right? Those soft voices and bottomless eyes?"

Vic was shaking his head slowly, but not in disagreement.

"And he made us to appreciate all of it. But I tell you what, Vic. I'm sick to death of appreciating women from afar." Trevor rubbed a hand over his eyes and dropped his head back against the cushion behind him. "Man, I sound like a fifteen-year-old boy."

"Nah. You sound like a thirty-something-year-old man who's holding out for the right woman." Vic picked up the tab the waitress had left at their table right before Carrie and her group passed by. He shook his head when Trevor reached for his wallet. "Let's get out of here. I got this."

SIX

"THERE'S SOMETHING ABOUT HER," Trevor began. They were in Vic's car, heading out to the range for an hour of target practice. Trevor often teased his police officer friend about shooting off duty, but it was something they both really enjoyed doing together.

Besides, they weren't using guns. They pulled into the Midtown Archers Club parking lot and Vic turned off the engine. "About Phoebe?"

"Yeah."

Vic stilled, both hands on the steering wheel. Finally, he spoke, his eyes narrowed in concentration. "Look. I agree, she's quite a woman. But she's... well, she's not on the same page as you are, my friend. You may have a tiger by the tail, but she's got the world eating out of the palm of her hand. Phoebe's life is dialed in, and she likes it that way. And I don't think she's looking to change any time soon, Taz." Trevor could tell Vic was being careful with his choice of words to describe the flamboyant woman.

"I don't mean it like that. Yeah, she's gorgeous. And that voice!" Trevor shook his head appreciatively. "She may have a whole different set of standards than I do, but then, that's not saying much, is it? Apparently, most of the world has a different set of standards than I do." He made a fist, his forearm bunching on the armrest of the passenger door. "It's just that I feel like I know her from somewhere. It feels like I *should* know her from somewhere. It's driving me crazy trying to remember, though. I can't place her, but I somehow *recognize* her."

Vic chuckled. "Maybe that's your testosterone *recognizing* her."

"Ha. You're a funny guy." Trevor pushed open his door. "Come on, Sheriff. Let's see if you've improved any since the last time we were here."

Trevor loved bows. He appreciated a well-built recurve, and he liked the efficiency of a compound, but he loved his collection of longbows more than any others. He'd been into archery since he was a kid, not for competition or show, not even for hunting. It was more the overall concept of the weapon, and he'd spent hours and hours constructing his own bows and arrows from a variety of woods. His latest masterpiece he'd crafted from yew in the classic English longbow style. The wood felt solid and sure in his hand, the riser settling into his grip in an organic way only wood could. His favorite bow, up until this one, had been a Tomahawk longbow—it fit his lean musician hands perfectly—but the more he shot this new one, this one he'd custom built to his standards, the more he liked it.

Vic, although almost as enthusiastic about shooting as Trevor was, only had two bows; a recurve that was his preference, and the sweet Bear Montana longbow he'd brought with him today. The two friends had spent more hours than they could count putting holes in targets, whether they were the foam-backed bosses at the club, or cheap paper targets tacked to straw bales out in the back forty at Trevor's folks' place in the canyon. The Zanders had almost three acres out there. His mother worked as a trainer in several of the local stables, and they boarded a few select horses on their property as well, but there had always been plenty of room there for Trevor to set up his range.

When they'd first met, Vic had been fascinated by the hobby and had joined right in. Now, years later, it was still something they did together when they could get their schedules to cooperate.

"Well, you're from around here and so are the Gustafsons," Vic suggested. "You've probably seen her around town." They pushed through the double glass doors of the club and headed toward the front desk to check in.

"Nah, it's not that. I feel like I *know* her, or at least something about her."

"Maybe you remember when their parents were killed?" Vic signed his name in the registry and stepped aside to let Trevor do the same. "It was big news around here, from what Juliette tells me."

"Not that, either. I think I was too young and self-absorbed when it happened. I didn't go to school with them and I wasn't personally affected by it, you know?" He paused. "I do remember hearing about it. And I remember the other girl involved, Angela something, I think. The one who was driving. But that's only because my mom knew her mom from one of the stables where she worked." He shook his head. "It's something else. And it's going to drive me crazy until I remember, I know it will."

Vic reached over and put a hand on Trevor's shoulder. "Just be on your guard, my friend, okay? She's going to be my sister-in-law, and I'll stand by her, no matter what, don't get me wrong. She loves her sisters like there's no tomorrow; I'd trust her with Juliette's life, and that's saying a lot." He frowned before continuing. "But her lifestyle is—well, just be careful."

"I didn't say I was going to pursue her."

"Maybe not out loud, but I can hear you considering it."

Trevor studied Vic's serious expression a few moments. Then he nodded. "Fine. Yeah. I'm considering it. I know I was supposed to stop at that Chevron today, and I know it was because of her." He rubbed a hand over his mouth. "And I don't think it was just because God wanted me to carry her gas can back to her Jeep for her."

"Fair enough." Victor dropped his hand from Trevor's shoulder and started forward again.

"But will you do something for me?" Trevor didn't want to ask. He wanted to think he was strong enough, manly enough, *godly* enough, to be able to handle this situation on his own. But he was well aware of his weaknesses, and even the thought of Phoebe tasted like temptation.

"Anything."

"Will you hold me accountable?"

"How?" Vic wasn't going to make this easy.

"I don't know. I don't even know what any of this is going to look like. But I want to at least figure out why I'm so—so *bothered*—by her. I feel like I should know her," he said again. "I just don't know if it's because I know her from somewhere in my past, or if it's because I'm supposed to get to know her. Or even because I just *want* to get to know her. Regardless, I feel compelled to move forward until God closes a door on this."

They'd reached the 70-meter line and chose two lanes side-by-side. It wasn't terribly busy, which made continuing their conversation a little easier.

"Okay. We can pray about it, and I'll do what I can to help."

"Thanks. God?" Trevor knew that Vic was accustomed to him breaking out in prayer at any time, so he moved right into it without explaining. "You know I'm yours. You know I want to live by your plan for my life. But you also know my heart, my strengths and weaknesses. Give me the courage to move forward, give me the discernment to recognize a closed door when—*if*—I see one. I'm asking for wisdom here, God, something I feel in short supply of these days. And thanks for Vic. Show us how to be the iron that sharpens iron in each other's lives."

"Amen," Vic said after Trevor fell silent.

Trevor braced one end of his bow on the ground and bent the top limb forward so he could loop the end of the string in place. He strapped a short leather guard around his bow arm because he'd never quite learned to bend his elbow out far enough not to get burned by the bowstring. Then he slipped a three-fingered shooting glove on his other hand. He made his own from pliable suede and had given Vic a couple, too. Selecting a hickory arrow from the quiver slung low on his thigh, he notched it, drew back on the bowstring, and released it. With a crackling thunk, it embedded itself into the target, only millimeters off center, the shaft quivering enthusiastically.

"Nice," Vic said before releasing his first arrow. He didn't even make the inner circle. Trevor may have missed the mark when it came to women, but at least here, on the range, he outshone Vic by a long shot. Or a short shot. Or any shot.

"You never finished telling me about this album you're working on."

"Right." Trevor selected another arrow. "I still don't know what I'm going to call it, but it's the theme of transformation. Not the stereotypical bad to good transformation, though. More of a 'works to faith' transformation."

"Why not call it 'Transformation? You just used the word three times,'" Vic asked, sending another arrow flying.

Trevor could see him from the corner of his eye, and he almost laughed. The man had perfect form, just like everything else he did in life. Vic was a walking paragon of self-control and being around him sometimes made Trevor feel like such a slouch. Although his faith was strong, a powerful living force inside him, Trevor felt more like the ruled-by-emotions King David of the Old Testament than the passionate self-disciplined Paul of the New Testament whom he so longed to emulate.

"Too cliche, too churchy. Too familiar. Makes it easy to write off, even though the concept of transformation, if we really considered it, would blow our minds. No," he shook his head slightly. "It has to be something the world would understand, and something that might make believers stop and take notice." He paused, considering how best to describe his project. "This is about the transformation of a Christian from being a guy who follows all the Christian rules and regulations to being a man who believes with every fiber of his being that his works amount to nothing without Christ in him. The kind of transformation that should come after we accept Christ, you know?"

"The kind that doesn't happen nearly as often as it should," Vic added, raising his hand in acknowledgment. "Speaking from experience, here."

Trevor nodded and set up another shot, then lowered his bow before releasing the arrow. He turned to face his friend. "This is a really personal project. I'm not interested in if it sells or not, except for the fact that higher sales indicates that the message is getting out to more people. Dude, I'd give it away if I thought that would help spread the word. It's that important."

"You know I believe in you, brother. You, of all people, can bring that kind of message to life."

SEVEN

THEY WERE THERE TO talk about baby showers and wedding plans. Not about Phoebe and Trevor. Or Taz. Or whatever his name was.

She had to move past this; get the others to move past this. She had to move past *him*. She wanted no part in his life, no matter how boy-next-door sexy he was.

But she couldn't stop thinking about the way he'd smiled at her, how he'd goaded her into letting him help her even after she insisted that she was fine. The guy *flirted* with her openly. Granted, he didn't ask for her number, but there were all kinds of 'come on' in that crooked grin. And she knew a come on when she saw it. But he'd pulled away from her when they were in front of everyone. And then back to smiling and teasing her from across the room. Good grief, the man was a basket of contradictions and complications. Something she wanted no part of.

"So, what did you think of Taz?" Gia asked, as though sensing the object of Phoebe's thoughts. "Isn't he awesome?" The youngest Gustafson sister dropped back down on the floor atop a pile of over-sized cushions. She leaned forward and scratched Bob's rib cage. He rolled onto his back, legs in the air, mouth falling open into a toothy grin. Mr. Bobo scampered into Gia's lap, vying for her attention, too.

After the guys left, Phoebe had settled into her customary seat on the sofa, at the opposite end from Juliette. She took a sip of coffee, delaying her answer. She was sure Trevor was awesome. Just not her kind of awesome. And she certainly didn't want to talk about what she thought of him. She wasn't even sure she knew herself.

"He's very kind. And insistent."

"I know, right?" Gia agreed, her beautiful amber eyes wide. "He isn't the kind of person to be put off, you know. If he wants something, he just goes out and gets it." She wiggled her eyebrows at Phoebe.

Phoebe laughed and shook her head. "I'm sure he does. But since that has nothing to do with me, how about we get on with the task at hand. Gia? You ready to get this thing started?"

"Wait a minute," Juliette interjected, holding up a hand. "You didn't answer her question. What do you think of Trevor?" She stretched a shapely leg across the couch cushions between them and poked Phoebe in the thigh with her bare toe.

Phoebe dropped her head to one side and scowled over at Juliette. "Seriously? You guys, I ran into him twenty minutes before I got here."

"Yeah, and a lot can happen in twenty minutes, Phoebe," Renata retorted, but she was smiling.

This new version of Renata didn't sit well with Phoebe. She preferred the arguing and bickering between them. It was comfortable. The norm.

"Look. I don't *think* anything of him, okay? He's a nice guy who helped me out at the gas station and who happened to be coming my way. And we didn't even talk enough to know that until we both stopped at the same place. Now drop it."

Ren's perfectly shaped eyebrows rose in response. Good grief, the woman looked amazing right now. Her hair was thick and shiny, the tips of it brushing her jawline. It had grown so fast in the last few months, mostly due to prenatal vitamins and the pregnancy hormones coursing through Ren's veins. Her eyes were bright and her skin, rosy and smooth. Pregnancy suited Renata Gustafson Dixon Larsen, Phoebe knew. She'd seen her sister look this way four other times before. But it was more than that these days. And Phoebe didn't think it was all about Tim—although Ren's new husband doted on her like she was the Queen of England. No, something inside her sister was shifting, changing, or just revealing itself for the first time. Had this version of Ren been there all along?

"You know, Phebes, he really is a great guy. I can vouch for him. And so can Victor. Maybe you should at least *think* about thinking of him." Juliette spoke quietly, not quite hesitantly, her statement almost more of a request.

"I agree. The two of you together? You know, that would be amazing. He's so cool. And his music. Have you heard any of it?" Gia gushed, sounding more like a fan girl than a personal friend of the man's.

"I haven't heard his music, but I have a feeling it's not really my cup of tea. And I also have a feeling that he and I might disagree on a lot of things. Things that would probably prevent us from... being *amazing* together." Phoebe took another sip of coffee. "So. If we are done with all that, can we please get on with the G-FOURce?" She looked pointedly at her little sister.

"Fine. But you really should give his music a listen," Gia acquiesced. "I think you might be surprised. In a good way." She moved closer to the rest of them as they all stood and gathered around the coffee table, even Renata.

As the youngest sister, it was Gia's job to officially open the meeting. "Welcome Empress Juliette, Empress Renata, and Empress Phoebe." She pressed her hands together in a prayer-like manner and nodded her head to each sister accordingly.

"Welcome, Empress Georgia." The other three spoke just as somberly, nodding back at her.

They clasped hands, then, forming a circle, they began the G-FOURce pledge, a time-honored tradition that had somehow survived adolescence into adulthood.

Let the words of our mouths
Be necessary, kind, and true.
Let the secrets we share
Be kept safe amongst us few.
Let the decisions that we make
Be brave, noble, and wise
Oogie-boogie-doggy-loogie
Wiggly-jiggly-fries!
G-FOURce unite!

They didn't collapse into giggles the way they used to, but none of them was quite grown up enough to give it up. The pledge was like an unbroken cord weaving through their lives, binding them together.

Everyone made it back to their seats and Renata pulled out her thick black planner. "So, my due date is officially November 7th, which is less than a month away. Does that give us enough time to plan anything?"

"Who's 'us,' Rennie? You're just here to approve the theme. We're the ones planning the shower for you," Phoebe teased.

"I know, I know. I just feel bad that we're on such a short time frame."

"Actually," Juliette picked up the open wall calendar she'd laid on the coffee table earlier. "What about having it after Charise is born? I'm just thinking if everyone knew there'd be a baby to fuss over, that we'd get a lot more people there, don't you agree? And since you've had pre-birth showers before, it's not like you'd be missing out on that experience. You already have the basic necessities, too, so—"

"You don't have to convince me, Juliette," Renata interrupted, holding her coffee cup aloft in agreement. She'd refused to give up her caffeine during any one of her pregnancies, and this time was no different. "I think it's a fantastic idea. Between getting married, and having a honeymoon, and trying to prep for a new baby, all while I feel a little like a beached whale, the thought of trying to squeeze one more thing in right now makes me want to go to bed for a week." She rubbed a hand over her rather large belly. "Oh!"

"Is she kicking?" Gia asked, pushing up off the floor again. "Let me feel her!" She hurried over and put her long hands on either side of Ren's stomach. "Hey, sweet baby girl, are you in there?" she cooed.

Renata rolled her eyes but smiled sweetly. "She's in there, believe me. Oh!" She stiffened again. "Ouch, little one. That hurts." She pressed a hand to her rib cage. "Feels like she's kicking me in the lung."

Gia's eyes widened. "Is that possible?"

Renata swept a hand over Gia's long copper curls, tucking a few behind the girl's ear. "She won't puncture my lung, if that's what you're worried about."

Phoebe watched the exchange with a growing sense of discomfort. She longed to race across the room and rest her cheek, her ear, against Ren's stomach, to whisper sweet nothings to that little girl who would soon be welcomed into a household of brothers and embraced by this family of sisters. But she couldn't bring herself to do it. Not just because it was Ren, either.

Without realizing what she was doing, she slid her hand over her own flat stomach, her fingers spreading out as though to cup as much of her abdomen as possible. She closed her eyes and imagined the fluttering and shifting, the hiccups, the fullness of a baby in her womb.

"Phebes? You okay?" It was Juliette, her voice soft, murmuring from the other end of the couch.

Phoebe's eyes snapped open, and she jerked her hand from her stomach, clenching it into a fist around the fabric of her skirt on her lap. "I'm fine."

Jules watched her for a few moments, her expression, as usual, open and inviting and clearly concerned. Phoebe glanced over at Renata, who was watching the two of them over the top of Gia's head. Gia was still gently prodding Ren's belly, and laughing when Baby Charise kicked back.

"I'm fine, really. I've probably had too much coffee today. Need to get some real food in my belly."

"Ouch. Stop poking, Gia." Renata's tone was rather sharp.

"Sorry," Gia said apologetically. She rose to her feet. "Granny G sent over some leftovers with me if you're hungry, Phebes. It's in the fridge."

Phoebe wasn't hungry at all, but she was glad for the excuse to duck out of the room for a moment. Fortunately, the Tupperware in the fridge held Granny G's mashed potatoes, something Phoebe knew would go down easy and stay put. She leaned against the counter while she warmed a bowl in the microwave, purposely standing where she couldn't see or be seen by her sisters. But she listened to their comfortable chatter, wishing, not for the first time, that she didn't have to try so hard to be the person they thought she was.

Not that she wasn't that person. She was. In fact, this version of her was the easiest role to play. The sexy sister, the sexy photographer, the sexy artist, the sexy single lady.... The list went on and on, all roles she knew well, and actually liked pretty well, too. It was the sexy part that got old sometimes, and today it seemed to weigh heavily on her. When was the last time she'd left her house in sweats and flip-flops? Ha! Had she *ever* left the house in sweats and flip-flops for that matter?

Her image always came first. The facade. The front. The cover. Because the truth was that people *did* judge a book by its cover, and if she could keep people distracted enough by her cover, maybe they'd never look beyond that.

The microwave beeped and Phoebe pulled the steaming dish of potatoes out, stirred in a dollop of butter and some salt, and headed back into the living room to join her sisters. She intentionally added a little extra movement to her hips, liking the way the hem of her skirt swished against her ankles.

· · · · ● · ● · ● · · ·

"WAIT. I THOUGHT YOU said she wasn't being paroled until next summer." Renata's voice was tight, but Phoebe was a little taken aback to see the grimace that seemed to be an attempt at a smile on Ren's face. "I mean, I'm glad she's getting an early hearing, for her sake, but...."

"I know. That was what her last letter said." Juliette pulled the folded yellow legal-pad paper out of the envelope in her lap. Phoebe could see lines of neat penmanship filling what looked like two or three pages. "From what Angela says, this kind of thing rarely happens. Usually, it's the other way around; things get pushed back time and time again. But I think it was nice of her to give us a heads up, don't you?" Her voice held a hint of false brightness; Juliette was desperate for the rest of them to be as okay as she was with Angela Clinton coming back to town.

Not that Phoebe wasn't okay with it. The girl had every right to want to come home after almost sixteen years of prison, but that didn't mean Phoebe—or any of them, for that matter—had to welcome her with open arms.

The girl—because that's what she'd been at the time—had killed their parents. She'd plowed into them in the middle of an intersection, going so fast there was no way she'd even slowed down for the red light. Drunker than a politician at a strip club, Angela had been headed to her high school graduation ceremony, late. The same destination to which Paul and Simone Gustafson had been going to see their eldest daughter, Juliette, graduate, too. None of the three in the accident had made it to the event, and only Angela had made it out alive.

And now, apparently, she had served her time for the double homicide, and was on her way home in just a few short months.

"From what she says here," Juliette continued, running a finger down the lines of Angela's writing, "it's possible she'll be back in Midtown as early as the beginning of May." She lowered the letter to her lap and paused, not looking at anyone for a moment. When she finally spoke again, Phoebe was surprised at the words that came from Juliette's mouth. "I'd like to get married before she gets here."

Renata chimed in her agreement without hesitation. "I agree. This isn't something you should have to face alone. I know you and Victor are already the real deal, but knowing you'll have him to come home to at the end of the day will make facing whatever you have to with Angela a little easier."

Phoebe knew Ren didn't mean to be insensitive, but she wanted to shout out, "What about me? Who do I get to go home to at the end of the day? Who will hold me when our past catches up to us?" Gia still lived with Grandpa and Granny G, Ren had her Tool Belt Tim, and Jules was getting her champion, too.

Phoebe didn't say a word, though. As far as her sisters knew, she was just fine on her own. It was exactly the way she wanted it. Why on earth would Renata think twice about Phoebe facing the future alone?

"So, Victor and I have set our date for the first Saturday in April. The weather should be perfect for an outdoor wedding and it will give us time to take our honeymoon and still be here when Angela gets back to town."

"Oh, I love weddings in the spring!" Gia chirped, obviously trying to focus on the bright side of the conversation. "Have you already booked a place? Steward's Mansion? Or somewhere else?"

EIGHT

PHOEBE PUSHED A SHOULDER into the cerulean blue door of her home and shoved. She'd have to take a wood planer to it before the rainy season started. The old wood warped more and more each year, no matter how much she did to try to salvage it.

Phoebe's whole home was actually salvaged; a refurbished packinghouse, one of the many buildings left over from the citrus groves that had been wiped out to make room for places like Midtown. She'd purchased the property with its ramshackle building using her portion of the life insurance left to her after her parents' death. She then moved out of the little apartment building she'd shared with several other artists to live in her grandparents' RV while she worked alongside the construction crews and handymen who converted the old warehouse into an artist's dream house.

It had taken almost two years, but it had turned out exactly the way she wanted it. The open great room on the ground floor was a combination of living space and art studio, sporting huge windows that let the soft north light in. The building's original office space had been converted into a guest room, but Phoebe now used it for a changing room for her clients. She'd mounted a bank of five lockers along one wall for personal belongings, had put in a hair and makeup vanity station, and had mirrored one whole wall. A small storage room next to it now housed costumes from a variety of cultures, eras, sizes, and colors, most of them made by Phoebe herself.

The kitchenette was open as well, and although Phoebe enjoyed cooking now and then, she rarely did much more than warm things up in the microwave or on a burner of the apartment-sized stove. She didn't like the idea of residual food smells tainting her work, and she couldn't remember the last time she'd actually stuck something edible inside the oven. Currently, it was being used to store her collection of *Gossamer Magazine*, all the issues with her work in them. Tucked away where no one would see them.

Her pride and joy, however, what made the place her sanctuary, was not the studio, although she loved it to distraction with its wild disarray of creativity, but the loft bedroom at the top of a spiral staircase. A huge, hand-hewn mahogany four-poster bed was the focal point of the room, draped with a down comforter with a white-on-white damask duvet cover, and matching shams, throw pillows piled high. White faux sheepskin pelt area rugs lay scattered around on the dark wood floor, and delicate white sheers hung from the windows. Everything up there but the flooring and bed frame were in varying shades of white, and although it wasn't stark and sterile by any means, it was clean and rife with possibilities. A sparkling fresh canvas. The few people who had seen it were always a little shocked by the monochromatic decor, but the furniture and textiles used were whimsical and feminine, giving the room an almost cloud-like feel. Even her silk pajama sets were white, and Phoebe liked the image she created in her mind of an ebony-haired, red-lipped angel, sleeping on a cloud at the edge of Heaven, finding respite after a long day's work.

She unbuckled her sandals and kicked them off just inside the front door, and then made her way across the open floor plan and drew the blackout blinds on the windows. In the near dark, she climbed the stairs to her bedroom, where she flung herself across her bed, relishing the feel of the fluffy comforter plumped up around her.

She was exhausted. She'd been exhausted for what seemed like weeks. No, months, if she was being honest with herself. Somewhere deep inside, she knew why; she just didn't want to think about it. Instead, she just wanted to sleep. And if she couldn't sleep, she'd lie there and try not to think. The desire to move as little as possible overrode any shame over how lazy she was becoming.

Phoebe wasn't sick. And she didn't think she was suffering from depression. Lethargy, maybe, but not depression, as far as she could tell. She wasn't exactly sad... but she was *weary*. She felt like she'd been waiting for something, or someone, all her life, but there was no end in sight, and she was tired of waiting.

Yet until she could figure out what she was waiting for, she had no idea how to go about finding it.

Which meant more waiting.

Today's G-FOURce had shaken her up; the conversations sat now like boulders on her chest. Ren had become increasingly uncomfortable throughout the afternoon, her late-stage pregnancy making her more irritable and impatient than she usually was. Or rather, than she used to be. Lately, Renata had seemed so much more at peace with the world, with herself, and with them, rarely rising to the bait Phoebe habitually threw out to her. Surely, it had a lot to do with her new marriage and the much-awaited arrival of baby Charise in the next few weeks. But still, when Ren didn't get her hackles up, Phoebe ended up just looking antagonistic and plain old mean. Juliette was justifiably excited about her pending nuptials, but even Gia had been a little more squirrelly than usual, prodding at Ren's stomach to get a reaction from Charise until Ren had grumpily called her 'Pokemon' and ordered her to sit across the room from her.

It was the discussion of Angela Clinton that had really unsettled Phoebe the most, though. The girl had changed the Gustafson girls' lives forever on that fateful day more than fifteen years ago, and the thought of her coming back to Midtown after all this time made Phoebe's stomach churn. If she never laid eyes on Angela Clinton again, it would be too soon.

Angela had started drinking hours before her and Juliette's high school graduation ceremony. By the time she got behind the wheel of her car to get to the event, the girl was plastered. And late. She never saw the Buick Park Avenue pulling into the intersection in front of her, she stated in court. She did see the light turn red, but not soon enough to stop for it.

Angela had plowed her El Camino into the side of Paul and Simone Gustafson's car, killing Simone almost instantly. Paul had died about an hour later, his hand clutched tightly in Grandpa's, who had made it to the hospital in time to say goodbye.

It had taken Angela several months to recover enough to stand trial, but when the time came, she stated she'd known what she was doing when she started drinking, and had gotten behind the wheel, also knowing she was too inebriated to drive. "My intention was to end my life that day," she murmured, her voice trembling, but clear. "I never dreamed I'd end anyone else's." She took full responsibility for killing the two beloved parents, accepted her sentence without recourse, and made a brief, heartfelt statement to the Gustafson family members who were in the courtroom about how terribly sorry she was to have caused them so much suffering.

But suffer, they had. Each of the four sisters grieved in their own ways, their individual strengths and weaknesses rising to the forefront of the battle to survive. Juliette, steady and quiet and thoughtful, had caved in on herself, at first falling into a depression so severe, their grandparents thought she might die, too. Once she finally came out of that dark period, she remained reserved and unassuming, almost afraid to really live, lest her happiness be once more taken from her. Phoebe thanked the God her sisters worshiped that Victor Jarrett had come along when he did, his love for Juliette breaking through the last of those barriers binding her to the past. Juliette claimed most of her change had actually stemmed from her acceptance of Christ, but Phoebe was pretty sure that was just church talk. She saw the way the two of them looked at each other, Victor and Juliette. Jesus couldn't hold a candle to the glow emanating off those two lovebirds.

The same could be said of Renata these days, but it hadn't always been that way. Born with maternal instincts and the rallying charisma of a cheer captain, Ren had stepped into the combined shoes of both their parents and Juliette's when the eldest Gustafson sister had disappeared inside herself. But those traits had morphed into something ugly and often insufferable, turning her motherly sister into a cantankerous shrew over the years. A good man in her life—John Dixon, devoted husband and father to their four sons—had taken the edge off in the early years of their marriage. But like a hedgehog, Ren's quills, although smoothed down by love, had remained intact and poison-tipped. Over the years, slowly, but surely, she'd become prickly and toxic again.

When the unthinkable happened, leaving Renata's world devastated, however, something had changed in her. The need to jab and judge, to poke and punish, seemed to have leaked out with her tears, leaving behind a softer, almost sweet version of Ren, a version Phoebe struggled to relate to after all these years of the love-hate relationship they'd shared.

Gia, darling Georgia, only four when their parents were killed, had borne up the best of them all, as far as Phoebe could tell. Perhaps the young are the most resilient in situations like theirs, although Phoebe felt certain Gia would be darling and effervescent and vivacious even if she'd been a teenager like the older three. But Gia carried a different burden than the others. Something Phoebe sensed was shifting, rising, becoming more of an issue in the youngest Gustafson girl's life. Gia had a tendency to float, to be whatever the circumstances and crowd of the moment demanded. She wasn't really a chameleon, at least not at this point. No, she tended to simply say less, demand less, *be* less, when she thought being fully Gia might make waves. Phoebe wasn't really worried yet; Gia was in that transition period from teenager to adult, having just graduated from high school and figuring out what it meant to be a grownup.

But Phoebe had made the decision to pay attention, something no one had really done for Phoebe when she was that age and desperate for someone to notice that she was disappearing behind the facade she'd created just to survive.

Because Phoebe, maybe more than any of the sisters, had missed her mother most of all. When her parents died, she was fourteen, and was in the process of embracing her individuality, her artistic expression, her identity, and Simone had been her loudest cheerleader. Her mother had encouraged Phoebe's flamboyant fashion, her vivacious thirst for living out loud, giving Phoebe license to resist the constraints of the accepted "norm" in a traditional hometown. Simone had urged Phoebe to push herself, to dig deep into the part of her that made her unique and courageous and powerful.

When Angela took the lives of Paul and Simone Gustafson, Phoebe had dug even deeper, not to expose and share her great gifts with the world as her mother had wanted, but to bury herself, to hide behind them so that no one would see the gaping hole the loss of Simone, her most stalwart champion, her truest believer, had left behind. On the outside, she retained her flamboyance, but it became distorted somehow, her flair for color and style transforming into something more provocative and grittier, the courage and power she'd unearthed with her mother's gentle guidance taking on a decidedly darker bent. Her eyes stayed open, but not as a window to the soul, as many believed. No, in Phoebe's bold gaze was a challenge to any who looked a little too long or too close, daring the beholder to draw back the inky blackout curtain draped across that window, to see the real girl sitting alone in the dark inside.

In order to compensate for her lack of transparency, she worked hard to make the outside look good, to draw—and hold—attention for as long as she needed it or could stand it. Although the act had backfired on her once or twice, she'd grown comfortable with the mask she wore, perhaps even addicted to it, and no longer thought of it as a separate version of herself.

And now Angela Clinton was returning to Midtown, dredging up old memories and secrets best kept buried, and the mask Phoebe wore might very well be exposed for what it was.

Phoebe didn't know if she could bear it.

NINE

Trevor stared at the monitor, the digital sound waves marching across the screen as he listened intently to the music playing through his headphones. The chord progression was perfect for the driving rhythm of the piece, and he nodded, satisfied at the sound he was getting.

The song ended and he jotted down a few thoughts on the legal pad beside his computer keyboard. He grinned sheepishly at the name spelled out at the top of the page. Phoebe Gustafson. And not just once. No, he'd written her name in print, then in old-school cursive, then in all capitals, and even in chunky, cartoon-style lettering.

"You are such a junior high girl, Taz," he muttered out loud to himself. But his pen moved, seemingly of its own accord, and traced the letters again. "Phoebe Gustafson." He said her name softly, his voice stroking the syllables.

He couldn't get her out of his head. All week long, he'd been distracted by thoughts of her. He'd known she was an artist for some time now. He'd asked Juliette about the paintings on her walls—he'd been emotionally moved by the depth and tone of the different pieces—and she'd bragged on Phoebe with gusto.

She certainly looked the part. Her long, wild hair and those smoky eyes that made him think of Monica Bellucci, her flowing skirt and chunky jewelry giving her that whole Bohemian vibe. He'd been considering asking Juliette for Phoebe's contact information for weeks now, ever since he'd first seen her work hanging on Juliette's walls. He was seriously contemplating purchasing a piece, or even a whole series of her artwork, for his new album. Sure, he could go to her website or look her up online, but anyone could do that. It was easy...and impersonal. He always preferred a personal connection when it came to his own work, so he presumed others in the arts did as well.

When he'd asked Vic if he thought she might be interested in working on the album art, he'd said, "I don't see why not. Until recently—maybe a year ago now—she worked for a magazine called *Glamour*, or *Glimmer*.... No, *Gossamer*. That was it. Some kind of fantasy art rag. But Juliette said it wasn't a good fit. She's indie now, so I'd think she'd be open to new clients."

"Not a good fit?"

Victor had shrugged noncommittally. "From what I gather, the job was bad enough, but the guy she worked for was worse."

"You've seen her work. What do you think of it?"

Vic frowned and hesitated for a moment before answering, but it had been enough for Trevor to realize he was probably asking the wrong person for artistic feedback. His response made Trevor grin. "I have. Several of the pieces on Juliette's walls are Phoebe's. The...splashy ones. With all the color and movement. She's good if you like that kind of thing. The stuff makes me feel a little uncomfortable, truth be told."

"Yeah. But then, a little discomfort isn't always a bad thing."

"No, no. You're right about that. Especially when you're talking church folk. We do tend to get a little too kicked back in our padded theater seats."

"My thoughts exactly."

Trevor had let the subject drop then, but he couldn't get rid of the idea so easily, and the more he thought about it, the more he felt compelled to follow through on it.

But there was also the little problem of his immediate and obvious attraction to Phoebe. How was he going to pursue her professionally without pursuing her personally? Every time he thought about her, it wasn't her artwork that made his blood heat up. Yeah, it was fantastic—exactly the emotions and expression he imagined for his album—but it was the way she'd looked at him, an alluring mixture of disdain and vulnerability, of curiosity and coy, of *come-and-get-it* and *approach-at-your-own-risk.*

Besides his own feelings, what about her? Hadn't Vic indicated that her problems with her last job were because of the guy she worked for? He supposed that must be status quo for her—he imagined she was constantly hit on by customers.... "No way. That's not going to be me." He ran a hand over the scruff on his jaw; he needed to shave. He closed his eyes and dipped his head a little. "God, help me to be an upright man. Help me treat her with the respect I owe any child of yours. Please show me your plan in bringing us together. I need your wisdom. I need you."

He stood and crossed to where his acoustic was propped up in a stand. He slung the strap over his shoulder and strummed a few chords, the rich sound making him smile just as it did every time that he played the thing. The instrument was one of his prized possessions; a 1968 D-21 Martin. When Trevor was in high school, he had discovered it at the back of a second-hand thrift shop, complete with its original case. The guitar was in great shape, and although the store owner had no idea what the guitar's history was, he had done his research and knew what he was selling. Even still, the price had been considerably below market value, and Trevor had snapped it up, emptying his bank account to buy it. His parents had reimbursed him half the cost of the instrument as an early birthday gift, and he had used much of that money to pay a qualified luthier to do a neck reset and fret job. The guitar played like a dream, the full sound resonating richly, the Brazilian rosewood sides and back—one of the rarer features of the instrument—creating a warmth in the tone that stirred his very soul.

His eyes darted around the room, his appreciation for what he had always at the forefront of his mind. He'd converted the second bedroom of his house into a state-of-the-art recording studio, complete with top-of-the-line gear and equipment. He'd always had the best of the best—not necessarily the most expensive, but the best money could buy—because money had never really been an issue for him. His parents weren't wealthy, but they lived comfortably, and he was their only child. They'd doted on him, he knew, and they'd bent over backwards to encourage and nurture his music. And not for them, either, as so many parents did. But for him, because he'd known music was his life's blood—there was no Plan B—and his parents had recognized it as such, too.

Not that he'd always been so appreciative. There'd been a time when he'd taken it all for granted, believing he deserved what he had, that he was owed the good things in his life. A time when he'd seen his good fortune as a direct result of his good behavior.

But pride is a duplicitous and seductive creature, luring men and women into traps of their own making, and Trevor had been no exception.

His fingers moved boldly over the strings, plucking out arpeggiated scales as he warmed up his hands. Even exercises sounded exquisite, almost divine, on the Martin. They came easily to him, and he closed his eyes and nodded his head like a metronome, keeping time with his steady pace. He forced his thoughts away from the woman and focused instead on the set of songs he was writing for the new album.

The message he wanted to portray had to come out exactly right, or he would end up looking just as pompous and self-righteous as he'd once been. Because, unlike his last album, the one he'd written for people desperate for peace, with this new one, he was preaching to the choir. This time, his message was for those already saved, already rescued, already adopted into the family of God.

God had laid on Trevor's heart a message about a man changed, not from a sinner to a saint, but the other way around.

A man who once believed he was a holier-than-thou saint bound for glory because of wise choices and good living... a man who now recognized his status as the lowliest of sinners. The chief of all sinners, as the apostle Paul declared. But because of God's unconditional love for him, the man was a sinner bound, not for Hell, but for Heaven.

Transformation. From a pompous, self-righteous Christian into a servant, a Christ-*follower*, walking in the footsteps of Jesus, the greatest servant of all.

Trevor wanted not only his songs to portray that message of transformation, but for his album cover to represent the same thing. And he felt certain that Phoebe Gustafson could do the job.

Pursuing her personally? He'd give that one a little more time. But hiring her to do the album art, if she was willing, felt like a sure thing.

So, what was this foreboding undercurrent that the path ahead might not be so clear?

• • • • • • • • •

HE HELD THE PHONE between his ear and shoulder, listening to it ring on the other end of the line, his hands busy working the large knife he was using to dice vegetables for stir-fry.

"Gia. It's Taz," he said, when the girl answered after the fourth ring. He'd almost hung up.

"Hey, Taz! Ricky's right here. You looking for him?"

The pot of Jasmine rice on the stove still had a few minutes before it was ready—plenty of time to sauté the carrots and zucchini, broccoli, garlic, and water chestnut. He tossed the vegetables in the skillet, shredded a leftover chicken breast from last night's meal into bite-sized pieces, and added it to the pan at the last minute so as not to dry it out.

"No, actually, I called to talk to you." From the fridge he pulled out the coconut curry dressing, and dumped a couple of tablespoons in, stirring quickly to coat, but not burn.

"Oh. Well, how may I help you, sir?" He could hear the smile in her voice, and for possibly the hundredth time, he wondered if the girl was ever sad. Trevor lifted the lid on the pot of rice and breathed in the heady aroma. He was suddenly starving.

"I'm thinking about your sister."

"Ohhh." The word was long and drawn out, and Trevor shook his head, realizing too late what kind of fodder he was handing over.

"Not like that," he back-pedaled. "I mean—"

"Sure, sure. Of course not." Gia giggled. "Like *that*, I mean. Whatever *that* is."

"Gia," he warned, but he was grinning, too. "Seriously, I was thinking of hiring her to work on my next album cover. I really like what I've seen of her work. At Juliette's," he added.

"You are speaking of Phoebe, am I correct? Or were you referring to the epic photo album scrapbooks on the end table? Ren makes those. She's the Scrapper Queen!"

Clearly, Gia was having a ball with this discussion, and he wondered briefly if the sisters had given Phoebe a hard time at their meeting the other day, after he and she had shown up at Juliette's place together.

"I don't think scrap-booking is really big in progressive rock these days, Gia. Yes, Phoebe. The artist," he confirmed.

"So…" Once again, she dragged the words out. "You like her…"

"I did not say that," he cut her off. "I said I like her—"

"Her work. Yes, I know. That's what I was saying before you interrupted me. Can I help it if I speak really slowly? So rude." Her voice grew muffled for a moment, as though she were covering the mouthpiece with her hand. "Ricky, your cousin is so rude!"

"Fine. I'm rude," Trevor retorted. "Can you give me Phoebe's number?"

"You didn't get her number from her last week when you rescued her on the side of the road? Slacker."

"Gia."

"Fine," she said, echoing his earlier tone almost exactly. "I'll give you her number… *if* you come with Ricky to dinner over here tomorrow. Sunday Family Dinner at the grandparents. The whole Gustafson gang. And friends," she added.

"You're inviting me to dinner?"

"Yes, I'm inviting you to dinner. Ricky's a regular, so you won't be the only guy at the table other than Grandpa."

"What about Vic? And isn't your other sister married with a bunch of boys?" He was actually entertaining the idea, and the more he thought about it, the more he liked it.

"I'm not sure if Vic will be there or not. He's pulling some overtime to cover for another officer who's on vacation. But Ren's guys won't be. Tim is taking them on one last boys-only camping trip before Baby Charise makes her debut."

Gia paused a moment to respond to something Ricky said to her, then she was speaking into the phone again. "Besides, Grandpa and Granny G have been dying to meet you, and Granny G always cooks way too much when it's just us girls." Again, she paused briefly, then tacked on a few more words in a cajoling sing-song tone. "Come on, Taz. Do it for Ricky."

"Do it for me!" Ricky sing-songed in the background.

"Do it for love, Taz. Familial love for Ricky, of course," Gia clarified with a giggle. "Unless…."

"Okay," he interjected, cutting off her trailing word, but her teasing made him smile. "Sounds good. Dinner tomorrow, then." He scooped a steaming spoonful of rice into a serving bowl and topped it with the vegetables and chicken. "And speaking of dinner, mine is ready, and I don't want it to get cold, so I'm gonna let you go. What time should I be there?"

"We eat between noon and one o'clock, but most of us just come back here whenever church is out for everyone. Grandpa and Granny G usually get home around ten—they go to the early service—so you can come any time after that."

"Perfect. I'll see you tomorrow."

He heard Ricky holler something else in the background. "Ricky says to remember to save us a seat," Gia repeated into the phone.

"I'll save you two a seat at church." His words were redundant in more ways than one; even though he was typically late, he always arrived before them, and he always saved them a seat.

"Excellent," she said, as though he'd just suggested a brilliant new idea. "See you tomorrow!" And with that, she hung up. It was only after he took the first delicious bite of his supper that he realized she hadn't given him Phoebe's number.

"I'll stop being such a slacker and ask Phoebe for it myself tomorrow," he declared, pleased at the notion. He took another bite and then carried his bowl and water bottle into the living room to look for something to watch on television while he ate.

Saturday night, home alone, thoughts of a beautiful woman weighing heavy on his mind. "Careful, man," Trevor muttered to himself as he flipped through channels, not finding anything worth settling on.

Saturday night television. It was like playing Russian Roulette with his imagination; he knew. "Movie night, methinks," he said, flipping over to Netflix. A good, *long* movie with an epic score by Hans Zimmer, or Danny Elfman.

TEN

PHOEBE WOKE WITH A start, gasping for air in the pitch black, her whole body trembling. She'd fallen asleep fully clothed, and from what she could tell, the night was well underway. She'd slept straight through dinner, straight through the evening, straight through her date with Stan—they'd made plans to go out tonight to celebrate landing another book cover contract, this one for a series of four books, all featuring the handsome mechanic.

Shaking off the elusive dream that had her shoulders tight and her jaw aching from clenching it, she rose and headed downstairs to find her cell phone. Had Stan called? Or stopped by when she didn't show up at The Tudor House Pub?

Switching on a few low-light lamps, she made her way to her bag where she'd dropped it just inside the front door. The screen on the phone showed no calls, no texts, no messages at all. Strange.

It was after 10 PM, but they'd planned to meet downtown two hours ago. She pushed redial, knowing his was the last number she'd called.

"Hey, Phoebe Gustafson. Where have you been?" His velvet drawl swirled through the phone after only one ring, but the noise in the background told her he wasn't really missing her. He'd just partied without her, as far as she could tell.

"Sorry. I fell asleep."

Stan laughed out loud. "You really know how to bolster a man's ego, darling."

Phoebe smiled ruefully and shook her head over her insensitive statement. "That didn't come out right. I did fall asleep, but not because of you. It's been a long week, and I'm just really worn down. I was out cold at about five o'clock this afternoon. But I'm wide awake now. Where are you? Want some company?"

Through the phone, Phoebe heard a female voice call out something too muffled for her to understand, followed by a cheer of appreciation. Sounded like he already had all the company he needed. His next words confirmed it.

"Nah, get some rest, beautiful. I'm getting ready to head out in about an hour, anyway. Got an early morning at the shop tomorrow."

Phoebe didn't miss a beat, refusing to let on that his rejection of her company stung just the tiniest bit. "Oh good. I'm glad you're all right with that. I've got a project due next week, and I could use the extra time to put into it." *Stop now, Phoebe girl. You're rambling.* She lowered her voice to a sexy purr and brought her mouth close to the phone. "Forgive me, big guy?"

"What was that?" Stan's voice rose as the noise around him did, too. "I didn't hear that last bit."

"Never mind," Phoebe said, grimacing. "I'll see you here on Tuesday, okay? Don't be late."

"Unlike some people I know, I always show up when I'm supposed to, woman." He said it with laughter in his voice, but Phoebe thought she might have caught a hint of disappointment in there, too.

She really liked Stan. He had a handsome boy-next-door face that made it hard to decide whether you wanted to tuck him in with a kiss on the forehead, or crawl under the covers next to him with a kiss on that full mouth of his. He had a steady job and good work ethic, he didn't seem to have a girlfriend, and from what she could tell, he was respectful to those around him. He made a good companion for Phoebe—they were each other's arm candy, if not exactly friends with benefits. Although if he ever offered, she might actually consider it... even though in the end, she'd most likely refuse him, anyway. People liked to think she was trashy, and she did nothing to contradict the assumption, but it was all part of the game she played. In some sick way, she liked knowing she had everyone fooled, that the rest of the world was so easily duped by a pretty face and feminine curves.

But the fact that he hadn't missed her, hadn't even bothered calling to check on her, to find out why she hadn't shown up when she said she would, told her something was shifting.

"I'm losing my touch," she murmured, her voice loud in the quiet room. Dropping into a chair, she rested her head against the seat back, stretching out her legs in front of her, and crossing her ankles. She let her hands hang limply over the padded armrests. Her phone slipped from her grasp to the painted concrete floor, but she didn't pick it up, not even caring if it was still in one piece or not.

In fact, right now, she didn't care about much of anything. A tear gathered in the corner of one eye, then another, and soon they were falling slowly, but steadily, running down over her angled cheekbones, dripping off her jawline, and dampening the neckline of the top she wore. She wept soundlessly, her breath catching only slightly now and then. The release felt good, though, and Phoebe didn't resist.

Finally, she stood and wandered over to the table that held her pottery wheel, running her hands over the surface of the bat, chalky with prolonged disuse. Her fingertips came away dusty, and she sighed and sniffed, swiping at her cheeks with the back of her knuckles, feeling the growing urge to create something new, to pour whatever this indefinable emotion was into something outside of herself.

Phoebe filled a bucket with water, lined up her tools—a few sponges, a metal rib, a wooden sculpting tool, and a wire tool—and straddling her stool, she slid up to the table, the wheel and its bowl wedged between her knees. She draped an old towel over her lap, then taking a deep breath, she drew a large cooler out from under the table, and pulled out a plastic bag of gray clay, a lump about the size of a softball. She was pleased to find it was still pliable and elastic.

She formed it into an egg and dropped it in the center of the wheel. She had no idea what she wanted to make, but she wanted to feel the slick, smooth texture of the clay beneath her fingers, against the palms of her hands, the motion of the wheel spinning and spinning, swirling away her heavy thoughts until all that remained was the sensation of inspiration pouring from her heart through her veins to her fingertips.

Less than an hour later, she slid the wire tool beneath her creation to separate it from the wheel, and carefully moved it to a shelf close by to set. She'd made a delicate tulip bowl complete with a scalloped rim, and she'd carved an intricate pattern of cherry blossoms around the inside lip of it, imagining Granny G's delight when she opened it at Christmas.

Her phone rang, and she glanced at the huge wall clock that hung near the front door. Who on earth would be calling her after eleven at night? Had Stan changed his mind after all?

Wiping her hands on the towel across her knees, she scooped up the phone from the floor where she'd dropped it earlier.

Ren? *Ren! Oh no. Oh no, oh no, oh no.*

Tim and the boys were out of town for one last camping trip before the baby was born.

Renata was home alone.

· · · · **·** · **·** · · · ·

"REN?" PHOEBE SPOKE BEFORE the phone was even up to her ear.

"Hey, Phoebe. Sorry to bother you so late. Are you busy?"

Phoebe released her breath in a whoosh, relief flooding through her veins. Renata sounded ridiculously calm and relaxed.

"It's not so late, *ma cherie.* What's up with you?" But the fact that her usually uptight sister sounded so chill at 11 o'clock at night *and* was calling her—the least favorite sister of the bunch—had Phoebe's radar on high alert. Something wasn't right.

"I'm fine. What are you doing right now?"

"Why do you want to know? And you're not fine. You wouldn't be calling me if you were."

Renata huffed and said, "Okay. Then I'm as well as can be expected, under the circumstances. What are you—" Her voice suddenly cut off, and Phoebe heard Renata's sharp intake of breath hiss through the phone.

"Ren?" Phoebe stood up too quickly and had to grab the table's edge, the sudden movement making her lightheaded. "Rennie?" she repeated when her sister didn't respond.

"I'm—I'm okay. But I need—" Ren drew in a long breath and then let it out into the phone like she was blowing out candles. "I need help, I think." Another breath. "I may need someone to take me to the hospital. I'm in stupid labor." The petulant words sounded like they were ground out through clenched teeth.

"Have you called Tim?" Phoebe interjected the man's name between Ren's heavy breaths, but she was already scurrying around the room, gathering up her bag, snatching her car keys off her desk, and shoving her feet into a pair of Mary Janes, shoes she knew would be comfortable for the long haul.

"Not home—until tomorrow. Can't reach him. No service or he's not answering."

"Jules?" Phoebe couldn't help wondering why Renata hadn't called Juliette. Or Granny G, or even Gia, before calling her.

"She's out with Vic. It's Saturday night, remember?"

Right. Saturday night was Date Night for Vic and Jules. Every week, like clockwork. Those two were made for each other.

Renata released a long, cleansing breath right into Phoebe's ear. Her voice relaxed again, and she said, "I didn't want to call Granny G, either. She hasn't been feeling well, and I don't want to get a cold right now. Besides, she's already agreed to keep the boys while we're at the hospital."

Phoebe tried not to read anything into her sister's statements, tried not to take things personally. It didn't matter that Phoebe was clearly Ren's last choice on the call list, other than Gia. Had she really expected any differently? The fact that she was on the list at all had to mean something, right? At least Phoebe came before Ren's church friends.

"I'll be right over. But let me call Jules anyway and see if Vic can't figure out a way to get a hold of Tim. Maybe call the Forest Service people or something. Don't all those departments know each other—law enforcement, forestry service, fire department?" She waved her free hand in a big circle as though Ren could see her. "He needs to be here."

"I know, I know. And I'm sure he could figure something out—you know Victor. I didn't want to spoil their date, though. It's not like I haven't been through this before. I kinda know what to expect, you know?"

"Ren, seriously?" Phoebe couldn't believe she was hearing the conscientious words come out of her sister's mouth. "Okay, listen. Sit tight. I'm heading over now, and I'll call Vic as soon as I get there. Unless you want me to call him now."

Ren didn't answer right away, and Phoebe held her breath, willing herself not to panic. "You alright?"

"I'm—fine. Sounds like a—plan." Her sister's voice trembled a little, making her sound young and vulnerable. Something tugged painfully in Phoebe's chest, and she pressed the heel of her palm to her sternum.

"I'll be right there!" Phoebe hung up the phone and jerked open her front door, snatching a denim jacket off the large coat rack as she passed by it. She slipped one arm into it, locked her door, and had Xena backed out into the street before she realized she still only had the jacket half on.

"Thank God for small towns," Phoebe muttered to herself as she slipped it on the rest of the way. The night air was a little chilly, and she was glad she'd brought it; the topless Jeep made for a brisk drive.

In less than ten minutes, she was pulling up outside Renata's home, her cell to her ear, waiting for Juliette to pick up.

ELEVEN

"Hey, Phebes." Juliette gave no indication that the call was interrupting anything, but Juliette always answered her phone that way.

"Jules! I'm glad you picked up. Sorry to bug you on your hot date, but I just pulled up at Ren's house. She can't get a hold of Tim—she thinks he's out of cell phone range—and she's in labor. Can you ask Vic if he can figure out how to reach him?" The words gushed out of Phoebe as she clambered out of her Jeep and hurried toward Renata's front door. It stood open just a bit, causing a shiver of alarm to race up her spine.

"What? Oh, no!" Juliette's gasp spurred Phoebe on a little faster, and she pushed open the door, gently, in case Renata was right behind it. "I'll let Vic know and we'll be over as soon as we can," Juliette finished.

"Ren?" Phoebe called out as she entered the house, the phone still pressed to her ear. "Where are you?"

"I'm here," Renata said, her tone grumpy and breathy. She poked her head out of the bathroom in the hall.

"I have Jules on the phone. You okay? You want her and Vic to come over, too?"

"No, no," Renata waved off the suggestion, her gesture impatient. She moved slowly, uncomfortably, out into the hallway. "I just need him to get a hold of Tim for me. Now. This baby isn't going to wait for him to get back tomorrow night."

"Did you hear that?" Phoebe said into the phone.

"Should we come over there or meet you at the hospital?" Juliette asked.

"Do you need me to take you to the hospital now, Rennie?" Phoebe asked. "They can meet us there instead."

"I don't know," Renata snapped, and then closed her eyes and leaned against the wall, both hands wrapped around her belly, her shoulders hunched forward, chin lowered. The pose made it look like she was holding herself up. "I need John," Renata moaned softly. "Oh God, I need John," this time in a broken whisper.

Phoebe stiffened at the name that escaped her sister's lips, shock and grief crashing through her in a tidal wave of surprise. "Oh, Rennie," she murmured, rushing to Renata's side.

"Jules," she said into the phone, "I gotta go. I'll call you in a few minutes and let you know what we've decided, okay? In the meantime, please have Vic do whatever he can to find Tim."

Phoebe shoved the phone in her bra and gently pulled Renata into her arms. Ren let go of her belly and slipped her arms up around Phoebe's neck and then sagged into her. It hurt a little, Ren's forehead pressing against her collarbone, but Phoebe didn't dare shift her position; her sister clung to her like she'd never let go.

Phoebe couldn't remember the last time she'd actually embraced Ren—any of her sisters, for that matter. Not real hugs, anyway; the kind that lasted for more than a simple greeting or celebration required. And as awkward as this felt with Baby Charise, a hard globe between them, Phoebe suddenly ached for what she'd been missing.

Renata pressed her head harder into Phoebe's shoulder and moaned again, her hands clutching the collar of Phoebe's jacket. "This is a strong one. Sorry." The words were muffled between them, and Phoebe held on, biting her own lip to keep from yelping in pain. She was certain she'd come out of this with bruises.

"John—held me—like this," Renata ground out between breaths. "He was so much better—at giving birth than I was." She half-sobbed, half-laughed, breathing in short, punctuated pants. "So strong—and patient—with me." Phoebe felt the wetness of her sister's tears on her chest. "I miss him so much."

"I know, Rennie," Phoebe murmured into her hair.

Standing there in the dimly lit hallway, holding her laboring sister upright, she closed her eyes and tried to look at life through Renata's eyes for a moment. John had died suddenly only a little more than eight months ago, leaving behind Renata and their four boys... and a baby girl on the way. It had taken Renata almost three months to realize she was pregnant, and then another three months for Tim, John's best friend, to convince her that marrying him—and loving him, and letting him love her and John's children—was the best thing for all of them. What a huge leap of faith it must have been for someone like Renata, who controlled everything but the weather in her world, and even that wasn't beyond the scope of imagination. To trust someone like Tim, even though she'd known him for years, someone who'd never been married, never had children, to step into John's superhero shoes?

"Oh, *where* is Tim?" Renata moaned, her breathing easing, her grip loosening. She straightened a little and took a deep breath. "Why did I let him go away this weekend? I promised him he wouldn't miss out on any part of this, and I should have known better. This little girl has been bouncing her head on my bladder for weeks, but over the last few days, I've felt like I was walking around with a coconut between my legs. What was I thinking, telling him to take off like this? One last *grand* adventure—ha! And with the boys, no less!" Her words came fast and furious, spiked with genuine frustration more than any real anger.

"There's the Renata I know and love," Phoebe quipped. The lines of discomfort etching Ren's forehead had eased noticeably. "So, do you want me to take you to the hospital?"

"Not yet. These contractions are still only about fifteen minutes apart, and my water hasn't broken. If all goes as it usually does, I figure I've got another hour or two before I have to think about going in." Renata's deliveries were historically by the book, lasting eight to ten hours, and transitioning from one phase to the next like clockwork. "Although there have been a few differences this time, and I'm a little afraid of being caught by surprise." She rolled her eyes and rubbed her stomach in slow, swirling movements. "Like now, Charise Olivia Larsen. You're not due for another two weeks," she cooed, her tone making the statement a caress rather than a reprimand.

"Well, I'm happy to keep you company," Phoebe said, meaning every word. Almost. Happy might not be the right choice of adjectives. She was honored her sister had called her, and she was glad it had worked out that she was available. But as the full scope of what might lie ahead began to play out in her mind, Phoebe felt a balloon of trepidation begin to inflate inside her chest. "But I'm going to bet on Vic and his ability to hunt down Tim, okay? He'll make it."

Renata took Phoebe's hand and pulled her toward the living room. "I'm glad you're here, Phoebe. As much as I hate to admit it, I really don't want to do this alone, even the waiting for Tim part, and I'm glad it's you here with me now."

Phoebe chuckled, not quite knowing how to take the rare compliment from Renata. "Are you sure you wouldn't rather I call Juliette? With Vic hunting down Tim, I'm sure she's available now." She intended it to be a joke, but it came out sounding sincere, maybe even a little pouty. Perhaps because under the jesting, the question was legitimate. Renata had never purposely chosen Phoebe's company over anyone else in all the years she could remember.

"No. You're the one I want. Juliette would be fine until she witnessed a contraction. Then she'd freak out and either cry or ask Victor to come help—no, thank you."

When Phoebe saw the sofa, she chuckled. "You're nothing, if not prepared, Ren darling." A large trash bag lay spread out on the cushions, several layers of thick bath towels on top, and one of the pillows from Ren's bed propped against the arm of the couch. On the coffee table sat a tray of refreshments, complete with a bowl of bite-sized fruit—grapes, blueberries, boysenberries, even cantaloupe cut into cubes—Ren's favorite vanilla-flavored Greek Yogurt, a ramekin of almonds, and a pitcher of fragrant herbal iced tea.

"I just didn't think I'd need backup, you know? Tim has been like a helicopter these last few weeks, hovering and swooping, making sure I had everything I needed at my fingertips. I suppose that's why I sent him off—I needed a little breathing room. But I never thought...." She waved a hand around, indicating the empty house, and then lowered herself onto her side on the sofa, making sure not to mess up the towels and plastic covering. She closed her eyes, took a deep breath and let it out slowly, her body deflating as she tried to relax. "You've always been my first choice, Phoebe. For back up," Ren murmured, almost to herself. "I should have asked you long ago."

Phoebe sat in a high-backed armchair and studied her sister in silence, a rush of intense emotion making it hard to breathe for a moment. Ren looked like she might even be drifting off, and Phoebe knew not to disturb her. If a laboring woman could get some rest between contractions, she absolutely should. Besides, it gave her time to attempt to wrap her head around all the things Ren had divulged in the few minutes since she'd arrived.

Things on the Dixon-Larsen home front weren't as idealistic as Phoebe had assumed. Tim was a helicopter husband, something John, Ren's first husband, had *not* been. Even when there were times he should have considered being so. No wonder his wife missed him, especially now. He had been the cool head of reason in their marriage, no matter where Renata's head had been, and now it seemed that Renata was being forced to step up.

Not that the notion was a bad thing. The downside to John's unflappability was that it allowed his wife to be somewhat unrestrained. Renata had always inferred that she led a perfectly ordered life, but in reality, she really was just a high-strung control freak who was judgmental and stuck up, to boot. For the duration of their marriage, John had cleaned up after Renata's meltdowns, and although he apparently didn't mind—his love for her seemed to transcend reason—he hadn't really made anything easier on anyone by not calling Renata on her behavior.

And now, although she had a man who rivaled any six-packed stud Phoebe had ever photographed, painted, or sculpted—real or imagined—Tool Belt Tim apparently had chinks in his armor, and maybe even a few missing tools in his belt. A few missing screws, too—what sane man would take on a grief-stricken, pregnant widow, and her four preteen boys?

Renata, dear coddled Renata, was having to think about the ramifications of her own actions. She was finding out what it felt like to be alone, even when surrounded by loved ones. How to be strong because no one else would be strong for her—or when no one else could offer her the kind of strength she needed.

No, it wasn't such a bad thing that the lickable Tool Belt Tim wasn't so perfect after all. Which meant Renata Gustafson Dixon Larsen's life wasn't so perfect after all, either.

Even more surprising, Renata had not only admitted, but insisted that Phoebe, of all the women in the family, was her first go-to girl on the list. The thought made Phoebe warm contentedly inside, and she wondered if she glowed just the tiniest bit in the dimly lit room. Never in a million years would she have imagined Renata would choose her to be her support over everyone else in the lineup. Something had truly changed in Renata, and in turn, it was triggering some kind of a reactionary change in Phoebe.

Phoebe wasn't sure she was ready for it, though. Happy to be here? No, still not the right word. But content with the way things were at the moment? Yes.

"That'll do, donkey," she whispered into the stillness, quoting a favorite line from the movie *Shrek*, one she'd watched a hundred times or more with her nephews. "That'll do."

Renata didn't open her eyes, but the corners of her mouth lifted in a gentle smile.

A few minutes later, she moaned softly and drew her knees up a little higher, rounding her shoulders forward again. "Here comes another one. Maybe you can help me get up."

TWELVE

An hour later, the contractions were definitely getting closer together, down to about every ten minutes. Renata was still putting off heading to the hospital, but they were also getting more difficult, and she'd begun to weep silently during the last one, the tears interfering with her breathing. Phoebe counted, rubbed, paced, and took deep cleansing breaths with her sister, all her senses tuned into the natural rhythm and rending of childbirth. She knew Ren was waiting to hear from Tim, but Phoebe was feeling quite unsettled about waiting any longer.

Her phone vibrated against her chest inside her bra just after midnight. Ren was on her knees on the sofa, her head resting on her crossed arms on the back of it, while Phoebe gently rocked her hips for her and swept long, slow strokes up her spine and over her shoulders, making soothing noises with her movements. She paused in her ministrations to answer the phone.

"Phoebe, Tim here." His uncharacteristically abrupt tone spoke volumes about his frame of mind.

"Hey there," she murmured, keeping her voice low, not wanting to say who it was until she knew what he had to say. "Where are you?"

"I'm about half an hour away. How is she?"

Phoebe glanced at the huge wall clock mounted above the mantle; she'd been monitoring Renata's contractions with it. It had been just over five minutes since the last one, but the woman on the sofa was beginning to make small, sighing moans again, a sound Phoebe was growing to recognize. She didn't think it wise to put things off much longer, especially now that they'd gotten a hold of Tim. "She's doing great, but I'm thinking we should probably head to the hospital shortly. Can you meet us there?"

"Is that Tim?" Renata asked, her words muffled against her arms.

Tim spoke at the same time. "The hospital. Yes. Can I talk to her?" Phoebe heard fear in the gravelly edges of his words.

"Of course. And Tim? She's doing great," she assured him again. "I mean it."

"Thanks, Phoebe." He had to clear his throat before continuing. "I'm sorry I'm not there right now, but I'm glad you are. Thank you."

"Of course," she said again. "Here's Ren." She reached out and touched her sister's shoulder. "It's Tim, Rennie."

Phoebe turned away and busied herself with straightening some of the items on the coffee table, giving the couple a moment to talk privately. The conversation was short out of necessity, and Renata grunted as she handed the phone back to her. "As soon as I get through this next contraction, we should probably go."

Phoebe took the phone and once more assured Tim that his wife was doing fine before hanging up. Renata began to rock back and forth on her knees, her head down, hands now clutching the back of the sofa, the singsong moans a little louder this time. Phoebe once again pressed the heels of her palms into Ren's low back, applying counter pressure against her tailbone.

Suddenly, a gush of fluid burst from between Renata's legs, and she cried out in surprise. Phoebe jumped back a little, her eyes wide, and let loose a startled curse.

"Bad word," Renata growled.

Phoebe giggled, fighting off the surge of hysteria clawing its way up her throat. "Are you reprimanding me, or are you saying 'bad word' in lieu of an actual bad word?"

"Bad word," Ren said again, making her intent quite clear. "Bad word, bad word, bad word." She took another deep breath and carefully rose up off the couch, making sure to stand over a towel as more liquid sluiced down her legs from beneath the soft knit maternity dress she wore. "My overnight bag is already in my car, but can you please grab some extra towels for my seat?" She grunted in frustration and clutched at her hard stomach. "Slow down, baby girl. Wait for Ti—wait for Daddy, okay?"

Phoebe made certain Ren was steady before dashing down the hall to the bathroom. The hospital was less than ten minutes away, but things had suddenly progressed much quicker than expected. A low moan from the living room had her madly scrabbling for towels, not bothering to close the cupboard doors behind her, as she careened back out to find Ren, once more on her knees on the sofa, caught in the throes of another contraction.

"Already?" Phoebe shot a look at the clock. Less than five minutes. "Ren?"

But her sister was breathing in short, sharp pants, her expression one of shock and fear. Her eyes bore into Phoebe's. "Help me, Phoebe. I can't—" A half-sob burst out between breaths. "Too fast."

"I'm calling 911," Phoebe muttered as she moved around to the back of the couch so she could get eye-to-eye with her sister. "Let's not do this here, okay?"

"They'll take—too long. You take—me to—the hospital." Renata punched the words out between clenched teeth. "Now!" Before the contraction was completely over, she was already pushing up off the sofa and grabbing at one of the towels in Phoebe's arms. "Call the hospital and tell them we're coming," she commanded, and then breathed in long and deep, her exhale shuddering on the way out.

They were in the car in less than a minute, Phoebe thankful she'd parked in the driveway beside Ren's SUV rather than behind it.

Halfway there, Renata had another contraction, this one intense enough to make her cry out.

"I'm sorry, Rennie. I'm going as fast as I can." At that time of the night, there was virtually no traffic, but she didn't want to get pulled over either, so although she was speeding, she made every attempt not to drive recklessly.

As they pulled up in front of the Emergency Room entrance, another contraction hit, and Phoebe laid on the horn before scrambling out of the car and hurrying around to the passenger side to open the door. Again, Renata sobbed out loud, but Phoebe sensed it was more out of frustration than just pain.

"He's not going to make it," she moaned as a uniformed woman approached quickly, pushing a wheelchair. "Oh, Phoebe, Tim isn't going to make it." Renata moaned again as she eased her bulk into the wheelchair.

Phoebe parked in the first open spot only a few yards away, yanked the overnight bag from the back seat, and caught up to them as the attendant wheeled Renata inside. The sisters held hands as they traversed through several sets of double doors and down the endless corridors to the Labor and Delivery ward where Ren was handed over to waiting staff who already had a room prepped and ready for her.

Phoebe stayed close while a matronly nurse helped her sister out of her maternity clothes and into a hospital gown, then up onto her bed. She held Ren's hand through another contraction. A doctor swept in, introduced himself as Dr. Adams and deftly put Ren's feet up into stirrups and performed a quick and efficient internal exam.

"Well, my dear, you're progressing nicely, I'd say. Dilated about eight centimeters, so it's a good thing you decided to come in." He removed her feet from the stirrups and draped the sheet over her with quick, sure movements. "Your doctor has been notified and is on his way, but we're ready when you and your baby are, okay?"

Phoebe liked this Dr. Adams. He looked to be in his fifties, his hair halfway between blond and gray, his features warm and open. He moved intentionally and confidently, a calm spirit exuding off him as he made his way around the room, communicating with his staff while they hooked Renata up to monitors, and prepared the necessary equipment for the pending birth. She knew Renata would prefer her own doctor, the man who'd delivered all four boys, and walked her through several miscarriages, but if he didn't make it on time—a distinct possibility—Phoebe thought Dr. Adams would do just fine.

For which she was glad. Suddenly, the enormity of the situation struck her, and she closed her eyes and held her breath to block out the sights and smells enveloping her. It was all she could do not to cover her ears like a child.

"Stay with me, Phoebe. Don't leave me," Renata murmured, still clutching her hand.

"I'm not going anywhere," Phoebe promised, opening her eyes and letting the words out on a release of air. She had to keep it together; for Ren, for Baby Charise, for everyone. For herself and her own pride, she had to step outside herself and focus on her sister.

Phoebe took a deep breath and eyed the monitor on the other side of the bed, grateful for something to concentrate on. "Looks like another one is coming, Rennie. Take a deep breath in through the nose and out through the mouth. Breathe with me."

• • • • • ● • ● • • •

LESS THAN HALF AN hour after they'd arrived at the hospital, Tim pushed into the room, a hulking mass of tightly wound man-flesh. In spite of the situation, Phoebe took a moment to appreciate the sight of him practically storming the gates to get to his woman and child. She smiled in welcome as he hurried to Renata's other side, where he bent over her and kissed her tenderly on the forehead. Then a nurse practically dragged him to the sink to thoroughly wash his hands before letting him back to the bedside.

Renata burst into tears of relief as her own Dr. Flynn bustled into the room only moments after Tim, a huge smile softening his sleepy features. He shook Tim's hand, patted Renata's shoulder, and then scanned the monitors as the nurse filled him in on any details not on the screen in front of him.

The room quieted as Renata's whimpers turned into a deep moan when a powerful contraction swept over her. Phoebe took a step back, suddenly uncertain of what her role now was, but Renata thrust out her hand and grabbed her wrist. Her pain-filled eyes zoned in on Phoebe's. "Stay. Please. I—need—you," she gasped out.

Tim nodded, his gaze wide with shock and concern, clearly unprepared to witness the woman he loved in such distress. "What should I do?" he asked quietly, stepping close to Phoebe. "How can I help?"

Phoebe took his hand and put Renata's into his. "Just stay right here, close, where she can focus on your face." She smoothed the hair back from Renata's forehead and leaned close to her sister. From a long-untapped source of willpower and courage, Phoebe spoke, her voice calm, her attention focused solely on Renata's eyes. "I'm staying right here. Don't worry. We're both here. Let's do this together, okay?"

At 2:32 AM, Charise Olivia Dixon Larsen made her grand entrance into the world, a euphoric Tim and exhausted Renata both shedding tears of joy over the tiny red-faced baby girl.

At 2:38 AM, Phoebe once more bent over her sister, kissed her tenderly on the forehead, and whispered, "You were amazing, Mama Ren."

At 2:44 AM, Phoebe congratulated Tim for the third time, and then slipped from the room. She stumbled only twice as she made her way back through the winding corridors to the Emergency Room, nearly blind with unshed tears of her own, and out into the parking lot where Renata's car was parked.

She kept it together until she had slipped behind the wheel of the SUV and pulled the door closed behind her. Then she covered her face in her hands and released the pent-up agony that had been building inside her, great wrenching sobs tearing through her body as wave after wave of memories washed over her.

THIRTEEN

Sunday morning, Trevor and Ricky sat shoulder-to-shoulder in the amphitheater seats of the big sanctuary where they attended church. Gia hadn't made an appearance, and Ricky's expression clearly showed his concern. He'd tried texting her when the service started, but she'd not responded. He kept checking his phone periodically throughout the hour of worship, and Trevor was sure the kid hadn't heard a word of the sermon.

The last song was sung, and the pastor dismissed them all with a prayer of benediction. Trevor felt a slight surge of adrenaline rush through his veins at the thought of the coming meal, the company he'd be spending it in.

It was just after eleven and lunch wouldn't be ready for another hour or so, and he'd hoped Vic and Juliette would come by to listen to a few of his new songs before heading over to the Gustafsons. But he hadn't seen them in their usual row, either.

Juliette had become one of his favorite beta-listeners; she loved his music, but it was her deeply sensitive nature and intuitiveness that provided him with exceptional feedback. She had yet to give him suggestions that weren't spot-on, and in fact, on this album alone, some of the changes he'd made because of her thoughts had turned good songs into great songs. He was anxious to see what she thought of his latest pieces.

Maybe Ricky was right to be worried. He glanced over at his young cousin, an eyebrow raised in question.

"Nothing. I'm going to try calling her again outside."

Trevor nodded in agreement and gestured for Ricky to go on ahead of him. He stopped and spoke with Tom and Michelle Peterson, the older couple who had dedicated themselves to mentoring the college-aged and young career adults in the church. They hadn't seen Vic and Juliette that morning, either, and when Trevor looked up to see Ricky hurrying back down the long aisle toward him, a knot of worry formed in his gut.

"They're all at the hospital," Ricky announced without preamble, the words bringing all conversations around them to a stand-still. Everyone collectively held their breath as they waited to hear what had the Gustafson family at the hospital. "Gia's sister had her baby last night."

Relief rode on the voices that rose in excitement and joy as Michelle pushed Ricky for details and a few of the other people clustered around them gathered close for information, too. But Ricky, being a typical eighteen-year-old guy, had no information to pass on, other than that Gia had said everyone was fine.

"Dinner is postponed until next week, and they still want us there if we can make it." He hesitated briefly, and then added, "Gia said we can go see the baby if we want to." His expression made Trevor grin—Ricky clearly had serious misgivings about the merits of the notion.

"Do you want to go?" he asked, a spark of excitement igniting in his belly where the worry had been only moments ago. "I wouldn't mind dropping in if she's serious about us visiting. Have you ever seen a newborn, Ricky?"

"Um, I don't know." Ricky's noncommittal response made Trevor want to laugh out loud.

"You don't know if you want to go? Or you don't know if you've ever seen a newborn before?" Trevor teased.

"Oh, leave the poor boy alone," Michelle interjected, reaching out to place a stilling hand on Trevor's forearm. "Why don't you two join us for lunch if your plans have changed? A bunch of us are meeting at The Griddle in about an hour." She cocked her head and peered up at Trevor, her eyes narrowing. "Unless you really do want to go see the new baby...." Her voice trailed off as she studied his face, her eyes seeing more than he'd intended.

He *did* want to see the baby. The thought lodged in his mind and held on. His fingers clenched tightly into fists in resistance to the urge to hold a warm bundle of life in his arms, to cup a down-covered head in the palm of his hand, to feel tiny fingers curl around his. *Baby fever.* The words sucker-punched him, and he swallowed hard. He'd heard countless women coo and sigh those words over babies in the last couple of years, as many of his peers had started families of their own. He'd never heard a man admit it, though.... *This is baby fever*, his mind insisted. *Oh God, I have baby fever.*

Not only was he going crazy without a woman in his life, but now he was imagining a child—a baby of his own—cradled in his arms, held securely against his heart, a soft cheek pressed to his shoulder. A longing so fierce it made his chest ache. *What is wrong with me?*

He cleared his throat and turned to Ricky to avoid the questions in Michelle's eyes. No, he did not want to go to lunch with the singles group, not after the startling revelation he'd just had. Even as he tried to push the desire from his mind, he couldn't help but wonder at the intensity of it. He didn't want a plate of fried food. He wanted to see that baby. "I'm thinking I'll take a rain check on The Griddle, Z-man. I'm game for heading to the hospital. What about you?"

Ricky lifted one shoulder in a noncommittal shrug. "I guess I'm cool either way. You got any food at your place? Or maybe we should call Gia and see if she's hungry. We can take her a taco from Titos—that's her favorite place these days."

"We can do that," Trevor nodded. "In fact, when you call, ask if anyone else wants anything. We can do a food run for everyone."

"My goodness. Aren't you boys thoughtful," Michelle mused, a curious smile pulling the corners of her mouth up as she continued to study Trevor. He wouldn't meet her gaze, but he felt her sizing him up. "You tell Vic and Juliette to give us a call, okay? And let them know we're praying for the whole family; thanking God for the gift of that new baby."

They extricated themselves from the group and headed across the parking lot to Trevor's four-year-old Dodge Challenger. When he was younger, he'd watched Dukes of Hazard religiously, yearning for a General Lee car of his own. But as an adult, he preferred the old school look of the newer Challenger SRT to the curvier body of the modern Charger. He loved the fuel-efficient muscle car—he kept it running as clean as it looked—and even though he secretly agreed the racing stripes were "a bit much" as his mother put it, he liked the black on orange color scheme, his not-so-subtle nod of acknowledgment to the Duke boys.

Once they were both buckled in, Trevor grinned satisfyingly as the car rumbled to life beneath them. It wasn't nearly as loud as his Harley, but the V8 growled like a hungry beast all the same. While Ricky made his phone call, Trevor let the car idle while he considered his unsettling feelings.

The gift of a new baby, Michelle had said.

"A gift!" Trevor stiffened in his seat and turned to look at Ricky, who was just ending his call. "We need to bring a gift, don't we?"

The younger guy looked bemused, and then with growing revulsion, he blurted out, "You're not going to make me shop for baby clothes, are you?"

"No, no!" Although, much to his chagrin, Trevor got a visual of the two of them perusing an aisle of miniature clothing together. Another glance at Ricky's horrified face, and he discarded that imagery without any difficulty. He'd much rather peruse baby clothes with a woman at his side. *His* woman by his side. *Lord, have mercy. Stop.* "No, I mean like flowers or balloons or something."

"Taz. Dude. I am not going to buy a bunch of flowers and balloons with you. Not cool." Ricky crossed his arms over his chest and stared straight ahead. "Can't we just get tacos? That's a gift, right?"

Trevor punched him lightly in the shoulder. "Don't worry. I won't make you carry anything too pretty. Besides, I'm sure there's a gift shop at the hospital. We can just grab something once we get there."

"I'm holding you to that. I'm not carrying balloons or flowers. It'd be one thing if they were for Gia, but Renata scares me a little. I'd rather she not notice me at all."

Trevor laughed outright and shifted into reverse, backing slowly out of the parking spot. Nothing like Sunday morning congregants loitering in the parking lot. "So, are we off to hunt down wild tacos for the women and children?"

"Actually, only for us and Gia. No one else wants anything."

"Oh. Okay." Trevor glanced at the clock on the dashboard. It wasn't quite noon yet, but surely, they hadn't all eaten already. "Okay," he said again, and pulled out of the parking lot, the car surging forward as he shifted gears.

They stopped at the taco stand and loaded up on a myriad of entrees anyway, enough to feed an army: two shredded beef tacos, an order of chicken taquitos, a couple of *carne asada* burritos, and a *chille relleno* burrito for Trevor. Ricky insisted that he and Gia could eat the majority of the food themselves, and Trevor agreeably doled out the money for all of it. It hadn't been that long ago when he could eat one of everything on a menu, too.

At the hospital, the gift shop was open, and a pretty teenager came out from behind the register to offer them help in finding the right gift to take up to the third floor with them. She spoke to Trevor, answering all his questions and making a few suggestions of her own, but her eyes rarely left Ricky's face. She seemed fascinated by the way his hair kept flopping over one eye, and when Trevor noticed her chewing on her bottom lip, he decided to put the poor girl out of her misery. He quickly selected a square glass vase filled with a short bouquet of sunburst-colored roses and a mishmash of greenery and opted not to wait for the girl—Brenda—to fill a bunch of balloons for them. Instead, he snatched up a little stuffed mouse with big ears and a pink bow around its neck.

"It plays 'Somewhere Out There' when you squeeze its ear," Brenda said, her eyes begging for some kind of a response from the oblivious Ricky. "See? You try it." She held it out toward him, and Trevor rolled his eyes when Ricky shook his head.

"That's cool. I believe you."

Brenda smiled bravely, took the credit card from Trevor, who cringed when she told him the total due, and said a sweet, sad goodbye to them as they hurried out of the shop. Ricky had his phone out and was texting Gia to let her know they were on their way up, so he didn't even notice the girl's tragic farewell.

• • • • • • • • •

THEY FOUND THE RIGHT floor, the right wing, and even the right room without mishap, mainly because the tall, willowy Gia stood in the corridor waving them down the minute they pushed through the double doors of the ward. When they slipped into the room behind the girl, they were greeted warmly by Juliette, Vic, and Renata.

A very large man sat on the side of Renata's bed, a beefy hand resting possessively on her thigh beneath the bed linens. *Renata's husband, Tim,* Trevor decided. And beside him, in a chair pulled close to his mother's bed, was Renata's oldest son, Reuben, a tiny, blanketed baby in his arms. Trevor smiled in greeting at the young teenager, lifting his chin in the universal nod recognized by men of all ages. Gia had brought the star struck kid over to listen to music a few times; Reuben now had a copy of every Trevor Zander album in existence, and digital files of a few unreleased acoustic numbers as well.

The grandparents weren't there, but since Renata's three younger boys were also absent, perhaps they'd already left for the day and taken the boys with them.

Phoebe Gustafson was also not accounted for, and the immediate and overwhelming disappointment caught Trevor unawares, leaving him feeling like a deflated balloon. He had to press his lips together to keep from asking where she was; they were there to congratulate the parents and their new baby.

Tim rose and introduced himself, but he didn't stray far from his wife's side. He, too, wore the satisfied smile of a man who recognized a job well done. Trevor considered Tim's role in the blessed event, and even though neither Reuben nor Baby Charise were genetically his children, there was no mistaking the look of a proud father and husband.

Trevor added his vase of flowers to the others lined up on the counter beside the sink, but handed the stuffed mouse to Renata, along with his congratulations.

The woman looked amazing, Trevor thought. The blue smudges beneath her eyes were the only indication she'd had an eventful night, but otherwise, Renata seemed to emanate a subtle glow, making him think of a Renaissance Madonna painting. A soft smile molded her pale lips, her cheeks were pink with happiness, and her gaze never lingered long away from the baby in her son's arms. As he watched her, she reached out and stroked the dark wisps of hair on top of the baby's head, then brushed the backs of her fingers against Reuben's cheek. It was an almost unearthly tableau, the purest love of a mother for her children. Trevor had to look away, an odd sense of guilt over having witnessed the intimate exchange.

"Would you like to hold her?"

He almost missed the question, having forced his attention away from the woman sitting upright in the bed. He turned back abruptly. "Me?"

"Yes, you," Renata said, her smile still warm, friendly. "Reuben was getting ready to hand her back right before you two showed up. She's perfectly content right now, so take advantage of the moment if you want to hold her. She'll be ready to eat again in about half an hour and you'll have missed your chance." She spoke with a teasing lilt, but Trevor realized she meant what she said.

"Well, yes. Yes, I'd like to hold her." He moved to the sink to wash his hands first and then circled the bed to sit down in the chair vacated by Reuben. Trevor swore he could feel the weight of Tim's measured gaze on him, but the need to hold the tiny girl in his arms was unrelenting, and he kept his eyes averted from the big man to his left. Instead, he focused on steadying his hands, on relaxing his shoulders, on making it appear as though this wasn't the first time he'd ever held a brand new baby.

Reuben laid the infant in Trevor's arms, his voice cracking a little when he spoke. "She just farted on my arm, so good luck with that. The nurse said that's a good sign she'll probably poop soon."

"Thanks for the warning," Trevor said, a flutter of nerves and excitement making his throat tight. But when he peered down into the tiny face, the closed eyes with only a hint of eyelashes resting against flower petal cheeks, a pointy little chin beneath a mouth no larger than the end of his thumb, the tightness moved to his chest, making it feel like his heart was too full to be contained within. The miracle in his arms moved him in a way he'd never experienced before, and he began humming softly, his soul overflowing with wonder, words of praise and worship finding their way into the lilting melody.

The room fell silent around him, but he barely noticed. He slipped his hand beneath the baby's head, marveling at the way the curve of her skull seemed designed to be held that way, and his thumb traced the half-circle of her ear.

Charise's nearly translucent eyelids fluttered, her lips fell open with a little smacking sound, and he felt the tiny body tense in his arms. He stopped singing, momentarily concerned, and the silence was replaced by the sound of the baby girl filling her diaper.

Everyone burst into laughter around the room, making the baby startle in his arms. Her eyes popped open, and she seemed to look accusingly at him, as if holding him responsible for the loud noise. Then she blinked slowly and began bumping her face against his chest in movements that reminded him of newborn puppies. Nonplussed, he lifted a questioning gaze to Renata, who grinned and held out her arms for Charise.

"That's my girl," she said, her voice ringing with pride. "Although, if we ever have any trouble with constipation, now I know who to call," she teased. But her eyes shimmered with what he could only assume were unshed tears. "That was beautiful, Trevor," she murmured as he leaned over the bed and handed her the baby. "Thank you. I don't know that anyone has ever sung a blessing over my newborn baby before today."

Trevor straightened, a lump in his throat as his eyes darted around the room. There were tears on Juliette's cheeks and she brushed them away with her fingertips, even while she smiled at him. Vic was dry-eyed, but he nodded his appreciation. Tim cleared his throat and stood to gather supplies for changing Charise's diaper. Reuben had joined Ricky and Gia in the corner, and the three of them huddled over the paper bags of food. But Gia caught his gaze, and her eyes were bright, her smile sweet.

"That was amazing, Taz. You should record that for Charise," she declared around a bite of taco. "Right, Ricky?" She elbowed Ricky and he grunted, nodding agreeably, his mouth too full to speak.

"You should," Reuben responded in Ricky's stead. "It was pretty cool."

"Where's Phoebe?" Trevor asked, the question slipping out unchecked, almost as though the words had waited until his guard was down and then made their escape.

The room stilled again. And then, as she efficiently unwrapped the lower half of the blanket swaddling Charise and changed the tiny, soiled diaper like she'd done it a thousand times before—*she probably has,* Trevor realized—Renata said, "She was here last night. She's catching up on the sleep she lost."

The response, as straightforward and sensible as it sounded, left a whole lot more unsaid, and Trevor raised a questioning brow in Vic's direction.

His friend shook his head, a movement so slight it was almost indiscernible, but Trevor knew the stoic man well. He'd just been strongly encouraged to drop the subject.

When he turned back to Renata, he froze. In a deft motion, the woman brought Charise to her breast, and even though she'd draped some kind of blanket over her shoulder, from where he stood, he could see the swollen mound of womanly flesh above the matching curve of the fuzzy head of the baby. He blinked, swallowed hard, and once again was filled with an overwhelming sense of awe over God's masterful design.

Trevor darted a glance at Tim. He appeared to be relaxed in his chair, his hand still resting on Renata's leg, but Trevor recognized the tightly leashed challenge in the way the man gazed up at him, clearly gauging his reaction to the scene before them. Trevor hesitated long enough to analyze his own feelings, decided what he was feeling was appropriate, nothing to feel guilty about, and he smiled, meeting the large man's gaze squarely. "Your daughter is beautiful. Congratulations, man."

"Hey Taz," Ricky called out from the corner of the room where the three teenagers sat on the floor. "Here's your burrito."

But Trevor wasn't really hungry anymore, nor was he about to slink off into a corner at that moment, even if he had been ravenous. He had his pride, by golly, and he'd done nothing to be ashamed of, felt nothing but innocent admiration over what he'd inadvertently witnessed. Besides, part of him knew if he did join the younger group and separate himself from those gathered around the nursing mother and child, he would only perpetuate the misguided notion that breastfeeding was somehow perverse or sexual, if not to those around him, perhaps in a subtle way to himself. "You guys can have it. I'll get something later."

"If you're hungry, Trevor, please eat. I don't mind," Renata urged.

Juliette laughed and dipped her head toward Gia, Ricky and Reuben. "You wouldn't know it by looking, but those two have already eaten, too."

"We're just keeping Ricky company, Jules. It would be rude to make him eat alone," Gia quipped, and then elbowed Reuben, who sat cross-legged beside her, unwrapping the *chille relleno* burrito Ricky had handed him. "Right, nephew-of-mine?"

Reuben bit off the end of the burrito before nodding. He chewed the bite maybe three times and swallowed. "Thanks for the chow, Taz."

"Chew your food, Reuben Dixon," Renata chided from the bed.

Reuben rolled his eyes at his mother. "Why don't you tell Charise to chew her food?" he retorted, and then ducked when Tim threw a little stuffed animal at him. It wasn't the mouse from Trevor and Ricky.

"Good comeback, Reub," Gia snorted, and nudged him again. The boy grinned smugly, but he did chew more.

And the tension in the room had dissipated, the young teenager's ready—albeit age-appropriately crude—acceptance of his mother's exposed breast putting everyone at ease.

Except that Trevor couldn't completely quiet the slightly unsettled feeling in his gut. A secret part of him—one he refused to give voice to—was worried about Phoebe Gustafson, and why everyone was tiptoeing around her absence.

FOURTEEN

Phoebe was drunk.

Going on her second day of it, to boot, if the early morning easterly sun peering through her windows was any indication. She squinted against the too-bright light and her eyes homed in on the nearly empty green bottle of Glenfiddich perched on the ugly clay stand she'd fashioned around it sometime in the middle of the night. She'd dozed at her potter's wheel, her head resting on her folded arms on the flat surface, and clay had dried and hardened on her hands, under her nails, sticking to the undersides of her arms. She straightened up slowly, groaning at the crick in her back. The mounting pressure behind her eyeballs foretold a hangover headache from hell whenever she stopped drinking long enough to let it kick in. When she closed her eyes, the room spun like a carnival tilt-a-wheel ride, so she pried them open again, and planted both feet firmly on the floor, lest she topple off the stool.

She reached for the bottle and wrested it from the clay that had hardened around it. It broke free, making her whole body lurch back with the release, and she whimpered into the mouth of the bottle before swallowing a long gulp of whiskey. Then she held the bottle aloft as the golden liquid seared its way down her convulsing throat.

"Hair of the Dog," she saluted, her eyes too bleary to focus on her reflection in the grouping of framed mirrors on the wall before her.

A few moments later, the additional alcohol not helping her balance any, but at least wetting her parched throat, she pushed to her feet and stumbled over to the sink. She turned the water on, pulling the spray nozzle from its base and lowering her head and arms into the deep basin. As the shockingly cold water sluiced over her, she groaned and braced herself against the counter. "Safer than a shower, safer than a shower," she muttered repeatedly, just sober enough to remember the last time she'd stepped into the shower in a similar condition, only to slip and fall, coming around much later with the water running cold over her, and a tender lump above her split left eyebrow.

She finally turned off the water, pulled her long hair around to one side, and grabbed a dishtowel from the stack folded on a shelf above the sink. She wrapped it around the ends of the loose, dripping strands, and straightened slowly, giving the wobbly world time to settle into her new perspective.

"I'm a wretched woman," Phoebe muttered to herself as she sized up the stairs leading up to her loft bedroom. Could she make it? She took a tentative step away from the counter, and although the room shifted with her, at least it seemed to be moving in the same direction as she was.

A chill shuddered through her as water dribbled down her back. Her shirt was soaked, the towel around her hair was too small to be very effective, and she needed her hands free to hold on to furniture. And since her left hand was busy holding the Glenfiddich, that meant she had to lose the towel. She left it lying on the floor and continued to the stairs, then mounted them, pausing every few steps to rest. She didn't look up or back down the way she'd come; either angle made her dizzy and a little nauseated. "One more step, Phebes. Then one more again."

Somehow, she made it to the top of the stairs, where she sank to her hands and knees to crawl across the floor toward her bed, pushing the bottle along ahead of her. "Come to mama, little angel cloud bed of mine."

FIFTEEN

Phoebe awoke to the incessant buzzing of bees, a pulsing rhythm filling the air around her. A thousand of them maniacally fluttered their wings without letting up. "Stop," she groaned, and then bit down hard on her lip to quiet the sound of her own voice rattling like a bag of rocks inside her head. "Oh, stop," she whispered, covering her ears against the buzzing that wouldn't let up.

She finally realized it was her alarm clock going off, the black plastic box with the LED numbers on her nightstand letting her know it was ten o'clock in the morning. And it was just out of reach.

Tears of frustration and pain began to build like hot lava behind her eyes, but she rolled onto her side and tried again. This time, her grasping fingertips found the edge of the table and the dangling electrical cord. She pulled the plug out of the wall socket with a quick jerk that made her head spin, but the angry bees fell silent.

"Thank you." She mouthed the words, not daring to actually speak again, and covered her face with her pillow. She wondered absentmindedly if she'd have the strength in her arms to remove it when the oxygen ran out beneath it. *Maybe it would be better that way....*

But Phoebe knew she didn't have it in her to harm herself, at least not physically. At least not with anything but alcohol, her throbbing head corrected her.

She'd tried. Oh, how she'd tried. But no matter what she did, she could never bring herself to make the final cut, take the step out into space, pull the trigger. *Slow and steady wins the race.* The words drifted through her thoughts, caustic and cruel. *You're going to die slowly and painfully after a long, lonely, miserable life.*

The need for air forced her to bat the pillow off her face with a sloppy swipe of her arm.

The buzzing started up again. "No," Phoebe moaned, squinting her eyes against the daylight to look for the clock. It wasn't on her bedside table.

But this time, it was her phone vibrating on the hardwood floor near the top of the stairs where it lay, face up, beside her shoulder bag. She vaguely remembered dropping them there when she'd come home from the hospital in the predawn hours of Sunday morning. She'd come straight upstairs to change out of the clothes that smelled like childbirth and hospitals, the reek of them assaulting her senses, and then burrowed under her covers, begging for sleep to take her far, far away.

There was no way she could get out of bed to her phone before whoever was calling gave up. She closed her eyes, swallowing hard against a sudden urge to vomit, and reached for the pillow again. This time, she kept one end elevated so she could breathe, and the fluffy down effectively shut out the intrusive piece of technology.

She must have passed out again, because when she next opened her eyes, the shadows in her home were long. The days were short this time of year, but if she was thinking clearly—ha!—she'd spent the whole day in bed. Where was the bottle of whiskey that she'd brought upstairs with her? Had she actually polished it off?

It took her quite some time and no little effort to haul herself out of bed and into her bathroom where she filled the tub, the sound of rushing water loud to her ears. While she waited, she rooted around until she found the box of Blowfish at the back of her make-up drawer. She tore open one of the pouches and dropped the tablets into a glass on the counter. The fizzy drink might not work the miracles it claimed to in the commercials, but it did help take the worst of the edge off the rare times she'd found herself under the crushing weight of a hangover.

On the vanity sat her electric kettle and coffee bean grinder alongside a wire basket containing the components of her Aeropress, appliances as necessary to her morning ritual as her blow dryer and hot rollers. She eyed the grinder, hoping she wouldn't have to run the loud machine, and was greatly relieved to find that the canister already held enough grounds for at least one or two cups of coffee. She plugged in the kettle and prepared the coffee press while she waited for the water to heat up.

By the time she'd brewed a strong cup of Italian Roast, the deep tub was full. She dropped a couple of scoops of an aromatic detox bath salt she'd purchased at Nettles and Nests, her favorite herb shop. She couldn't remember all the ingredients, but along with Epsom salt and finely ground green tea, it included a selection of essential oils, like lavender, vanilla, and frankincense. She didn't care for the smell of lavender by itself, but the blend was quite soothing. She usually used it to help her relax sore muscles after a long stretch of work—it always surprised her how tightly wound she could get when she was in the throes of creativity—but she figured it might be just as effective in this situation. It certainly couldn't hurt.

As she replaced the jar on her vanity, she spotted a watch bracelet and picked it up to check the time. Almost six o'clock PM. Was it still Monday? Or was it Tuesday? It felt like she'd been asleep for weeks. Her phone still lay on the floor by the stairs and nothing in the bathroom gave her any clue as to what day it was.

"Bath first. Then find out how much of the week you've lost." She didn't even want to think about who had called her; she wouldn't be answering or returning calls anytime soon, that was for sure.

Phoebe was beginning to feel a little more human, albeit a trembling and wobbly human, but the tub was drawing her to it like a magnetic force. She sank down into the water, the heat at first making her gasp, turning her skin bright pink, but as she grew accustomed to it, she began to relax. She laid her head back and peered up through a skylight above her, strategically placed there for this very purpose. The sky went from turquoise to peach to diamond-studded indigo velvet as she let the bath work its magic on both her body and her soul.

Lying there, she ruminated on all that had transpired to bring her to this moment, this place of complete isolation. Most of the time, she liked the hours she spent alone, but more often than not, she found she was lonely.

Today, she wasn't just lonely.

Today, she was afraid she might always be lonely.

SIXTEEN

Monday morning came and went while Trevor poured his heart into his music. His visit to the hospital the day before had inspired him in completely new ways, and he found himself tapping into emotions and ideas he didn't even know he had.

By midday, he'd laid down tracks for two more new songs and over the course of the afternoon, he edited and mastered one of them. When he sat back and listened to what he'd worked on, he nodded in time to the tempo, pleased with the near-finished production. The lyrics spoke of the longing he was experiencing, not for a baby, but for a connection that mattered. A deep intimacy between a man and his God, between a man and those around him. It was something he knew many people never experienced in their relationships.

As the last notes of the song faded out, his thoughts drifted to Renata and her new baby. They'd have been discharged from the hospital by now, according to what she'd said Sunday afternoon, and he sent up a quick prayer that all had gone smoothly, and that mother and child were safely home.

He selfishly wished he could pay them another visit, hold that baby again, but no matter how hard he wracked his brain, he simply couldn't come up with a sound enough excuse to do so. Especially now that they were home. Tim Larsen had been perfectly polite at the hospital, in spite of the awkward moments, but Trevor had sensed the man sizing him up, and something about the way he did so made Trevor think Tim would find it especially odd if he showed up on their doorstep with anything less than a really, really good reason. As well as he knew Gia, Vic, and Juliette, he was still virtually a stranger to Renata and Tim. He'd simply have to wait until Sunday when, come hell or high water, he was going to be at the Gustafsons' for the family meal. Surely, the Dixon-Larsen gang would all be there, Baby Charise included.

And surely, Phoebe Gustafson would be there, too, and he'd be able to talk to her about commissioning her to work on his album art.

The thought of Phoebe—the memory of her driving that topless jeep beside him, her skirt mocking him as it billowed around her long legs, the huge sunglasses that hid most of her face, those lips—he sat back in his chair and laced his fingers behind his head, his eyes closed so he could focus on the mental images longer.

"She's beautiful," he murmured, his voice husky with appreciation. But he didn't mean just on the outside. Yeah, she carried herself with the confidence of a woman who knows what she's got and knows how to work it, but what drew his eyes to her memory again and again was the slight hesitance in her gaze, the fleeting flash of vulnerability that showed itself when he first came around the pump at the gas station. She'd been embarrassed at her circumstances, he could tell, and he'd done everything he could to put her at ease.

But he was glad he'd first met her that way; had he been introduced to her in her own element, he might not have caught the glimpse of *that* Phoebe, and he might not have felt the earth shift under his feet the way he had in that moment.

Trevor knew people. He studied them. He watched how emotion played across features and how human nature responded to circumstances and events. He spent much of his time evoking responses from people and then amping up on those responses and going deeper, deeper, until his audiences *became* their feelings, even if just for a moment. He knew how to use his voice, his eyes, his body language to push buttons, to touch those triggers, and he knew how to tap those places in himself, too, how to simply release himself in the moment, like he'd done when he held Charise and poured out his heart over the baby in his arms.

And he knew, just by spending those few minutes with her, that Phoebe knew the same things he did—how to elicit a certain response, how to manipulate with a look, a movement, that voice. But he'd caught a glimpse of something more, something deeper that she kept tucked away, clutched tightly to her where she didn't think anyone could see. He didn't know what it was she kept so close to her heart, or why she kept it hidden, but he was sure that whatever it was had the potential to destroy her... or make her even more beautiful.

More than that, though, he *remembered* her beauty. The more time he spent thinking about her—she'd not been far from his thoughts in over a week now—the more he knew it to be true. It was a visceral knowledge of her, like something about her had been stamped on his heart and mind long before he'd stepped around the gas pump to offer her his help. Sure, Juliette talked about her—quite often, in fact—and so it was possible he just *felt* like he knew her already. But that wasn't it, he was certain.

He'd *known* her... in another time, another place, another life. Try as he might, though, he could not conjure up the memory that would tell him how.

He leaned forward and shoved his rolling chair backward as he stood, not caring that it careened off the wall behind him. He had to figure this out before it consumed him. With an urgency that matched the one he'd felt yesterday about meeting the new baby, he needed to know. He would just come right out and ask her when he saw her again.

When? *When?* Sunday dinner was still almost a week away.

"I can't wait that long," he growled to himself as he paced in a tight circle in front of his desk. "Why didn't I get her number from Gia yesterday?" And now, if he asked her for it, the girl and his cousin would certainly turn it into something it wasn't. But then, who was he trying to kid? The draw to Phoebe was far more than just the desire to have her create his album art.

He stopped and braced his hands on the edge of his desk, his eyes on the huge monitor that still displayed the tracks he'd been editing. Pulling the keyboard forward, he minimized the digital audio workstation, opened his search engine, and typed Phoebe's name into the address bar.

He hadn't done this before because he'd disciplined himself to be so careful about going on random searches online when he was alone, and part of him worried what he might find under her name. From what Vic had told him about her, from what he'd seen of her himself, from the flamboyant artwork displayed in Juliette's home, he could tell

Phoebe lived passionately... which wasn't a bad thing. So did he. But he lived passionately for Christ, and Phoebe, well, Phoebe appeared to live passionately for herself.

And that meant it was possible he might see more of her than he wanted to if he searched her name online. He wasn't being judgmental or self-righteous. He just knew his own weaknesses, and now that he was acknowledging the draw to her was more than just professional, he knew he had to tread carefully, respectfully. For her sake, as well as his.

The first page of the search engine flooded with site after site attached to Phoebe's name, the majority of them art related. When he clicked on the images tab—he narrowed his eyes and prayed for protection—image after image of dazzling artwork filled the screen, interspersed with pictures of Phoebe. Close-ups of her startlingly beautiful face that took his breath away, and snapshots of her in evening attire, pretty little dresses at fancy events. There were also a few family pictures of her and her sisters that looked like they'd been pulled from one of the social network sites, several candid shots of her out on the town with varying groups of people, often with an arm around some smiling man—who wouldn't be smiling with Phoebe Gustafson pressed up against you?—and page after page of stunning photographs obviously taken during professional photo shoots. Not of Phoebe herself, but of other people, all attributed to her.

Mixed into the bunch were images of several bodice-ripper type romance novels from a publishing house called Vineland Press, but Trevor assumed the connection to Phoebe was through her photography. Several of the models from her photographs, the male models, especially, looked like they also graced the digitally enhanced covers of the Vineland novels, and the company's address had it based out of Monrovia, not more than an hour's drive away.

If Phoebe designed book covers, surely, she'd be open to working with him on his album cover.

He clicked on a link to *Gossamer Magazine* because Phoebe's name was listed as a contributing artist. He closed it quickly when he saw the content warning stating that it was for adults only.

But other than the candid images of the beautiful woman in her sometimes really racy clothes out on the town, and the curious connection she had to *Gossamer*—"Which is none of my business anyway,"—he was thrilled to see how renowned she was in the industry as an artist. He was also pleased to see that she didn't seem to be attached to one particular man… at least not that he could tell by the pictures or headlines. He reached for his chair and pulled it up to the desk, a nervous flutter behind his sternum.

"Okay, God," he said as he lowered himself into the black leather seat. "I should have started this with a conversation with you. Sorry. So tell me. What do I do now?" He moved the mouse, so it hovered over the link to Phoebe's professional website. It wasn't that he was afraid of what he'd find there. It was just that opening it meant he was pursuing her of his own free will. It wasn't a blind date like he'd had with Juliette last year. It wasn't Gia trying to hook him up with another one of her sisters. It wasn't a chance meeting on the side of the road.

If he opened Phoebe's website in the state he was in, he'd be intentionally pursuing her, both professionally… and personally.

"Is this what I'm supposed to do, God?"

Pray for her.

"I will. But what about contacting her?"

Pray for her.

"Fine. Then can we talk about contacting her?"

Pray for her.

Trevor sighed. He rubbed at the back of his neck with one hand, his other lingering on the mouse. Phoebe's China doll features studied him, her thoughts indiscernible behind her eyes in the portrait next to her website link. He let go of the mouse and scrubbed both hands through his hair. He grabbed the mouse again and moved the cursor to the upper right-hand corner of the screen. It hovered there… close out altogether or just minimize until later? After he'd prayed for her.

Once again, he rose and paced, his eyes going back to hers again and again.

Pray for her.

With a growl, Trevor shut down the Internet and walked away from the desk to stand at his west-facing kitchen window. The sun was making its way toward the rick-rack line of mountains, and the sky was catching fire. Southern California sunsets in autumn were almost always glorious, and he stood there watching the shifting colors for a few moments longer, willing his thoughts of Phoebe into prayers. Then he snatched up his keys, his helmet, and his flannel-lined denim jacket.

"Better than a cold shower, any day," he declared as he swung a leg over his Harley and knocked the kickstand up. Nothing like a twilight bike ride to clear the head. "Pray, I will. Fine. But I'm going to have a good time doing it," he grouched, sounding like a petulant child. He wasn't sure if he was trying to convince God or himself of the fact.

And running through the back of his mind was the memory of what had happened the last time he'd taken the bike out... was that only a little over a week ago?

SEVENTEEN

When Phoebe finally picked her phone up off the floor, she was amused to find more than a dozen calls from family members. Four of them were from Renata, the last one less than an hour ago. And there were that many more texts, too. She didn't bother listening to the voice mails everyone left, but she did scroll through the texts.

Meeting at the hospital for lunch—see you there. Yesterday morning. From Jules.

Dude. Phebes. TAZ IS ASKING ABOUT YOU! Come to the hospital NOW! Gia, Sunday afternoon.

Charise wants to see you. Last night from Renata.

Gia last night: *Where WERE you? Charise is soooooooooooo cute and squishy. And TAZ WAS ASKING ABOUT YOU!!!!!* The text included ten rows of hearts.

I want to see you. Late last night from Renata.

Heading home in an hour. Renata this morning. *Come over later. Tim will be picking up the boys from school and taking them to his shop for the afternoon.*

Did Renata think Phoebe had left because Tim showed up? She stopped reading the texts and dropped her phone into her purse. She left them both upstairs and headed down to her kitchenette for a bottle of cold water and to see what kind of food she had on hand. She was parched and ravenous, and although she would have preferred greasy fries and a huge burger, right now, anything would do. It was almost eight o'clock, and she hadn't eaten anything but pretzels with her whiskey some time yesterday—the empty bag beside her potter's wheel was a testament to that—and a red velvet Pop-Tart from the box of midnight snacks she kept stashed in a sweater box under her bed, sometime after her bath. The strong coffee she'd had earlier made her stomach feel like it was trying to chew on itself, and she knew she needed something in her belly as soon as possible.

The refrigerator was loathed to cough up anything convenient. A green apple, but Phoebe had no idea how long it had been in there. A tub of plain Greek yogurt. Half a loaf of whole grain bread Granny G had made last week. No butter, and she already knew there was no peanut butter in the cupboard, either. A head of cabbage... "I can make some coleslaw." But the idea of cabbage at that moment made her stomach flip-flop. "Maybe not."

The freezer wasn't much more forthcoming. Frozen pizza rolls Gia had stuck in there months ago. A packet of chicken breasts. A bag of mixed berries. A yogurt smoothie?

"Too healthy. Too sweet. I need salty." She downed a huge swig of the cold water bottle. "And I don't want to cook." Her legs still felt unstable beneath her.

Phoebe didn't hate cooking, but she didn't love it, either. And she really didn't enjoy cooking just for her. It wasn't the eating alone part that bothered her; it was the time it took to prepare a meal just for herself when she could just pay someone else to do the work *and* the cleanup. She picked up the phone and dialed The Fat Greek. For a few extra bucks, they delivered within a five-mile radius. Phoebe's home, although on the outskirts of Midtown, was within that radius, and she never had a problem getting someone to run her food over while it was still hot and fresh. It probably helped that the two servers who did the delivery runs were young men, one of whom often lingered to talk about the food, the weather, Phoebe's art, *anything,* even after she tipped him. But she was accustomed to that kind of attention. She usually just took it all in stride.

Not tonight, though. Tonight, Phoebe hoped it was Nate who showed up at the door, because he would smile longingly as he handed over her food, accept her payment and generous tip, and then leave.

Twenty minutes later, the iron knocker thunked against the outside of the solid oak door, and Phoebe opened it, cash in hand.

"Hey, Phoebe. How's it going?"

"Hey, Jason." Of course. "It's going great," she said, not quite making eye-contact with him so as not to encourage conversation. Fortunately, she knew exactly how much she owed him. She handed him a couple of bills. "Here you go. Keep the change."

She tipped the other guy, Nate, more than Jason, because Nate never counted it in front of her, nor did he act all self-effacing over her generosity the way Jason did. She also knew Jason only responded that way so that he'd have an excuse to linger a little longer. Tonight, she'd kept the tip at 18% and change, so there would be no reason to discuss it, but to no avail. Before he even finished counting the money, he was already opening his mouth to argue.

"This is too much, Phoebe. As usual. You already pay for delivery." Jason didn't offer her the money back, though, she noted. He had the bills folded into his zippered money pouch by the time he had finished the statement.

"It's worth it to me, Jason. It's my way of saying thank you. I'm glad to do it." She reached for the door handle and started to pull it closed. The kid looked like he wanted to say more, so she thanked him again and ducked inside before he could get anymore out. Then she opened the bag of food and breathed in the tangy aroma of *tzatziki* sauce and roast beef.

"I don't ever have to leave the house if I don't want to," she said aloud. It wasn't such a bad idea in her estimation. "I'm turning into Juliette," she muttered as she unwrapped her meal and laid it out on her bistro-style dining table.

The old Jules, she mentally corrected herself. The Juliette who had all but stopped living when she and her ex-boyfriend split up. The Juliette who had put her life on hold more than fifteen years ago when Maman and Papa were killed by Angela Clinton. The old Juliette. Not the new one.

The new Juliette seemed to wear a perpetual blush, as though she couldn't stop thinking about the man she loved. This Juliette laughed easily and stood up for herself. This Juliette fought for what was right, even when no one else stood with her. She was still fragile in a way that spoke of wounds newly healed, but she seemed to have tapped into a new inner strength... one that had come along before Vic did. One Juliette attributed to her newfound faith in Jesus Christ, and all that she was learning about God in church on Sundays and her weekly Bible study group she went to with Vic on Tuesday nights.

Phoebe shook her head as she took a too-big bite of her gyro wrap. Cucumber sauce dribbled down her chin and she snatched up a paper napkin to wipe it away.

Jesus Christ was *not* the man for Phoebe. She didn't need some ethereal being in the sky keeping track of her sins for her. She did that well enough on her own. And she didn't need another absent father to try and please, either. She had a fine replacement for her father in Grandpa, and she didn't need any other. And she certainly didn't need some self-sacrificing, self-righteous, parable-wielding, Rastafarian guru god making her feel guilty for being self-indulgent or not going to church.

No, Phoebe needed a man she could touch, a man to hold. A man who would converse with her when she wanted to talk. A man who would appreciate her outer beauty and still accept her inner flaws. A man who treated her like an angel and wouldn't abandon her when she fought her demons.

"Ha." She took another bite. "There's no such man," she said around the food, not bothering to practice good manners. There wasn't anyone around to impress, after all. "And I certainly won't find one like that in church." She knew that from experience.

In an act of outright obstinacy, she got up and poured herself a glass of Moscato d'Asti, her go-to wine that paired well with almost anything. "Maybe not with a hangover," she muttered, but she stubbornly sipped on the dry, zippy drink.

The thoughts of men and church and Jesus Christ, however, brought to mind Trevor Zander, and her sister's texts. Why was the guy asking about her? *What* was he asking about her?

Had he remembered her? Because sometime yesterday morning, probably right around the time the rest of her family was heading to the hospital to visit Renata and the new baby, right before Phoebe popped the cork on the Glenfiddich, she had remembered him.

EIGHTEEN

"You think you're so wonderful, don't you? You think your looks and your perfect little body are going to get you anywhere in the real world? You're a slut, Phoebe Gustafson, a smear on the good name of this family. You're just trash." Renata's words ricocheted off the walls of the living room, slamming into Phoebe again and again as they careened and crashed around the shocked and silent witnesses. "Your looks and your body and the way you barely keep it covered are going to get you somewhere, I can assure you. On your back, that's where!"

She'd been right. Renata had been right all along....

The Homecoming party was supposed to be fun. It was supposed to be wild and crazy and good old teenage fun. A little booze, maybe some pot if she got lucky, and some slow-dancing with upperclassmen who wouldn't remember her name in the morning. She liked a good party because it helped her forget, too. At least for a couple of hours.

It had started out that way. Fun, a little wild and crazy, although she'd only scored one hit off a guy's joint because she wouldn't make out with him. But the night was still underway, and she'd known a lot of people there, at least by name, even though she didn't run in the same circles at school. Parties often laid waste to social barriers. Or at least the alcohol at parties did.

Then she'd seen Brad Haley saunter in, Renata nowhere in sight. Phoebe had almost run into them earlier—she'd ducked out of the way just in time. She didn't need any flak from Renata about being there. Her sister would accuse her of crashing the party, of trying to act like she was older than she was, of being trashy. Ren might even try to make her leave.

Phoebe hadn't cared if Ren was there or not. In fact, she'd actually felt a little rush at the sight of her. Maybe Ren would lighten up a little. But the look on her sister's face evidenced that Ren was more uncomfortable at the party than Phoebe had ever been sitting in church next to Granny G each Sunday. So, Phoebe had made herself scarce, avoiding the group she usually gravitated toward, a group that often included Brad Haley.

Brad Haley. Phoebe couldn't understand what her sister had seen in him, except that he was the first guy who'd ever shown a real interest in her. But Brad was a slick beast. He came across as a gentleman, and the ladies fell for it hook, line, and sinker.

Not Phoebe. She had stumbled upon him a few too many times pressed up against different girls at different parties, mouth usually too busy to talk, hands out of sight. Once she'd bumped into him coming out of a closed-off bedroom behind a woman who must have been a good ten years older than he was. He'd just winked at her as he'd passed.

But Renata wasn't going to hear about any of it from Phoebe. Not only would she not believe a word of it, but she would also most certainly accuse Phoebe of trying to ruin her life. Or worse, of trying to take Brad for herself.

So, when Brad strode through the room without Renata, Phoebe's antennae had gone up, and she'd hurried over to cut him off. Where was Ren? They hadn't been gone long enough for him to have taken her home. And besides, she knew Brad drank heavily at these parties and shouldn't be allowed behind the wheel.

"Where's my sister?" Phoebe had demanded, her voice raised over the loud music and conversation around them. "I just saw her with you a minute ago."

"Phoebe Gustafson. And I was just looking for you." The smug expression on his face should have warned her to be careful, but her concern had been focused elsewhere.

"Is Ren okay? What did you do to her? Where is she?" Maybe Brad was looking for her because Renata was upset and needed her. "Did she ask you to find me?"

He had stared down at her for several moments, his eyes narrowed, one side of his mouth quirked up in just the hint of a smile.

"Brad! Where is Renata?" She'd clutched at his shirt with both hands, pulling him closer to make sure he heard her, picked up on how serious she was.

"Come with me," Brad had said, taking her hand and pulling her away from the melee, down the hall toward one of the rooms. "She's fine, really. But you should come talk to her, just in case."

And Phoebe had followed Brad without reticence, anxious to come to the aid of her sister, to be *needed* by someone. She'd even rushed ahead of him into the darkened bedroom, an avenging angel sweeping in to rescue the damsel in distress.

Not an angel, but a stupid, naïve lamb, being led to slaughter.

She hadn't realized what was going on until she'd heard the door close firmly behind her, like the sound of an ax blade falling; not until she'd felt Brad's arm snake around her from behind, one hand closing gently, but securely over her mouth, the other hand sliding insistently up the front of her thighs beneath her skirt.

She hadn't screamed. She hadn't cried out or begged him not to do it. Oh, she'd resisted fiercely at first, but when he'd dug his chin into the bend of her shoulder, making her whole arm tingle, when he'd growled into her ear that he knew she wanted it, that no one would believe her if she said differently anyway—they all *knew* she was a slut.... "Two Gustafsons in one night," he'd murmured salaciously. "I'm going to call this one a win-win."

It had been the thought of Brad forcing himself on Renata in the same way as he was with her that had turned Phoebe to stone; her sister would not have had sex with Brad willingly. Phoebe knew she was strong enough to endure the horror of Brad's assault, but Renata? How would she endure? How would Ren even survive?

She'd barely noticed when Brad left the room. Sometime later, she'd gotten up off the floor, straightened her clothing the best she could, and had slipped out a window into the balmy night. Then she'd walked the two and a half miles home, her heart broken, not for herself, but for Renata.

The moment she'd set foot in the house, Renata had gone after her, shrieking like a banshee, hurling accusations at her until Grandpa had stormed into the room to shut Ren down. But instead of coming to the aid and comfort of Phoebe—sick at heart, bruised in spirit, her body aching in places she didn't know she could hurt—he'd gone to Renata and embraced her, offered his solace to her as though Renata had been the victim in all of it.

And Phoebe had stood in the doorway trembling and silent, desperate to keep it together long enough to escape the room full of people looking at her. Alone in a room full of people.

Oh, so alone.

• • • • • • • • • •

By Christmas, Phoebe had known she was pregnant.

By Valentine's Day, she'd changed her style completely, telling everyone she was embracing a bohemian lifestyle. She'd worn blousy shirts and big poncho-style wraps over leggings and fuzzy boots. She took long afternoon naps in the RV in the backyard; she'd turned the camper into her own little pad, complete with incense burners and beaded curtains. She'd even learned to play the ukulele.

During the Good Friday service, the first week in April, Phoebe had wept silent tears as the pastor talked about the death of Jesus and the grief and fear that surrounded his followers over the next few days. Phoebe hadn't been mourning the death of Christ, but of her parents; oh, how desperately she needed her mother. She grieved because they weren't going to rise again like Jesus had and make everything okay.

She'd never felt more alone than she had in that moment, sitting tightly packed between her sisters in a crowded pew, surrounded by a whole congregation of people who talked a whole lot about saving the lost and feeding the hungry and turning the other cheek, but they didn't ever say anything about unreported rape and unplanned pregnancies.

By the end of April, Phoebe had taken to wearing too-tight sports bras and gimmicky weight loss girdle things under her clothes, not to get in shape, but to mask her fuller breasts and the cantaloupe-sized baby bump pushing against the skirts of her flowing dresses.

Then on the second Sunday in May, on Mother's Day, when Phoebe was exactly seven months along, she sat in church and listened as the pastor spoke about how important mothers and mother-figures were in the lives of everyone, especially young women who were soon-to-be mothers themselves. He told the story of Mary, the mother of Jesus, her pregnancy still hushed, going away to stay with her older cousin, Elizabeth, who mentored and encouraged and stood by Mary. A mother figure in Mary's life.

Was it possible Phoebe could find an Elizabeth in her own life? Was there someone right there in that church who would be a mother figure to her? She knew in her heart Granny G would find a way to embrace her, but her grandparents already had so much thrust into their hands when Maman and Papa had died, leaving the elderly Gustafsons with four girls to raise.

The next day, Phoebe ditched school and slipped inside the double doors of the church. She stood in the cool shadows for a few minutes while her eyes adjusted, a little surprised to find the building unlocked and unattended. But she was glad. She wasn't quite ready to explain her presence there; she wasn't even sure *how* to word her request, or who to ask in the first place. And now that she was there, she suddenly realized she'd have to tell whoever she spoke to about *that night*. She'd made every concerted effort to not think about *that night* ever again, to the point where she could almost convince herself there was no connection between *that night* and the baby growing inside her.

She only thought of it as *that night* and nothing more.

Phoebe skirted the back row and moved quietly up the side aisle, keeping as low a profile as possible in the quiet building. It was so peaceful, so unlike the busyness of church on Sunday morning. The silence felt almost reverent, like she was walking on holy ground, and she was loath to make any kind of a disturbance. Still. Quiet. No one else around.

But she didn't feel alone.

She slipped into a pew about halfway up the aisle and sat down. She automatically propped her huge shoulder bag on her lap to camouflage her baby bump, but then set it aside, realizing she didn't have to hide it today. She even went so far as to rest a hand around the curve of her belly, smiling when the baby inside bumped against her palm like he or she was acknowledging her touch.

She had no idea how long she'd been sitting there when a door off to the side of the stage opened and two men came in, their conversation loud and cheerful.

"—parent meeting went really well last night. There were lots of questions, but I think most of them are really glad their kids are getting this opportunity."

"Well, it's good to have you on board, young man. We need young men who are fired up about discipleship taking charge on programs like this. I know you're inspiring many of our high school students to think more deeply about going into full-time ministry. The harvest is ripe, and the workers are few."

Phoebe rolled her eyes. She hated hearing Christians talk that way. It was so... *elitist*, as though they spoke in a special Bible code. And what the heck did it all mean? To her, it just sounded like words to appease themselves with. *If I say the right thing, use the right words, the right phrasing often enough and loudly enough, maybe no one will notice I don't actually act any differently than anyone else.*

"I'm just grateful for the opportunity to come alongside the high schoolers this way. I think it's so important that we set Timothy up as an example. Paul discipling him didn't just change his life, but it continues to change lives generation after generation, because we have so much of his discipleship training in the Word," the younger guy replied. He looked like a college frat boy in his khaki Dockers and tucked-in green polo shirt... or a pastor in training, she decided, averting her gaze as though he might feel her eyes on him.

"It's all right there for us to replicate," he continued, clearly unaware of her presence. "As the Good Book says, 'Train up a child in the way he should go and when he is old, he will not depart from it.'"

"Amen. I hear it all the time. That early foundation of faith is so important. Even the prodigal son knew where to go when everything else had failed him. Why? Because his father had trained him up to understand unconditional love. It took him a while to embrace it and accept it, certainly, but deep in his heart, he knew where home was because he'd been trained up to recognize it."

Phoebe hunkered down low in the pew and kept her head lowered as the two men made their way down the center aisle toward the back of the church and the double doors she'd come in. *Please don't notice me. Just keep walking. Please, please, please—*

No such luck. The conversation broke off and the footsteps stopped.

"Excuse me," the older man said, his voice friendly but curious. "Is there anything I—we can do for you?"

Phoebe lifted her head, but kept her eyes downcast. "No, that's all right. I'm just—just praying," she said, knowing that was the perfect response to give in a church.

The young guy cleared his throat softly, then said, "Would you like us to pray with you? Or send someone else—a woman, maybe?—out to pray with you?"

Phoebe hesitated. Was it that simple? Was it possible some woman would slip into the pew next to her and be Elizabeth to her? "Um, I don't know. Maybe." The last word came out in a whisper, but the men heard her, anyway.

"I'll go see if Ruthie is available," the guy in the polo shirt said to the older man. "You go on ahead. I know you're running late already." Then he turned back to Phoebe, and she forced herself to look directly at him.

He was much younger than she'd expected. In fact, he didn't look much older than she was—early twenties at the most? He had soft, curly hair that flopped forward over his forehead, and he actually seemed to smile with his eyes. He wasn't conventionally handsome in a male model way, but he definitely had that boy-next-door vibe that made him come across as surprisingly approachable.

Which made the Bible code jargon he'd just been spouting seem incongruous, almost duplicitous to her. She felt her guard rise, but she wanted to trust that she was in the right place. She needed this to be the right place, and she needed him to be the right person, at least until he could round up this Ruthie person.

Ruthie. Even the name sounded motherly, didn't it?

"My name is Trevor. I'm a youth pastor intern here. I work with the high school group, but I don't think we've met. You're a high school student?" He asked the question, but it was clear he assumed she was.

"No. Yes." She fumbled to find the right words. He had slipped into the pew in front of hers and was close enough to notice her belly, even in the dim lighting. She hunched forward a little and fluffed her skirt out, so it formed a camouflaging tent over her lap. Let him think she was obsessed with her appearance. Better that than a pregnant teen. "Yes, I'm a high school student, but no, I don't go to youth group here. We do go to church here, though," she amended.

"Oh? Have you tried our Tuesday Teen Nights?"

Had he forgotten he was going to go get Ruthie for her?

"No. We do youth group at a different church." It wasn't exactly a lie. Renata still went to the group at their old church. They'd only started attending this church after Maman and Papa had died because this was where Grandpa and Granny G went. Phoebe hadn't ever gone to any high school church group. Her parents hadn't forced her to go, and neither did her grandparents.

"Well, that's good to hear. Okay. I'm going to go see if I can round up Ruthie. She's in charge of our women's ministries. Sit tight, okay?" He started to move away, and then paused and turned back to her. "I'm sorry. What's your name?"

Without premeditation, in a moment of sheer panic, she gave him her middle name. "I'm Jo. Josephine. Call me Jo."

Trevor leaned over the bench and stuck out his hand. "Good to meet you, Jo. I'll be back shortly, hopefully with Ruthie in tow, okay?"

Several minutes passed and the door at the front of the church opened again and Trevor returned, a warm smile on his face. "Ruthie is just wrapping up a meeting, but she promised to join us as soon as she was finished. About fifteen minutes, is that okay? Or do you have somewhere you're supposed to be?"

I'm a high schooler. On a Monday morning in May. Where do you think I'm supposed to be? Phoebe bit back the snarky retort. "That's fine. I can wait."

Trevor was silent for a moment, and then said, "Are you all right, Jo? I mean, would you like me to wait with you? You don't have to tell me why you're here or what you're praying about, but I feel bad just leaving you here alone." He eased into the row ahead of her again. He sat down close enough that he could speak quietly to her and still be heard, but far enough away that she didn't feel like he was crowding her. He turned sideways in the pew, propping one leg up on the bench beside him and looping an arm over the back so he could look at her. "My schedule is wide open for the next half an hour, so if you need company while you wait for Ruthie, maybe this is where I'm supposed to be."

Phoebe considered his offer, and to her surprise, she found she didn't mind his presence. He exuded sincerity despite the Bible talk, and there didn't seem to be anything threatening about him. "I don't really feel alone in here, but I don't mind the company," she said.

Trevor smiled and nodded. "Yeah, this place never feels completely empty to me. I come here a lot when I need to clear my head, when I need to sort things out with God." He turned and faced the front of the sanctuary for a few moments, his expression suddenly distant, like he'd momentarily slipped away to another time and place. She wondered what he was thinking about.

"Sort things out with God, hm?" she repeated, her voice low. "I suppose that's what I'm trying to do today. I'm not very good at praying, but I thought if I came here and just hung out, maybe God would whisper something to me. Give me some good advice." She laughed softly. "That sounds so stupid."

"No, actually," he said, looking back at her again.

She couldn't meet his eyes, but she could feel them on her face. She lowered her gaze to her knees, letting her hair fall forward to hide her features from his open scrutiny.

"Sometimes that's all praying is. In Romans Chapter 8, the Bible says, *In the same way, the Spirit helps us in our weakness. We do not know what we ought to pray for, but the Spirit himself intercedes for us through wordless groans. And he who searches our hearts knows the mind of the Spirit, because the Spirit interceded for God's people in accordance with the will of God.*" Trevor paused and glanced away briefly, as though carefully measuring his words. "I think this is the perfect place to be if you don't know how to pray or exactly what to pray for. The Holy Spirit is accessible anywhere and everywhere, but there's nothing like physically sitting in a place of worship when you're desperate to meet with God."

Everything he said made such perfect sense, and she felt tears beginning to form behind her eyes, burning at the bridge of her nose.

"You know how you can smell perfume even after a person has left? Or sometimes a crowded room seems to echo with the sounds of what was going on in it even after it's cleared out? That's kind of what it feels like in here to me. It's almost as though the fragrance or the echo of worship hangs on even after everyone leaves on Sunday." Trevor's voice had quieted to the point where he almost seemed to be talking to himself. "Sometimes I think I can actually hear God breathing in here on mornings like this. Like he's walking the aisles gathering up the burdens people laid down on Sunday, sorting through the prayers that were offered up."

A tear fell from Phoebe's eye and landed on her stomach. Without thinking, she spread her fingers wide over her rounded belly and left it there. "I don't know what to do," she whispered. "I need—I need help."

NINETEEN

SHE HADN'T PLANNED TO talk to him. She needed a mother figure, not a buddy. Especially not a buddy who was young enough that he might actually know Brad Haley. But the words kept coming.

"My parents died in a car accident almost two years ago and now me and my sisters live with my grandparents. They have so much to worry about with all of us. My littlest sister is only five and my oldest sister is just getting through some major depression over everything. My other sister is dealing with everything her way—she's a control freak and she makes everyone crazy. And I—I—well, I'm pregnant."

She gasped at the sound of the words. She'd never said them out loud to anyone before, and the shock of them made her whole body tremble. Her fingertips moved in slow, circular patterns over the rounded shape beneath her skirt. "And I don't know what to do," she repeated, her voice shaking. Tiny lights flickered at the back of her eyeballs, and she realized she was hunched over and holding her breath. She straightened a little, swiped at the tears spilling down her cheeks, and took some slow, deep breaths, in through the nose, out through the mouth.

Trevor didn't speak. In fact, he barely moved in the aftermath of her little rant. *Say something,* she cried out in her mind. But he seemed completely stumped by her admission, and when he still didn't say anything, she tried a different approach.

"Yesterday, the pastor talked about Mary and Elizabeth. About how Elizabeth was like a mother to Mary, even though her circumstances—Mary being pregnant and not married—would have been good reason for Elizabeth to turn her back on her. The older woman was there for Mary when she needed that mother-daughter relationship.

Well, my mom is de—dead, and my grandmother has her hands full." She paused, hating how childish her request now sounded. "I was kind of hoping I might find someone here who could be Elizabeth to me," she finished lamely.

"Ah. I see. Well, that makes sense." His voice remained low and gentle, but she heard the censure in it, anyway. Her head was still down, and she peered surreptitiously over at him through the waterfall of her hair that still hid most of her face from him. His eyes were narrowed, downcast, and he wasn't looking at her. In fact, the longer she watched, the clearer it became that he was making a concerted effort to look everywhere *except* at her.

Phoebe's heart sank. She straightened, pushed her hair back from her face, and made a show of glancing around the shadowy room. "Is there a clock in here? I may not be able to wait for Ruthie. I have a class starting soon and I don't think I should miss it."

He did look at her then, but the expression on his face only disheartened her more. He seemed closed off. Like he'd pulled back, separated himself from her on some level. He hadn't moved in his seat. He still smiled, but the warmth was gone. He pointed to the wall at the back of the church. "There's a big clock there. So the pastor can keep track of how long his sermon goes."

"Oh. Okay. Thanks." In the blink of an eye, her tears had dried up, and she now felt awkward and uncomfortable, her skin prickling with anxiety. "Yeah, it's almost ten." Was it only ten o'clock? "I have a class. I need to go." Phoebe stood up and slung the strap of her bag over her shoulder. "Tell Ruthie I'm sorry I couldn't meet with her. But thanks for sitting with me." She started to shuffle down the pew, feeling clumsy and foolish.

"Wait. Please wait. I—I'm sorry." Trevor stood, too, and stopped her with a hand on her arm. "You just kind of surprised me, that's all. I—well, this is the first time I've had to deal with something like this, and I'm admittedly kind of at a loss. I honestly don't really know what to say to you. Or the best way to help you."

Phoebe tried not to be offended, but she couldn't bite back the words in time. "The first time *you've* had to deal with this? *Deal* with this?" She waved a hand at her stomach. "Sorry, Mr. Youth Pastor In Training, or whatever you are, but you're *not* the one dealing with this. I am." She tugged her arm free of his and pushed past him and out into the aisle.

"Please, Jo. I'm sorry. Really, I am." He, too, had scrambled out into the aisle and was now walking backwards in front of her. He didn't touch her, but he was clearly hoping to prevent her from leaving. "Please wait for Ruthie. She'll know what to do. What to say."

Phoebe stopped and crossed her arms, glaring at him. "You're a youth pastor intern, right?" The question was redundant—he'd proudly introduced himself as such, and she'd already thrown it in his face once. She waited for an answer, anyway.

"I am. Yes."

"Well, a word of advice if you're going to turn this internship into a career. You might want to come up with something other than silence to say to the next teenager who comes to you with an unplanned pregnancy. Or does that not happen in your Tuesday Teen Nights?" She waved a hand in a wide motion, indicating the expanse of the room. "Is your congregation full of perfect people who don't have bad things happen to them, who never make mistakes?"

Trevor cocked his head at her, and she could tell she'd stung his ego a little. He spoke quietly, but firmly, and with great conviction. "There's no such thing as an unplanned pregnancy, Jo. If you don't want to get pregnant, you shouldn't be having sex."

Phoebe felt her jaw drop and her eyes widen in stunned amazement. For a moment, she couldn't even speak.

Trevor filled the silence. The kindness in his eyes and in the timbre of his voice belied the condemnation he pronounced with his words. "God designed sex to be between a husband and wife for a reason, you know. Because other than the virgin birth, pregnancy is a result of only one thing. Sex. So, if you're having sex, you're planning—even if only in theory—a pregnancy."

Phoebe knew if she didn't leave at that very moment that she might commit a crime. She stepped forward, nearly plowing into him. "You pompous, self-righteous, *arrogant* windbag," she hissed as she pushed past him.

"Hey, hey." He didn't reach for her, but he followed close behind her. "Jo, please. I was just trying to explain my point of view." He had longer legs than she did, and he moved ahead of her to stand in front of the doors, blocking her exit. "I don't mean to sound self-righteous or arrogant, really, I don't. I just get weary of hearing people talk about unwanted or unplanned pregnancies because it doesn't make sense, not when you really think about it."

Phoebe stopped in front of him, not wanting to touch him, either. She felt like she was on fire, she was so angry. The child in her belly seemed to tap dance in response to her elevated heart rate.

But Trevor wasn't finished. "We humans are so ready to make excuses for doing the things we want to do, and then when they don't turn out the way we want them to, or when we're faced with the consequences of our bad choices, we're so quick to point fingers at someone else. Or we simply refuse to take responsibility for our actions."

Why wouldn't he just shut up? Did he really think what he was saying would make her warmup to him? Feel contrite? Stick around so some other self-righteous windbag could speak condescendingly to her in the guise of prayer?

She took a step closer and lifted her face, so she looked him eye-to-eye for the first time. "I'm quick to point my finger at you, Mr. Youth Pastor in Training, because I want you to get. Out. Of. My. Way." She punctuated each word by jabbing him in the chest with her finger. "And I refuse to take responsibility for the bad actions of the man who *raped* me and left me with an *unplanned* pregnancy." She shoved a shoulder into him, effectively pushing him through the door ahead of her. "I'll go find help somewhere else, thank you very much. Besides, it seems to me that God left the building when you started spouting your religious vitriol. The only one left here is you. And you can explain that to your church lady pal, Ruthie." Then she bid him good riddance, using the foulest language she could think of, wondering—hoping—God might strike her dead for swearing in his house.

A week later, Phoebe explained her situation to a doctor at a free health clinic. When she insisted that she did not want an abortion, that she wanted to give the baby up for adoption to a family who wanted a child, the woman connected her to a non-profit program that would help her do just that.

She somehow managed to keep her pregnancy hidden until the school year was over, then she informed her grandparents that she had signed up for a summer work program on an organic herb farm up near San Jose in northern California. She gave them the name of a real farm in that area, just in case they looked it up—she made certain it was a place that actually had summer work programs—but the phone number she gave them belonged to the folks she'd be staying with, for emergency's sake. She made her grandparents promise not to call unless it was an emergency, and in turn, promised she'd check in with them at least every other night.

On June 10th, two days after Renata's graduation ceremony, Phoebe got on a bus and headed up north to San Jose where she would spend the last five weeks of her maternity with the couple who would be adopting the baby. They would participate in all the remaining doctor visits, take a series of childbirth classes with her; they would be present at the birth so they could witness their child coming into the world, and they would see to it that Phoebe had the best follow-up post-natal care, including counseling. The program also paid Phoebe a small stipend since she wouldn't be able to have a job during the two months she stayed with the family. By the end of the summer, Phoebe would return home with a little cash in her pockets and no baby, and everything would go back to normal.

And Phoebe would never set foot in her grandparents' church again. Or any other church, for that matter.

TWENTY

For more than an hour, Trevor rode. He headed out of town and zig-zagged lazily along Rim of the World Highway up through the San Bernardino mountains. At night, sections of the road could be treacherous for inexperienced and impatient drivers, but Trevor was neither, and he loved this route. Once he rose above the traffic and noise of the foothill cities, the road meandered higher and higher, until the panoramic view of the valley stretched out as far as the eye could see. On rare smog-free days, one could see all the way to the Pacific Ocean, and at night, millions of lights covered the valley floor like lakes of fireflies frozen in time.

He pulled over at his favorite turnout, got off the bike and approached the guardrail that he was certain would do little to prevent an out-of-control motorist from tumbling over the drop-off. He removed his helmet and shivered in the chilly mountain air—it might be a pleasant 65 degrees in Midtown, but up here, it couldn't be above 50 degrees, and as night fell, thick and heavy around him, he knew the temperature would drop, too.

He climbed nimbly over the guardrail to the narrow lip of earth beyond it, and then leaned against it, settling his backside against the cold metal. It wasn't the most comfortable perch in the world, but a little discomfort might keep him from getting too relaxed, help him stay focused on the task at hand.

Praying for Phoebe.

"Lord, Phoebe Gustafson." He paused and stared out at the lights below. His eyes followed the moving trails of cars that sped along the streets and highways like ants with flashlights.

How would Phoebe's artist eyes interpret the scene? Would she add color to the cobalt velvet and gold chromatic scheme? Would she paint it as she saw it, perched there on the mountainside beside him? Or would she, too, turn it into some kind of a magical otherworld? Maybe he should bring her up here one day....

"Stay on track, man." He tried again. "Phoebe Gustafson." He closed his eyes and her face drifted into his mind, the sound of her voice teasing him, assuring him that she wouldn't steal his virtue. His eyes popped open. "Help me, God. I'm not doing so great, here."

Why was he so overwhelmed by this woman he'd only met—and spent maybe half an hour with—a week ago? Why did she stir such a deep response in him? He understood attraction and chemistry and the impulse of the flesh to lay claim to a prize before anyone else did, and although he was most certainly physically attracted to her in a way that he hadn't been toward a woman in some time now, it was more than that.

There was something else. Something he was missing. Something he—

"This is about Phoebe, not me," he muttered, his frustration making him growl. "Okay, God. What do I pray? How can I pray for Phoebe? I know she's 'not like me', as Vic so blatantly put it. A bit of a party girl, I suppose. Probably not a churchgoer, either. Is she a Christian? Is that it?" He stayed silent for several minutes, listening, attentive.

A year ago, at Gia's pleading, he'd agreed to go on a blind date with the eldest Gustafson sister, Juliette. It was an agreement that actually went against his dating guidelines—he'd made the decision not to date anyone he wouldn't be interested in marrying. It didn't mean he would only date the one person he'd marry someday, but that he wouldn't treat dating like entertainment. He had friends he could hang out with for entertainment. To him, dating was all about romance and learning to love someone. He considered it more of an investment into a future, lifelong partnership, so to speak. His buddies often teased him mercilessly about it, but only because they didn't share his convictions. He didn't mind, nor did he judge anyone else by the standards he set for himself.

So, when Gia approached him about Juliette and the intervention plan the sisters had put together, he'd said no at first, partly because of his standards, but also partly because he saw it as a little cruel and slightly twisted to both Juliette and the various men they were planning to throw at the poor girl. He wanted no part in it.

But Gia had told him to pray about it, and even though her voice had held a hint of jest in it, he'd done just that. And the next night, he'd called the girl up and agreed to take Juliette out.

It was one of the best decisions he'd ever made, a perfect example of how God stretches his people to move beyond self-imposed limits to experience life God's way. Trevor strongly believed in the importance of having high and clear standards, but also in the value of being willing to make exceptions when the Lord nudged him. Because he'd obeyed God's very clear directing—he'd awakened in the middle of the night with an absolute certainty that he needed to say *yes* to the date—Juliette had allowed him the privilege of sharing Jesus Christ with her. He'd also been there to intercede on her behalf when Victor Jarrett had shown up under ridiculous misconceptions, confused and disconcerted by love, and had made an utter fool of himself. Because Trevor had prayed, listened, and obeyed, he was slowly, but surely, being embraced into the circle of Gustafson girls—first by Gia, then Juliette, and now, tentatively, by Renata and Baby Charise. And maybe, soon, by Phoebe....

"Am I supposed to lead her to you? If so, then show me how. Create opportunities for me to talk to her about you, the way you did with Juliette—" That thought brought him up short as he imagined taking Phoebe out on a date. To dinner. On the back of his bike. Her lean, petite body pressed against his back, her arms wrapped around his waist, her thighs— "Aaah!" he groaned. "No. Please don't make me take her out on my bike. Not until after we're married."

And that made him laugh out loud at himself. "Trevor Aidan Zander, you are a desperate, hopeless fool." He braced his gloved hands on the steel rail and hunched his shoulders up around his ears a little. The breeze was gentle, but it nipped at his skin with a taste of winter, and whispered secrets to him he longed to know.

Pray for Phoebe. NOW.

The thought crashed through him so forcefully, that he stood up and held his breath, waiting for more. The urgency of it had his hands shaking; he knew it wasn't the cold, because he was suddenly flushed with supernatural awareness.

He raised his arms above his head and began to pray. "Lord God, I don't know what's going on, but I'm standing here before you, asking for the life of my friend, Phoebe. Holy Spirit, protect her from whatever it is that has her in its grip tonight." The words poured out of him as he lifted her up to God. "Crush the head of Satan right now, Jesus. He wants to steal her heart, to kill and destroy her. Take away his power and show Phoebe the truth of who you are, Jesus, and the freedom only you can give her."

He fell silent for a moment, the breeze no longer nipping at him, but soothing him instead, calming him.

A fleeting thought had him hoping no one would drive by and misinterpret what they saw; he must look like some kind of modern-day druid trying to call down powers from the moon and stars scattered across the night sky. He smiled at how close to the truth it was, in fact. Trevor claimed his priesthood as a believer, and he was standing on the side of the mountain, calling on the power of the one true God who ruled over Heaven and Earth. Not for himself, but for the life of a lost lamb named Phoebe. He began to hum an old hymn from his youth, all but a few of the words forgotten. "There is power, power, wonder-working power in the precious blood of the Lamb...."

Jesus knew what it was to be a lamb led to slaughter. He knew how it felt to be disregarded, to be betrayed, to be denied, and something in Trevor sensed that Phoebe had experienced much of the same thing in her own life. He'd met so many people in the last several years who had suffered at the hands of people they loved, who had been abandoned by those who'd promised never to leave. He couldn't count the times a broken person had shared how they'd been so desperate for help, only to be turned away by those they sought help from. And more often than not, by those who claimed to be Christians. By people who represented the gracious and merciful and loving God.

Trevor had heard it said far too many times that Christians were notorious for shooting their wounded. And he knew it to be true—he'd been justly accused of holding the gun of sanctimonious contempt himself. Back when he was a new college graduate, all fired up about turning the face of today's generation toward God. A Jesus freak—and proud of it!—who had practiced what he preached and had all good things in his life to show for it. An idealistic holy roller who was quick to wax eloquent about the marvelous grace and mercy of the God he loved—and he truly did love God with every fiber of his being—but even quicker to draw heavy-handed and immovable lines in the sand that kept him safe from the blemishes of the world.

In his desire to be like Jesus, Trevor had elevated himself to godhood rather than godliness. He'd measured his worth—and the worth of all those around him—by their right or wrong living, creating a standard that no one, not even he, could possibly measure up to... and then doling out placating and empty messages about asking God's forgiveness and what would Jesus do, and taking responsibility for our own actions by repenting and trying harder to do what was right.

It was everything he preached *against* these days. Everything he never wanted to be again. The message in the music of his new album was that of humility, of servanthood, of raising others up and not himself.

Oh, yes, he'd been rightfully accused. And found guilty beyond a shadow of a doubt. Not by a judge and jury of peers, but by the whisper of the Holy Spirit as Trevor's eyes and ears were opened to the truth.

Trevor had been called out by a young pregnant girl who'd thrown his own pious words back in his face, and he'd stood there, stunned by the validity of her words. He could still hear her tight-throated snarl: A pompous, self-righteous, arrogant, windbag of a Youth Pastor in Training, she'd called him... as she'd flipped her long, dark hair over her shoulder... jabbed him in the chest with a finger again and again... and stared down his disdain with eyes the color of misty moors, skin like a porcelain doll, and a mouth that made a man forget how to form complete sentences.

"Oh... God," Trevor groaned as he went to his knees, his legs giving out beneath him. "Oh, God. Oh, dear Jesus. Help her. Help me. Help us both." He fell forward, his arms wrapped over his head, his nose nearly to the gravel, as he groaned out his prayer, asking God to make a way for him to undo what he'd done. He knew God had already forgiven him—he'd repented of his pride long ago—but now he begged God to help Phoebe to forgive him, too.

When the words ran out, he just moaned, remembering the scripture verse he'd shared with Phoebe—not Jo—all those years ago. *In the same way, the Spirit helps us in our weakness. We do not know what we ought to pray for, but the Spirit himself intercedes for us through wordless groans.*

"Search my heart, Jesus," he whispered. "Help me."

TWENTY-ONE

ALL THE WAY BACK down the mountain, Trevor kept praying, asking for wisdom, for the right time and place, the right words to say to Phoebe. And he prayed for her protection and peace.

No one had mentioned a child of Phoebe's.

What was in the woman's past... because of him? Or in spite of him. Had she had the baby or had an abortion? The thought twisted his gut painfully. Had she had the baby and given him or her up for adoption? Or had Phoebe raised the child? A teenager. The baby she'd been carrying would be a teenager now. That was almost fourteen years ago.

But surely Vic would have brought up a teenager the other day when he was all but warning Trevor away from Phoebe. Surely, he would have made the single parent thing one more point for him to consider. And none of the photos he'd perused online had given any indication of the presence of a child other than Renata's boys.

He needed to talk to someone. There was absolutely no way he could rest tonight with this burden sitting heavily on his chest. Was he supposed to go straight to Phoebe tonight? Pour his heart out to her and beg her forgiveness? But that seemed insane. What if she didn't even remember that day?

Or worse, what if she did?

But her behavior toward him the day he'd carried her gas can for her led him to believe she'd been unaware of his identity, that she hadn't recognized him.

He ended up in front of Vic's house around nine PM. He hadn't bothered calling, and he hoped for all he was worth that his friend would be home and alone.

Victor was home. But he wasn't alone.

Juliette came to the door before he even had a chance to knock. "I heard you pull up. Recognized the rumble." Her smile was warm and welcoming. "Come on in. We just finished talking wedding stuff and were getting ready for a bowl of ice cream and brownies."

Trevor would have liked to refuse; he didn't know if he could play nice right now. He thought he might just jump out of his skin if he couldn't talk to someone about his revelation. But there was no way he could spill to Vic, not with Juliette present. He had no idea what she knew, and he wasn't going to be the one to tell Phoebe's secrets.

If they were secrets, that is.

Trevor took a deep breath and let it out slowly as he followed behind Juliette into Vic's kitchen, where his friend was laying out the spread. The air was thick with the aroma of fresh-baked chocolate, and Trevor suddenly realized he'd forgotten to eat dinner. His stomach grumbled in anticipation so loudly Juliette turned to grin at him over her shoulder.

"Hungry?" she teased.

"Haven't eaten since early this afternoon."

"We've got leftover spaghetti if you want some of that before dessert." She pulled open the refrigerator door and pulled out a container of pasta. "You know where the plates are. You okay to just microwave it?"

Trevor accepted the offering gratefully and made short work of the meal preparation. When he sat down across from Vic with his steaming plate of food, his friend eyed him curiously.

"So, what brings you here tonight?" Not that there was anything that unusual about him showing up unannounced.

"Out for a ride and needed some company," Trevor said, not willing to deny that he was miserable, but not quite ready to expound yet, either. "Thanks for the grub."

"Are you alright?" Juliette asked, laying her spoon down and stretching a hand across the table toward him. She didn't quite touch him, but the gesture was meant to be comforting.

"I'm not sure." He decided to be as forthright as he could, knowing he could trust the two people across from him implicitly. He wouldn't divulge the pregnancy, just in case Phoebe had managed to keep it secret, but he thought maybe Juliette might have some insight into how he could approach her sister.

"I just spent the last two hours praying. For Phoebe. God put her on my heart tonight in a way I couldn't ignore." He snorted at the grin on Vic's face and shook his head. "It wasn't like that." He paused, held up a finger, and then amended, "Okay. It wasn't *all* like that. I was thinking about her, and about how to ask her out, and then felt this overwhelming impression that I needed to pray for her instead, okay?"

"Wow. Really?" Juliette studied him, her forehead furrowed in consternation. "You want to go out with Phoebe?"

"Yes, I do," he said, his voice quiet, but sure. Trevor understood her befuddlement. She knew personally about his feelings on dating. He'd openly divulged his standards to her the night he took her out. And he was pretty confident that if Vic didn't think Phoebe was a good match for Trevor, then neither would Juliette. And Juliette knew Phoebe far better than Vic did.

She cocked her head a little and reiterated her question. "As in *date* her, take her out? I mean, you just met her, right?"

"Yes, as in *date* her. Ask her to go out on a date with me." He hedged around the second part of the question; he still was trying to figure out exactly *how* to explain the whole situation to his friends. "I had originally just planned to possibly hire her to do my album art for me, but now I know it's more than that. I want to get to know her, to spend time with her." He swallowed, closed his eyes tightly against his shameful memories, then added. "I want her to get to know me." *The new me.*

"Wow," Juliette said again, picking up her spoon to stir the softening ice cream in her bowl. Her movements were slow and distracted, like she wasn't even aware she was doing it. "I guess when you know, you know, huh?"

Trevor took a deep breath in, feeling his lungs fill inside his chest, expanding his rib cage. He straightened his shoulders and released the breath slowly. "Well, there's more to it than just magically knowing."

Vic's dark eyebrows rose at the serious tone in Trevor's voice, but he didn't say anything. Juliette took a bite of her dessert, her eyes wide with curiosity.

"This evening, while I was praying for Phoebe, I remembered something. I remembered Phoebe."

"Wait. What? You two have met before? Well, that's cool." Juliette set her spoon down again and leaned forward, a smile lighting up her features, but just for a moment. "Isn't it?" Doubt flickered in her eyes as she studied Trevor's face. "How do you know her?"

Victor reached over and placed a hand over one of Juliette's. He didn't say a word, but Juliette turned to him and then back to Trevor. "Sorry. You talk. We listen."

"Almost fourteen years ago, I was working as an Intern in the Youth Department of a little church here in Midtown. I was actually fairly new to the church—I was there because of the internship—so I really didn't know many of the congregation, but I'd been working with the youth for almost the whole school year and pretty much knew all the faces, if not all the names, in our group. One day—it was a Monday—I was heading through the empty sanctuary toward the youth building and there was a girl sitting in the dark near the back. I was with one of the pastors, talking about some new program I was all gung-ho to launch to the kids. We stopped to ask if she was all right, if she needed anything."

"Phoebe? Was it Phoebe?" Juliette's voice was tiny, hushed.

Trevor nodded, not caring that she was rushing him. This wasn't story hour. He wasn't on stage performing, and definitely not out to impress anyone. "At first she said no, but then when I offered to get one of the ladies to come out and pray with her, she agreed to the idea."

"It was Phoebe? Are you sure?"

"Jules." Vic's voice was more caress than reprimand.

"Sorry. Go on."

Trevor took a steadying breath. Now that he'd gotten started, the words seemed to come easier. "I went to get one of the female staff members, but she was hung up for a few minutes, so I headed back in to wait with—with your sister until she got there. I was worried she might bolt; she had this desperate glint in her eye, and I sensed her decision to even be there at all was hard won. She said she wouldn't mind my company, so I sat, and we talked. She told me her name was Jo."

Juliette frowned for a moment, then her eyes widened in understanding. "Josephine. That's her middle name. Phoebe Josephine Gustafson. Daddy always called her Phoebe Jo, but she didn't let anyone else. Especially not after... after my parents' accident." Anyone who didn't know Juliette wouldn't have caught the slight catch and pause in her statement, but Trevor recognized it for what it was. It didn't matter that more than fifteen years had passed since that fateful night. The Gustafson girls still grieved the loss of their parents.

"It was only a year or two after your parents' accident, if I remember right. I'd heard about it in the news, but because I wasn't working there at the time of the tragedy, I didn't know that your grandparents went to that little church. From what Phoebe indicated that day, you and your sisters still went to the youth group at your old church?"

Juliette nodded. "Renata did. We all went to Sunday service with Granny G and Grandpa, but not the youth group. And Gia was too young. Phoebe didn't go at all." She frowned, concentrating, remembering. "In fact, I think she stopped going to church altogether a year or two after the accident."

Trevor sighed, trying to push back the guilt that made him feel like crawling in a hole. "Well, I didn't make the connection back then, even when she told me you guys were living with your grandparents. I was pretty caught up in my own self-importance and purpose, I suppose. I had these really elevated ideas of who I was and what my role was as a youth leader. So, when she started opening up, I listened—I really did—but I was so focused on my own ideals and truths that I didn't *hear* what she wasn't saying." He emphasized the word with a fist over his heart. "She needed help. A mother figure, she said. And I gave her religious vitriol—her words, by the way—about right and wrong and taking responsibility for our actions."

"Oh, Phoebe," Juliette whispered, her voice catching again, but this time for her sister's pain, not her own.

"It was the day after Mother's Day and one of the things the pastor had touched on was how God had designed the church as a family, and that the older generation needed to be father and mother figures to the younger generations. That's why she was there. Not to hear me go all holier-than-thou on her."

He sighed and ran his hands over his messy hair, lacing his fingers at the back of his head, wishing he could share more. But if Juliette had known about the baby, surely, she would have said something; he'd left a door wide open for her to bring that information through.

He sighed deeply, despairingly. "She left. She called me on the carpet for being, essentially, a Pharisee. Her words were much more descriptive and flavorful, mind you." He felt one side of his mouth lift in what might be called a wry grin, but he was too disheartened to make light of the situation. "And I felt every one of her words like nails in my coffin. I was everything she'd accused me of. I may have been *right*." He lifted his fingers to make quotation marks. "But I certainly didn't speak the truth in love. I wasn't Jesus to Phoebe that day, and she knocked me right off my puffed-up soapbox." He shook his head, remembering how brutally her words had deflated him. "Then, to make matters worse, I was too ashamed, too humiliated to go after her. I let her leave... and then I lied to the woman who came looking for her, told her Jo—Phoebe—had gotten help from someone else and had already gone home." He unlaced his fingers and his head fell back. He pressed the heels of his palms against his eyes and groaned. "I helped her, all right. Helped her right out the church door. Oh God, let it not be too late for me to get out of your way."

When he straightened up, he groaned again. Silent tears tracked down Juliette's cheeks. She sat still as a stone, staring into her bowl, clutching tightly to Victor's hand as though afraid to let go.

"Juliette. I'm so sorry." He reached forward across the table, but Vic gave him a quick shake of the head, so Trevor didn't touch her. "I'm so sorry for what I did, for who I was, for how I treated your sister." When she only nodded, he continued. "I looked for her every Sunday after that. I knew her grandparents attended—she'd said as much—but she hadn't told me their names. I asked around about a girl named Jo, but hit dead ends there, too."

"It wasn't your fault," Juliette whispered, dabbing at her cheeks with a paper napkin. "It's all right, Trevor."

But he shook his head. "It's not all right. In the Book of James, it says, '*Those who consider themselves religious and yet do not keep a tight rein on their tongues deceive themselves, and their religion is worthless. Religion that*

God our Father accepts as pure and faultless is this: to look after orphans and widows in their distress and to keep oneself from being polluted by the world.' It was like God had the apostle James write those two verses to me. I had the whole 'keeping oneself from being polluted by the world' part down, but I'd somehow missed that little word 'and' between that part of the statement and the 'look after orphans and widows in their distress' part. *And.* Not *or.* And." He thumped the table with a fist. Not hard, but with obvious frustration. "And the tight rein on the tongue?"

"Sounds like you used yours more like a whip than reins," Victor stated. His words hurt, but his tone was gentle. "I've been in your shoes, my friend. Juliette can attest to that."

Juliette nodded again, a sad smile tugging up the corners of her mouth. "Yes. The words that come to mind are pompous, self-righteous, judg—"

"I think he gets the gist, Jules." Victor ducked his head, but he was smiling now, too.

"Well, at least you saw the error of your ways, Vic. And look what came of it." She kissed him on the cheek. "You won my heart."

The air in the room seemed to lighten, and Trevor found it a little easier to breathe. "You know, those are some of the same words Phoebe used to describe me. I seem to recall windbag and arrogant, along with a few other choice words that would likely make a sailor blush."

"Oh, Trevor. Were you really that bad? It seems so out of character for you." Juliette's eyes were still bright with tears. "I can see Phoebe behaving the way she did—that girl was born with a chip on her shoulder—but you have never come across to me as judgmental and arrogant."

"Ah." Trevor shook his head and looked down at his hands. His head hurt a little over all that had gone through it this night... over the knowledge that this was only the beginning of things. "My arrogance—my pride—continues to be a problem. I actually convinced myself that God wanted me to take you out last year so I could introduce you to Christ. Makes me out to look pretty snazzy, right? I mean, if I'd not acted in obedience, you'd still be a sinner bound for hell. Thanks to me," he reached for his glass of water and lifted it in a mock toast. "Thanks to me, you are now saved and redeemed and going to Heaven. Please." He glanced around the room as though he had an audience. "No, please. Hold your applause. It was nothing. Nothing."

"Trevor." Juliette's voice was kind, soothing.

He wanted none of it. "But tonight, guess what I discovered. I discovered that this wasn't about me saving you, but about me being in the right place for my comeuppance. Taking you out was just the fork in the road that led me to this place. This hall of shame, where I'm now faced with the girl I all but tossed out of heaven because of my arrogance."

"Trevor, please."

"Tell me something. Is Phoebe a believer? Does she go to church with your grandparents these days? Or on her own somewhere?"

Juliette didn't respond; her silence was answer enough.

"When did she stop going to church? Think back. Could it have been after that Mother's Day about fourteen years ago?" Trevor leaned forward, lacing his fingers tightly together on the table in front of him as he watched Juliette.

She opened her mouth, closed it, then opened it again. "It was Mother's Day. I remember now. I remember because I cried for two days after that same sermon. Because I didn't want another mother. I didn't want someone to be a mother figure to me; I wanted my own mother. Phoebe just shut down altogether." Her voice had dropped to a whisper and Trevor bent closer to hear her words. "I thought—I thought it was because of Mother's Day. I thought she stopped going because she didn't want another mother, either. I didn't know. I was too wrapped up in my own bitterness and grief to notice her needs."

Juliette laid her head on Victor's shoulder and released a long sigh. "You two aren't the only ones with selfish arrogance in your pasts."

TWENTY-TWO

Phoebe ate the whole gyro wrap, along with the large bag of fries she'd added to the order last minute, and she drank two more bottles of water. Her headache was waning, and the food in her stomach helped relieve the shakiness in her limbs, but she headed back upstairs to lie down again, anyway. She wanted to forget about the last two days, forget about the memories that had emerged out of the inebriated fog she'd been in for days.

Most of all, she wanted to hide away a little longer, put off answering phone calls and text messages and doorbells as long as she could. Baby Charise may want to see her, but Phoebe wasn't ready to see Baby Charise yet.

The tiny cries that made everyone in the room coo pleasurably. The flailing, angry limbs as the little girl was thrust into the great big world—"Put me back! Put me back!" Renata's whimpers of joy and her obvious accomplishment over a job well done, the prize placed victoriously in her arms. Tool Belt Tim hovering, stroking, kissing, holding, whispering words of adoration and pride over both his girls.

"I can't bear it," Phoebe moaned, lowering herself gingerly to the side of her bed. "I can't bear it."

But the memories would not be held at bay.

• • • • • • • • •

Fifteen years earlier...

Exactly one month later, on the morning of July 10th, Phoebe's water broke in the middle of the kitchen while she made pancakes with Theresa Rogers.

After a few hours of hard and fast labor, she was wheeled into Delivery. The room thrummed with activity in chaotic contrast to the hollowness of Phoebe's soul. She breathed rhythmically—long and slow, in through the nose, out through the mouth—as her muscles worked to rid her body of the tiny bundle of life inside her. She focused on filling her lungs, on expanding her chest until she couldn't take in any more oxygen, and then letting the air flow out between her lips, steady and constant, but not forceful. She thought of the candle game she and her sisters played, where they had to blow hard enough to keep the flame dancing, but not enough to actually extinguish it. Phoebe imagined a dancing flame hovering in the air in front of her face. *Don't blow it out or you lose!*

Each inhale and exhale tore loose another thread from the cord that bound her to her baby. With every contraction, another strap of the bond broke loose. With every soft moan, Phoebe felt the dull, serrated edge of separation ripping and tearing her baby from her.

She would not look at the man and woman who stood close—kind, loving, precious strangers—who watched and waited, tears of joy coursing down their faces as they witnessed her child—no, *their* child—braving the rite of passage that is called birth.

Phoebe's eyes remained dry. Her tears would come later; she kept her anguish wedged inside the chambers of her heart, her rib cage a tightly latched prison. She embraced the pain that twisted and tore at her, bore down into it like a guilty woman taking her just punishment.

The doctor, a soft-spoken woman—Phoebe only remembered her first name, Melissa—touched her with gentle, but intentional hands. She exuded confidence, not just in her own medical knowledge and experience, but also confidence in Phoebe's intuition and instincts as a birthing mother. Not once did she look on her sixteen-year-old patient with condescension or judgment. In fact, at one point—it was one of Phoebe's sharpest memories of the ordeal—Melissa came around to the side of the bed and took Phoebe's hand in hers. She leaned close, so she was eye-to-eye with her and said, "You are brave. You are strong. You are amazing. I believe in you."

No one had said those words to her since her mother had died.

Phoebe still didn't cry. She didn't look at Jeff and Theresa. She didn't think about the baby she wouldn't nurse, the infant she wouldn't bathe, the child who would grow to look like her—would she have the gray Gustafson eyes? The inky black curls? Would she paint pretty pictures?—the girl who would never know her real mother. Instead, she kept her gaze trained on Melissa's face, the doctor's smiling eyes her focal point.

When Melissa told her to slide down on the table, helped lift her feet into the stirrups, and then instructed her to push when she felt the urge, Phoebe did as she was told, barely aware of the nurse who stood beside her, coaching her as she breathed, held, pushed, breathed, held, pushed....

Lily Grace Rogers slid into the waiting arms of a glistening-eyed doctor. "A beautiful baby girl!" Then she was laid on the trembling abdomen of the dry-eyed teenager while her umbilical cord was cut by her teary-eyed new father. Lily's new mother—the one who would adopt and raise her as her own—placed one hand of blessing on the back of the head of the squalling, squeezed-shut-eyed infant, and one hand on top of Phoebe's head, and thanked God for bringing them all together.

Overwhelmed by an immediate and crushing love for the baby resting slippery and naked against her own flesh, Phoebe cooed, "Hello, baby girl. It's all right. It's all right." Lily quieted just for a moment; her flailing movements stilled. Against her own better judgment, Phoebe touched one fingertip to the tiny lips, gasping at the immediate rooting response from Lily as the baby turned toward the feathery touch, her head bobbing, mouth wide.

Phoebe heard Theresa's breath catch, too, and when she glanced up at the woman beside her, she saw a gut-wrenching combination of possessive fear and gratefulness in her eyes. Phoebe recognized it for what it was. *Don't worry. She's yours.* She let her hand slip back to the crumpled sheets she'd been clutching only moments before; she would not intentionally touch the baby again.

She turned her face away from Theresa, from Jeff, from Lily. Away from Melissa's too-aware gaze and toward the wall. She closed her eyes, thought about her favorite beach at sunset, the way the sand ground between her toes as she walked, how the water was always surprisingly cold, even on the hottest of summer days.

A single, searing tear slipped from the corner of Phoebe's eye and burned a track across her temple and into her hair. Surely, it would leave a puckered scar, a mark that would forever brand her as a mother who had abandoned her child.

TWENTY-THREE

"I'm not going to tell you to pray about it," Vic said, sitting back in his chair, an arm holding Juliette to his side. "I figure you're going to be doing a lot of that without me having to suggest it."

Trevor stood and took his plate to the sink, washed the dish, and then took his time loading a bowl with ice cream and a brownie. He wasn't really hungry for dessert, but he needed to keep his hands busy.

"Thanks. So other than praying, you two have any suggestions on how to go about approaching Phoebe? I'm not going to wait until she brings it up. I'll be careful, but I'm not going to even try to pretend like it didn't happen if she doesn't remember me. I know if our roles were reversed, it would only tick me off more to have her know something like this and not say anything. Especially if she finally worked up the courage to tell me days, weeks, or months down the road, and all along she knew and was hiding it. That's the same as lying, right?"

Juliette straightened. "Trevor, if I know one thing for sure about my sister, it's that she's very good at keeping people out and keeping her real thoughts and feelings in. I don't know why she went to the church for help back then—it was a strange year, now that I look back. I'd already graduated, but I still lived with my grandparents, too afraid to leave the family I still had, too afraid to move past my parents' deaths. I was pretty shut down in those first few years, but I do remember some terrible fights between Renata and Phoebe. It seems like it was about boys most of the time, but I don't remember boys coming around the house at all. Not in those early years."

"It must have been so hard on all of you," Trevor murmured. "Those transitioning years into adulthood can be brutal even with great parents around to help you through it. I can't begin to imagine."

Juliette took a long drink of water and then sat forward a little, her forehead furrowed in thought. "You know what? Phoebe went away the summer before her senior year. She left on some kind of a summer work program—I think it was one of those sustainable farming programs where students learned while working or something like that. I figured it was just to get away from us—from the animosity between her and Renata. I thought it would be good for both of them." She smiled wryly. "For all of us."

Trevor lowered his eyes. He was pretty sure she hadn't gone to a farm to learn how to plant crops year-round. He was pretty sure she'd found someone who would help her with her pregnancy in whatever capacity she needed. He just prayed that the baby—the teenager now—was alive somewhere, being loved on by good parents.

"She came home in time for school to start and seemed much better, partly because of the time away, I'm sure, but also because Renata headed off to college that year, so Phoebe had the high school to herself. Gia started first grade that year," Juliette added, still lost in her memories.

"What do you mean by *better*?" Trevor asked, only glancing at her briefly.

"Just calmer. More aloof, too, like she'd grown up a little. I suppose you would have to grow up and be responsible at a place like that."

Trevor nodded. "I suppose you would have to." But he kept his head down. Oh, the burden that Phoebe had apparently carried alone for all these years.

"My advice is to take it slow. I don't know why she came to church that day, except that, like I said, it had been a really tough year for her and Ren, but the fact that she told you she came looking for a mother—" Juliette's voice broke, and she bit back a half sob, then tried again. "The fact she asked for help at all tells me she was really, really desperate. Things have never been easy between Phoebe and Ren, as far back as I can remember, in fact. At first, it seemed to get better after my parents died, but that year? I don't know, Trevor. I was still so caught up in my own head, I just didn't pay enough attention. Even though we have all remained close, something changed that year. In all of us, but mostly in Phoebe, I think. I guess I just figured it was an inevitable change because we were all becoming adults and figuring out our separate paths." She let the sentence trail off, but Trevor could tell this whole thing had her rethinking the way things were and why they went the way they did.

"I understand the need to tread carefully. I promise I will. God knows I don't want a repeat. But I know—I *know*—this is a second chance for, well, for us. For Phoebe and me. In whatever capacity. I want to pursue her heart, but I have a feeling once she finds out who I am—" He broke off, refusing to say what he feared might happen. "So, I'll focus on her soul for now. And maybe, in time, she'll open her heart to me."

"She's not a flowers and chocolates kind of girl," Juliette said. "I mean, she likes that stuff as much as the next girl, but she's so accustomed to men trying to woo her in all the cliché ways. You're going to have to get creative."

Trevor grunted, feeling overwhelmed all over again.

"Especially if you're going after her soul first," she added.

Victor chuckled. "Good luck, my friend. I think you're going to need it."

Trevor eyed his friends. "But you give me your blessing? Both of you?" He saw the uncertainty on their faces, but it was important that these two people—his best friend and Phoebe's sister—agreed and supported him in this. "If either one of you tells me I'm wrong or even off about this, I'll pull back. I trust you, and I would really appreciate knowing you're in agreement."

Victor leaned forward, resting his elbows on the table. He covered one of Juliette's hands with his own and cleared his throat. "Well, Juliette can speak for herself, but I will say this. Don't do anything tonight except pray. We'll pray with you now, and then I'll commit to praying for you tonight, too. But while you're doing so, maybe ask yourself a few questions. Are you pursuing Phoebe for the right reasons? I mean, if you're going to be obedient to the Word of God, you can't pursue a romantic relationship with her if she's not a Christian. Are you prepared to walk away if she says 'no' to God?"

Trevor cringed inwardly at the question, one he'd not wanted to ask himself—or perhaps one he hadn't wanted to have to answer—but he nodded slowly, knowing he would have to do just that.

Victor held up a hand. "I don't want you to answer me right now. I'm challenging you to talk these things over with God tonight and tomorrow if you don't have clear answers, or longer if you need to. In fact, maybe take tomorrow and fast while you pray. You're talking about not only preparing to address what seems to have been a major turning point in Phoebe's life—one you potentially played a pretty significant role in—but you're also considering making a huge step toward both your futures, if indeed, you decide to try to win her heart, too."

"All right," Trevor agreed. "That makes sense to me. I'll start with prayer tonight. Then I'll spend the day tomorrow fasting and praying before I take any other action." He caught the bemused expression on Juliette's face and realized that as a fairly new Christian, she may not quite understand the concept. "And Vic, after I'm gone, fill your fiancée in on how this whole fasting thing works."

Victor squeezed Juliette's hand and continued. "You believe God has asked you to take your music to a new level, a new place, and you're neck deep in that project now, right?" He didn't wait for Trevor to confirm. "Well, does pursuing Phoebe right now line up with this project? Or will it take you away from it; will she distract you from this calling on your life?"

"These are tough questions, honey," Juliette murmured beside him.

"Yes, they are. But I think because of the magnitude of the situation, they're questions that need to be asked."

"I agree," Trevor said. "It's all right. Anything else?" he asked, his gaze shifting back and forth between them. "Anything at all?"

"Are you willing to wait? Would you be willing to wait if God wants you to wait for His timing? If he says it's not the right time now?"

"To talk about our history together? Or to go after her heart?"

"Both. Either."

Trevor nodded, mulling over the notion. It didn't feel right to even consider waiting—he wanted to charge over there right now, at this very moment, crash through her door and tell her how sorry he was, what a fool he'd been, and beg her forgiveness, then plead with her for a fresh start.

Now! Not after a day or two or more of praying and fasting. So the thought of not doing anything felt almost suffocating. He made a little grunting sound that might have been a laugh. "He'd better make that pretty darn clear, if that's what he wants."

"I have a question," Juliette said. Her words were soft, tentative, and Trevor cocked his head to look at her. "Or two. But I actually do want answers tonight, if you can give them. And they may be selfish."

"Ask away." His tone remained modulated, but his heart rate accelerated. He wasn't sure he wanted to hear what she had to ask.

"Okay. First, let me start out by saying that I fully support you talking to her about whatever happened in that church. It's obvious to me that the air needs to be cleared between you two. I wish I could remember more about what was going on around that time, but I don't, so I have to trust your instincts on this." She pointed at him as she added, "And I do. I trust your instincts on that part."

"Good," Trevor nodded slowly. "That part is priority right now and if it weren't for the rest of it, I'd be there tonight, talking to Phoebe, instead of you two." He rested his elbows on the table. "Go on."

"Why?" she asked without any more preamble. "I mean, I love Phoebe beyond anything that you can possibly imagine. I want the best for her. And honestly, in some strange way, I think you might be the best person in the world for someone like her. You'd understand her flamboyant and creative side better than any of us do. You don't seem to be afraid of anything, and believe me, Phoebe has scared off more than one good man in her life."

Trevor bit back a grin; Juliette Gustafson was picking up speed. She did that when she was passionate about something... or just nervous. He wasn't laughing at her—Juliette was one of the most transparent people he knew, and it was one of the many things he appreciated about her. He forced his features to remain neutral and kept his eyes trained on her face as she continued.

"You're not judgmental and you don't beat people over the head with your high standards, but you have them, and you live them. You might actually be strong enough to take on someone like my sister and survive. Even thrive."

"Well, thank you. I think." Trevor did smile at that, but his eyebrows rose in question. "And yet, I hear a *but* in there."

"Yeah. *But.*" Juliette nodded. "Those are all reasons why you would be good for Phoebe. But what about the other way around? How is Phoebe good for you? Why are you drawn to her? Why Phoebe, of all people?" She turned to Victor, her expression troubled. Trevor realized she was looking to her man for confirmation—they were already a closely knit team. Either they'd already discussed this, or she was asking him to reassure her that she wasn't just being unkind. Her next words confirmed it. "I know that sounds awful of me, but because I care so much about both of you," she looked Trevor's way again, "I just feel like I need to know before I can fully get behind you. I don't want either of you to go into this with false hope."

Ah. He remembered Juliette's experience with the man she'd been in a relationship with for ten years before Victor. She'd been deeply hurt when she'd learned their expectations of each other, and the future of their relationship was quite different.

"And..." She hesitated, but he waited, giving her room to get the words out on her time. "You just met her. I know you officially met her ages ago, but it doesn't seem like it should count. I mean, she wasn't even an adult yet."

Trevor almost corrected her—*she was certainly dealing with situations no child should have to deal with alone*—but he held his tongue.

"And I know I talk about her all the time, so it may *feel* like you know her, but I admittedly have a rather biased opinion of her, so it's probably not very wise to base your perception of who she is on what I say."

Trevor nodded, not breaking eye contact with Juliette. He had a good hunch where this was all heading.

"Which means, technically, you met her for the first time last Saturday, spent half an hour with her at best, and now, here it is, a little over a week later, and you think you want to marry her?"

TWENTY-FOUR

"Help me understand, Trevor. Why Phoebe?" Juliette took a steadying breath and pulled a curly lock of her long hair over her shoulder to toy with the ends of it.

Trevor had seen Phoebe do the same thing all those years ago in that shadowy church, and he'd noticed she'd also done it while standing on the sidewalk waiting for him to get her car started. It made his chest tight to realize how much he'd noticed about the woman in such a short period of time. He swallowed back the discomfort and considered a moment before answering.

"Okay. So it may be a little over the top, but go with me on this." He leaned forward, and gesturing with his hands, he tried to explain. "Imagine a thirsty man—let's say he's a homesteader looking for the perfect place where he can build his home and raise his family—who stumbles upon the most spectacular mountain spring. After a moment—just a moment, mind you—of stunned awe and gratitude, he plunges his hands into the crystal-clear water and downs that nectar of the gods with great exuberance, taking his fill of it within moments." He cupped his hands together and pretended he was scooping water to his mouth. "It's love at first sight. The spring is lovely, the ground around it is lush and the trees are choice for building with. It will require some work, sure, but he's not afraid of hard work."

"If Phoebe's the spring in this story, and you're the homesteader, you'd better have his same work ethic," Juliette warned.

Trevor grinned but continued his tale. "He sits by the water's edge, overwhelmed by the beauty of it all, grateful for the path that led him to it. He's fully aware that there may be more springs, more streams—maybe bigger, clearer, deeper—out there, but from his perspective, this one is everything he could possibly need or want. The water is so delicious, so refreshing, so... *sparkly.*" He chuckled at the word that came to mind because it made him think of Phoebe and all her chunky shiny jewelry and flashing eyes. "And he knows he'll never be satisfied with any other water ever again."

Victor shook his head, one side of his mouth crooking up in a slightly mocking grin. "Oh boy. You've got it bad, my friend. Worse than I thought."

Trevor threw his crumpled napkin at him; the officer caught it out of the air and tossed it back, hitting Trevor in the chest, directly over the heart. *Touché!* thought Trevor, but he focused on Juliette again and continued. "Even so, the urgency has passed. And now, he simply wants to sip, and savor, tasting every drop, the texture and temperature of the liquid as it passes over his lips, his tongue. He wants to dip his whole face in it, his whole body. He wants to raise his banner over the spring and claim it as his own. And with every swallow, he prays not only that the spring will never run dry, but also that he will never be taken from it again."

"A little over the top, ya think?" Victor quipped. "Just a smidge, maybe?"

Trevor sat back, folding his hands on the table in front of him, dogged in his intentions. "Maybe. Sure. But would you ask that man *why*? *Why* the spring? *Why* does he want to stay there forever after having only discovered it? I doubt it—the reasons seem pretty obvious. It's a beautiful spring. It meets his needs and more. It's unclaimed. The list goes on and on. Sure, you might ask him for details about his plans for the spring. For instance, what if there are wild animals in the woods who also drink from the spring? Will he be willing to share with those who need the water? What happens in winter? Will the spring freeze over? And what if the spring gets tired of offering the man the elixir and it dries up one day? What if the man gets tired of the same old water every single day? These are all valid questions to ask him, especially since he wants to stake his claim on the spring, but you wouldn't even think to wonder *why* he wanted to stay, would you? He's a homesteader looking for a place to call home and he's found one. In fact, the more likely question would be *why not?* Don't you think?"

"You're crazy," Juliette stated after a glaringly silent pause, shaking her head in tandem with Victor beside her. They looked like they were both watching the same cuckoo clock pendulum. "That is the craziest, most insane, most bizarre, over the top thing I've ever heard anyone say." She closed her eyes and placed the hand not being held by Victor over her heart. "But in a strange way, it's also pretty stinkin' romantic, if you ask me." Her eyes popped open. "But crazy."

"What? You don't believe in love at first sight?" Trevor asked.

"Seriously? Or are you just being facetious?" Juliette laughed out loud. "Because I totally believe in chemistry at first sight. Absolutely. But love at first sight?" She shook her head brusquely this time. "Nope. Too many people are fooled by their hormones, my friend. Just because there's chemistry; it doesn't mean love is a given."

Victor turned to her; his head cocked to one side a little. "Actually, I might have to argue that point with you, Jules."

Trevor grinned broadly and kept his mouth shut, curious to see how this would play out.

"Ha. Really? You? Officer Dot-Every-I-and-Cross-Every-T? You really believe in love at first sight?" Juliette leaned back and looked down her nose at Victor, her eyes dancing with humor. "No way. Much too impulsive and unorganized for you."

The two of them locked gazes, and for a few moments, Trevor thought they wouldn't even notice if he got up and left the table. But then Victor reached over and cupped Juliette's cheek with a large hand. She blushed prettily and shot a quick glance at Trevor, as though suddenly remembering he was there.

"I'd be willing to stand before a judge over this one. I fell in love with you the first time I pulled you over." Victor spoke softly, his words intended for Juliette's ears, but clearly not caring that Trevor heard him. "Granted, it took me awhile to figure out what was wrong with me—"

"What was wrong with you?" Juliette squawked indignantly, but she didn't pull away from his touch.

"I'm just teasing you, baby. But I knew. I knew, even when I didn't think it possible—"

"You didn't think it was possible to be in love with someone like me?" This time she did pull back a little, but Victor still had a hold of her hand and wouldn't let her go too far.

"You know, man, you might want to quit while you're ahead," Trevor guffawed.

"Yeah," Juliette agreed. "You're starting to sound like Mr. Darcy again."

"But that's a good thing, right? Isn't he the hero of the story?"

"Oh, you're hopeless," Juliette sighed. "And I love you for it." She nestled back against his side and turned to face Trevor. "And you're apparently hopeless, too. I'm still not sold on the love at first sight thing, but it seems to have worked out well for him," she quipped, reaching up behind her to pat Victor on the jaw.

"Quite well, indeed," Trevor agreed, his chest filling with happiness for the couple across the table from him. "But in all seriousness, Juliette, it's not much different than that silly scenario I just painted for you." He paused for a moment and carefully considered his next words. "I've been alone for ages. I've had two girlfriends—one I thought might turn into something serious, but didn't—and a few dates with women who were just friends." He dipped his head toward Juliette in acknowledgment.

"And a lovely date it was," she quipped.

"Moving on..." Victor prodded. Juliette giggled and patted his cheek again.

"But I've spent my whole life praying for the woman God intended for me to marry, at first because my parents taught me to do so, but then because I thought it seemed like a good idea, especially in my early adult years when I didn't think I was ready for a wife and family. I prayed *for* her, not about her. I wasn't asking for her to be dropped into my lap. I never really asked God to *reveal her to me*." He hooked his fingers into quotation marks at the cliché phrase. "I didn't ask to know who she was or where I might find her." He shot a grin at Victor. "I admit to complaining to God about being lonely and impatient, and even a little jealous, as I've watched so many of my friends get married and start new lives with someone they love. Vic knows. He's heard it all."

Victor nodded, but didn't give him a hard time about it.

"I've been praying *for* her. Because for years now—*years,* Juliette—I've felt God urging me to cover her in prayer. I've never felt so strongly about praying for someone, at least not for such a prolonged period of time. And certainly not for someone I haven't—or hadn't—met yet. But every time I'd start bugging God about how much longer he was going to make me wait, I'd feel the overwhelming need to pray for her. Not for me, for her."

Juliette studied him, her gaze now serious, as she listened.

"It was the same urgency I felt today, you guys," Trevor continued, his voice dropping, growing more intense. "I *recognized* it. I recognized the same spirit inside me, pushing me to go to God on behalf of this woman, Phoebe, whom I just met—and was immediately and overwhelmingly chemically attracted to, fair Juliette—and to pray for her in the same way I've been praying for the woman I knew would someday be my wife."

"Wow." The word wasn't one of disbelief or amazement, not really. It sounded more like acceptance, even though it still didn't all make sense to her. "Okay. Wow."

"And here's the thing. It isn't love at first sight, not in the Hollywood sense of the term. I know that. Yes, there's chemistry or hormones or electricity—whatever you want to call it—and she'd be lying if she said there wasn't any on her part. It was like live wires snapping between us. I had to stand on the other side of the room once we got to your place, because the current buzzing between us had me pretty much incapacitated."

"I wondered what was wrong with you." Juliette's eyes widened in understanding. "You hardly said a word and practically hid behind Victor until you two left."

Trevor grinned sheepishly. "There's no *practically* about it. I unabashedly admit to hiding behind Vic. I was scared. Not of Phoebe herself, mind you. The whole encounter scared me. It freaked me out how intensely I'd responded to her. You have to understand, Juliette. I'm not immune to women, and because of the job I do, I get lots of attention, lots of opportunities to respond, if you get my gist. I'm not being a vain braggart, please understand. It just comes with the territory."

Juliette snorted, waving a hand at him dismissively. "I know that."

"I mean, I've met some amazing women on the road, in different churches over the years. But I haven't felt that—that—"

"That zing?" she suggested.

"Yeah. That zing," Trevor agreed. "I haven't felt that zing in a while. In a long time." He shrugged one shoulder and spoke around a half-smile. "And then to learn that the woman at the gas station wasn't just some stranger I was responding to, but someone already loved by people I love?" He lowered his gaze then, almost afraid to look at them as he stated what to him seemed so obvious. So validating. "It was like an *Aha!* moment to me when I figured out that she was a Gustafson Girl. I half-expected choirs of angels to burst into song and a beam of light to shine down from heaven, the voice of God himself saying, 'Here she is. Here is the one I made for you.'"

"Sure would be nice if he'd do that kind of thing," Victor muttered. "Especially for us thick-headed men."

"Amen to that." Trevor grimaced and lifted his eyes to Juliette again. "All I got, though, was 'Pray for her. Now!' So, I did. And I'll keep praying for her, just like I've been doing for as long as I can remember."

"Which is pretty cool in my book," Juliette whispered. "Very, very romantic."

"Good. I'm glad. Because here's the deal. I believe she's the one for me; I really do. But I also believe that her soul takes priority over my heart, period. I don't want to, but I'm willing to put aside my feelings—" He broke the sentence off and started again. "That's stupid. Not even possible. Anyone who says that is a liar, just for future reference."

"Noted," Victor grunted.

"Let me rephrase that. I don't want to, but I'm willing to hold off on acting on my romantic feelings, no matter how much they torment me, in order to focus on cleaning up the mess I made of things all those years ago. I'm willing to even walk away from her if that's what she wants. It might kill me, but I'm willing. However, I'm going to need your prayers, your support, and your accountability, both of you, so here I am."

"Here you are," Juliette echoed. "And wow, I say again. Just wow." She curled her bottom lip between her teeth and worried it a bit, pondering all he'd said. Finally, she said, "Okay. Well, I don't want to jinx anything, but I feel like we should hug or something."

Trevor eyed her curiously. "Oh, yeah?"

"I mean, since we're going to be family for real and all." She stood and came around the table as he stood, too. She wrapped her arms around his waist and squeezed him tightly. "I'll go to bat for you, Trevor Aidan Zander, but you'd better do things right or I'll use that bat *on* you instead. Starting right around the kneecaps."

"Ahem. You might want to curtail the threats until the officer is out of earshot," Trevor said *sotto voce.*

"Ahem, yourself. I'll be the one actually swinging the bat, my friend," Victor retorted as he came around the table and clapped Trevor on the shoulder.

Juliette stepped back and patted Trevor's cheek. "You know, you may not yet be *in* love, but you're definitely acting *on* love—or at least the decision to love—so who am I to argue with the whole love at first sight thing? I've heard even prearranged marriages between strangers work when the couple *chooses* to love each other, when they choose to act on love rather than waiting to be in love." She stepped to Victor's side and slipped an arm around his waist. "I'm behind you on this, Trevor. If there's anything I can do, any way I can help facilitate anything, let me know. I'd love to have you as a brother-in-law one day."

Victor still had his hand on Trevor's shoulder. "I've got your back, too, Taz." He grinned, teasing again. "You're a hopeless romantic, my friend. You always have been. Just a fool finally in love." Then he grew serious again. "Can we pray for you now?"

"Absolutely, yes! I thought you'd never ask." The relief that washed over him at the offer was something akin to that moment he imagined when the thirsty man discovered the mountain spring. "Please."

Oh God, he murmured in his heart as Victor began to pray over him. *I really am a hopeless fool, aren't I?* Was it possible he was actually in love, too?

TWENTY-FIVE

IN THE DARK STILLNESS of her room, Phoebe could almost hear Lily's squeaky little cries; the whisper of memory made the very marrow of her bones ache. She drew her knees up to her chest, curling into a ball on her side beneath her billowy white bedding. Crying only made her headache worse, but her mind refused to turn away from the images she'd conjured up from the darkened chambers of her heart.

When she awoke again, the sky was a pale, early-morning gray, and her pulse pounded behind her eyes. She lay still—today would be Tuesday, right? She had nothing pressing scheduled until Friday when she had to turn in her first round of three book cover options to Vineyard. She already had two ready to send over and a third just needed font work. As much as she disliked working with the arrogant Brandon, he was remarkably photogenic, and she had yet to have to do a re-shoot on any of the projects he modeled.

Free to spend the day as she wanted, she decided she wanted to do nothing. She got up to use the bathroom, took one look at her reflection in the mirror, and headed straight back to bed.

The clock still lay on the floor where she'd dropped it after pulling the cord from the wall. She plugged it in, but when she went to set it, she realized she had no idea what time it was, so she just left it sitting on the nightstand, flashing its changing numbers at her. Her comforter reflected the electric blue glow, and she watched it, mesmerized by the pulse of color in her otherwise white sanctuary.

When a new wave of grief and guilt caught her by surprise, wrenching her out of her semi-trance, she burrowed down under the blankets again, hugging one of her pillows tightly as though she might be able to plug the gaping hole in her chest with it.

Lily had turned thirteen on July 10th this last summer, only two days after Renata had told Phoebe, Juliette, and Gia about her pregnancy. The day the four sisters held hands and watched Baby Charise dance inside Renata's womb during the ultrasound, almost as though she knew she was being filmed. Phoebe had somehow managed to keep it together, had smiled even though she could hardly catch her breath, and had celebrated with her sisters over tostada salads and iced teas.

Phoebe remembered her own thirteenth birthday. Maman had made a chocolate hazelnut dacquoise cake—a family tradition from her own upbringing in France. "Every little girl who becomes a young lady must be celebrated with a real grown-up cake of the finest textures and flavors," Simone always said, patting her daughters' cheeks with flour-dusted hands. She'd made one for each of her three older girls on their thirteenth birthdays, and when Gia had turned thirteen, Phoebe, Juliette, and Renata had taken over Granny G's kitchen and made one for their little sister in their mother's absence.

Phoebe's stomach growled; she could still taste the layers of meringue and buttercream melting in her mouth. "Oh, Maman," she whispered. "I need you."

Phoebe stayed in bed all day, getting up only to use the bathroom and to refill her water glass. She slept off and on as her system recovered from the abuse of the alcohol, but only fitfully, her mind toying with her vulnerable emotions. Her empty belly played along, and she dreamed that she'd swallowed something invasive, something seemingly insignificant at first, like a tiny seed, but it had taken root inside her. And like Jack's beanstalk, it was now growing voraciously, out of control, tendrils twining round and round her bones, grinding them to nothing, piercing her heart, crowding and unfurling at the back of her throat, pressing against the inside of her skull until she thought it might shoot through the top of her head and straight to the sky where murderous hungry giants awaited her.

She awoke to her own whimpers and pushed back her covers in a panic. The clock on her nightstand flashed dutifully, the time on it contradicting the broad daylight flooding the room. It took her a moment to remember she hadn't set it, had just plugged it in and let it run.

She crawled out of bed, feeling hollow and weak, and made herself a cup of coffee. Her hangover headache was gone—*never again*; the pressure behind her eyes was likely due to all the crying. She couldn't breathe through her nose, which made her extra grumpy as she was having a hard time appreciating the rich aroma of the freshly brewed java.

Phoebe could sense the coming of winter in the chill of the early morning. She took a quick shower and changed into leggings and a long-sleeved thermal tee, then added a feathery-soft fleece hoodie to the ensemble. The floor was cold under her bare feet, so she pulled on a pair of thick wool socks before heading downstairs with her cup of coffee. She needed something to eat—maybe a piece of toast.

While she waited for the heel of bread to pop up—she really needed to go shopping—she eyed the mess she'd made at her potter's wheel during her binge, but she couldn't work up the energy to clean it up. It would require a good amount of water and elbow grease, and she just didn't have it in her right now. She grimaced at the ugly, misshapen stand she'd made for her bottle of Glenfiddich—where was that thing? For the life of her, she couldn't remember where she'd left it.

The toast popped up, and she slathered it with too much Nutella she found at the back of a cupboard, and then took her meager breakfast to her desk to check her emails. She wouldn't bother turning on her phone—she knew she'd have dozens of calls and texts to respond to, but she wasn't ready to face anyone yet.

Phoebe particularly wasn't ready to face Baby Charise yet, and she knew that would be the reason for most of the calls.

The clock on her monitor told her it was almost noon on Wednesday. She couldn't believe she'd been out of commission for so long. No wonder it felt like her stomach was trying to gnaw on itself. Over the last three days, she'd had a gyro wrap and fries, a couple of Pop Tarts, and a piece of toast in between a bottle of fine Scottish whiskey and a couple of mugs of rich Italian coffee. She went online and ordered pizza for delivery so she wouldn't have to talk to anyone, and then opened her email, releasing a cynical bark at the number of new messages waiting for her.

TWENTY-SIX

Interspersed between all the junk mail and posts she subscribed to was email after email from Renata, Gia, Juliette, Renata's Reuben, and even one from Granny G. Most of them were politely phrased requests to see her, wondering if she was all right, hoping she wasn't sick. They all knew her tendency to disappear when she was under project deadlines, so a day or two without hearing back from her wasn't uncommon. She always made certain to let someone know after the second or third day on a project, though, just so they wouldn't show up unannounced and worried about her and chase away her muse. They'd all gotten used to it and were usually content to just prod at her from their end until she surfaced enough to notice she was being addressed. With a new baby in the family, however, she could imagine they were all starting to worry about her, even if they hadn't yet made a big deal about her absence.

Renata seemed to have no such reservations this time. Phoebe opened Ren's most recent email from only an hour ago with the subject heading: *Where ARE you?*

PHOEBE JOSEPHINE GUSTAFSON!

Yes, I'm using your full name and in all caps. You won't answer my calls. You won't respond to my texts. You won't come and visit. What is wrong with you? And don't tell me you got sick from being at the hospital with us. You haven't been sick a day in your life, so I'll know you're just lying to avoid me.

ARE you just avoiding me? Did I do something or say something to make you hate me? I know I'm not the nicest person in the world, even on a good day, but I can't be held completely responsible for anything I said in the throes of labor. That's not fair, and you know it. If it's a project, just tell me, okay?

I'll be offended about your priorities, but at least I'll know why you're not coming around.

But come on. A new baby,

Phoebe! Another Gustafson Girl!

Please, Phoebe. Please come visit us. Come hold Charise. Come laugh at how wobbly my belly is—the boys have had quite a hoot over it. Tim, of course, won't allow us to make fun of it in his presence; he says it's disrespectful. He's right, I know, but part of me wants to push his buttons a little, test him, I guess. See if he still thinks it's so great to suddenly have the responsibility of a ready-made family. But the man might be as stubborn as I am—he insists I'm still beautiful! He says I'm radiant - ha! Can you believe it? I know he's just blinded by love for this precious baby girl who's taken up residence in our throng of boys.

The boys are so cute with her, even Jude. He keeps hugging her head and whispering something in her ear. He won't tell me what he says, and although he's really quite gentle with her, every once in a while, I wonder if I should be worried. He gets this look in his eye... I mean, he's been the baby around here for a long time now. You and he have a connection, Phoebe. What do you think? Should I intervene?

Phoebe, I didn't get to thank you properly for everything you did. I didn't even say goodbye—you left without saying goodbye. I'm sure it all must have been overwhelming, but you should have stayed, at least long enough to let me tell you that I love you.

I'm not mad, okay? I just want to know you're okay.

Phoebe closed her inbox; she didn't want to read anymore emails from family members asking if she was all right. For one thing, she wasn't all right. And in the state that she currently was in, she didn't know if she'd ever be all right. She just wanted to stay hidden away in her customized art-studio bungalow, have people bring her food—*when is that pizza getting here?*—and wait for the world to end so she wouldn't have to pretend anymore.

The doorbell rang.

"Pizza!" she cheered, the exclamation a little louder than she'd intended, making her laugh nervously. Hopefully, the person on the other side of her blue door hadn't heard.

She wound her hair into a loose knot at the back of her neck, smoothed the front of her shirt, and shoved the sleeves of her hoodie up her arms a little. She looked like the walking dead, but surely, even the dead had a tiny bit of dignity to uphold. It was possible Phoebe knew the person on the other side of the door.

She slid back the tiny cover from the old-school peephole and saw a teenage girl holding a pizza warmer in one hand, a cell phone in the other, her thumb working the keypad effortlessly. Good. The exchange would be quick. She didn't recognize this delivery driver, and today was not a day for introductions and niceties. If the girl kept her job long enough, she'd have plenty more opportunities to get to know Phoebe.

She opened the door and squinted, holding up a hand to shield against the late afternoon sun, even though it wasn't shining in her eyes. She knew it wouldn't conceal how terrible she looked, but at least she could avoid meeting the girl's eyes and seeing the pity there. As much as she'd like to convince herself that she didn't care, there was a part of her that hated being seen without her hair done and her makeup on—her armor in place. Even by a complete stranger in an over-sized polo shirt and a misshapen baseball cap.

"Pizza for Pho—um, Phoebe?" The girl stumbled over her name, pronouncing it *Fohbee*.

"Phoebe," she corrected, smiling kindly at the nervous teenager. "It looks different than it's pronounced, I know, but yes, that's me. What do I owe you?" She already knew, but she hoped the change of subject would put the girl at ease.

Phoebe wondered if Lily would one day deliver pizzas to people's homes. She hoped not. She thought it was a rather dangerous job for pretty young girls like the one on her doorstep.

The exchange made, she couldn't hold in the words that pushed up the back of her throat. "Um, Josee?" The girl's name was on the plastic tag clipped to her collar. "I noticed you were texting when you got here. May I make a suggestion?"

The girl reddened noticeably. "Sorry. I know I'm not supposed to be on my phone while I'm at work, but my mom makes me text her every time I make a delivery." She paused, clearly trying to determine how much more she needed to say.

"I'm glad," Phoebe said, smiling encouragingly. She was relieved for both their sakes; the girl had someone on the other end who cared, and Phoebe didn't feel like such a freak for worrying about her. "I was actually going to suggest you let someone know every time you pull up at a house. No matter how many times you've been to the place. Every time."

Josee cocked her head at Phoebe and grinned. "That's what my mom said, too."

"And if I were you, I'd take it one step farther. When your customer opens the door, don't hide the fact you're on the phone. Instead, make a big deal of putting it away and say something like, 'Sorry about that. Just letting my boss know I made it.' That way, your customer knows someone else knows exactly where you are and what time you arrived."

Josee laughed outright at that. "Wow. You sound just like her. You must be a mom, too."

Phoebe felt the words like a knife twisting in her heart, but she didn't flinch. "I'm a big sister," she said. "And I've been in your shoes, too. Just be careful out there, okay?"

The girl nodded. "I will. Thanks." She smiled and waved and hurried down the walk to her car. Phoebe waited until she pulled away from the curb before closing her door.

She lifted the lid on the top box and breathed in deeply; her nose was clearing up and the delicious aroma made her salivate.

Yes, she'd bought two large pizzas just for herself. Thick crusts with extra cheese on both, one a meat-lovers, the other a standard pepperoni. She'd also had them throw in an order of bread sticks and extra marinara sauce for dipping, so she was set. Enough food to last a couple of days if she was careful.

Before she sat down to eat, she jotted off a quick group email to her sisters and grandparents, explaining that she had come down with a nasty cold and was going to lie low for the week so as not to expose anyone to her germs.

She sent a separate email to Renata, congratulating her and Tim, confirmed that she was, indeed, not well, and that she hoped to be completely better by Sunday so she could join everyone for Family Dinner at the grandparents.

She just hoped her bold-faced lies would be enough to hold them all at bay, at least for a few more days.

TWENTY-SEVEN

Two days later, Phoebe still had not left her sanctuary. She'd stepped outside to check the mail, to breathe in the smell of rain coming—the weather channel had predicted an early winter deluge over the weekend—and had held the door open for the mustached man from Cal's Grocery who seemed surprised when he saw her. He'd even had her confirm twice that she was indeed Phoebe Gustafson.

It was *the* Cal Masters, Phoebe learned after he introduced himself. The mom-and-pop grocery store did a thriving business in Midtown, partly because they had a gorgeous website and had offered home delivery for as long as they'd been open, long before the big chain grocery stores in the area had added delivery service options. What set Cal's apart was the quality of their goods, and the personalized care they gave each customer. They had a dedicated staff just for their home delivery service, so each order was processed as it came in, then immediately filled and delivered within an hour to Midtown residents.

Phoebe loathed grocery shopping and was a regular at Cal's online—she'd only set foot in the actual store once to scope out the quality of their produce before ordering—and she hadn't met Cal until today.

"Forgive me," he explained after setting her order on her counter. His eyes politely scanned the open floor plan of her home, taking in the potter's wheel, the photography corner, and the huge canvas mounted on an easel in the middle of her workspace. Behind it, several more canvases were lined up, side-by-side, pencil sketches on each giving evidence that they were all part of a series in its beginning stages. "You're the artist." He didn't act flustered, just pleasantly surprised.

Phoebe smiled and held up her hands as verification of the fact. She'd been painting when he arrived, and she'd wiped them clean enough to pay for her delivery and put the food away, but her fingers were still splattered with the rust and cobalt hues she'd been using. She was intrigued by the fact that he knew her, though—although her artwork was in several different studios and businesses in Midtown and the surrounding metropolitan areas, she rarely received personal recognition outside the artist community she belonged to.

Cal crossed his arms and nodded thoughtfully. "Well, isn't that something. We have a piece of your artwork hanging in our front entryway." He seemed almost careful in his choice of words, which made Phoebe pay closer attention. "The painting means a great deal to my wife. It's called *Cerulean*. It's a pregnant woman."

"Oh?" She smiled, hoping he'd say more. Her heart lurched when he told her the name of the piece. It was a painting she'd done when she'd turned twenty-five, when Lily would have turned nine, during a period when Phoebe especially missed her mother—and her daughter, who was someone else's daughter—fiercely.

A nearly naked woman with her arms wrapped around her distended abdomen, her face lowered, eyes closed in an expression of longing and serenity. She had dark hair like Phoebe's that cascaded down her back, but her features were Theresa's, the woman who had adopted Lily. Standing against a cinnamon and caramel textured background, her face and neck transposed from skin tones into swirling hues of blues and greens over her chest and limbs, the colors separating into landforms over the orb of her belly, so that it looked like she cradled the world in her arms. And instead of depicting the excitement of a mother-to-be, Phoebe had painted the swirling blue and green ache of uncertainty—*am I woman enough to be a mother?*—almost eclipsing the golden halo of anticipation and joy.

There were times, like the woman in the painting, when it seemed to Phoebe like she'd been pregnant and waiting her whole life... just as there were times when the knowledge that the baby that she'd given birth to would never be her own to hold. She would ache with cerulean longing; instead of the weight of a child, she felt like she carried the weight of the world in her arms.

She'd embraced the color as her own; she'd even matched the blue in the painting to the blue on her front door. *Welcome to my cerulean world,* it declared to any who would notice.

Creating the masterpiece—it was visually stunning, one of Phoebe's best—had been cathartic, but it had taken so much out of Phoebe emotionally that she'd auctioned it off through a local gallery, unable to bear looking at it. She'd donated the proceeds to the organization through which she'd met Jeff and Theresa.

Cal's eyes lingered on the new painting in progress. When he didn't speak right away, she added, "Thank you. My work is very important to me, so I'm glad to know it has a good home."

Cal cleared his throat, now a little abashed. "Would you mind if I told her—my wife, I mean—that I'd met you? She—well, she would be honored, I'm sure, as much as I am."

Phoebe thought it an odd choice of words. His wife would be honored by the fact that Cal had met Phoebe? But she nodded agreeably. "Please do. I'm honored to have met you, too." She grinned, and then added, "And not just because of the art. I'm glad for the chance to tell you personally how much I appreciate you and your store. Your service is stellar, and the folks who deliver my groceries are extremely helpful and polite. I get a lot of stuff delivered to my home, and sometimes I'm wary. A single woman out here on the edge of town, if you know what I mean. But your staff is always a joy to have in my home. And I love the fact that you, as the owner, make deliveries, too."

"Thank you," he said, a satisfied smile on his face. "However, I must admit that although I oversee the shopping portion of each order, I don't usually get out on deliveries. I like to be on hand at the store at all times, but for some reason, we've had more delivery orders than usual today—and we're short a few staff members because of a flu bug going around, so I'm helping them out. I'd like to think Providence has played a hand in things in allowing me to meet you. You're a household name in our home."

"Wow." Phoebe felt bolstered by the man's kind words, and although she didn't have any plans to leave her home in the near future if she could help it, she handed him one of her business cards. "Perhaps one day I'll have the chance to meet your wife. In the meantime, my email address is there if she'd like to sign up for my calendar updates or my newsletter. I know that seems rather impersonal, but most of the time, I don't know where I'll be until I tell my subscribers." It was true. Phoebe's schedule was mandated by her next showing, her next customer, her unpaid bills.

"Alice would love that. In fact, I'd be surprised if she wasn't already on your mailing list, but I'll certainly give this to her." He hesitated only a moment before grinning sheepishly. "Would you mind signing the back of it for her?"

Phoebe smiled. "I'd love to." She took the card and scribbled her name across the back of it. "I can do you one better, too." She had a stash of desk calendars that she'd ordered for Christmas gifts for the family—she made them every year with her own art, and she always ordered several extras for occasions such as this. She explained as much to Cal after signing *Cal & Alice - From my heart to yours - Phoebe* on the inside of the cover. "You let her know she won't find this in any store or anywhere online, okay? It's a twenty-of-a-kind calendar," she added with a grin.

Cal's eyes were bright as he accepted it. "You have no idea what this will mean to her, Ms. Gustafson."

"Phoebe. Please."

"Phoebe." Cal picked up the plastic carton he'd carried her grocery bags in and headed for the front door. "This has been the highlight of my day." He paused on the front stoop and cleared his throat. "I feel compelled to tell you something else."

Phoebe stood in the entry and nodded.

"You might not understand at this moment, but I'm going to pray that God opens doors for you and my wife to meet one day. I want you to know that it might not be easy for either of you, but I have a strong notion that this meeting—" he waved a finger between the two of them. "—is part of a much bigger plan."

Phoebe's hackles rose a little. She didn't need God setting her up to meet anyone. The last time she'd asked for his help, he'd left her high and dry. He'd stood her up in his own house, instead, making her deal with the likes of Trevor Zander.

Who is suddenly back in your life like a bad penny, a small voice murmured inside her head.

A thought occurred to her. She gestured to her outfit, her hair she had swept up into a messy bun and covered in a tie-dyed scarf. "I hope you don't think I'm one of those recluse artists. You know, the kind who stay locked inside their own homes and only talk to their agents and delivery people and wash their hands a thousand times a day." She held up her hands again. "I'm messy and outgoing and I usually love meeting people, in case you're worried about that."

Cal chuckled and shook his head. "No, no. The thought hadn't crossed my mind." But he didn't expound on why he thought the two women might find meeting to be difficult, and Phoebe was finished trying to wheedle it out of him.

"Okay. Good. Thank you for the groceries. I'll see you or one of your other guys in a couple of weeks then. I shop about twice a month." She snorted. "Or rather, I make you shop for me about twice a month."

"It works well for both of us. You do what you do, and I do what I do, and everyone is happy, right?" He waved without waiting for an answer and headed down the walk to his van.

Groceries put away, she paused at her computer. She hadn't checked her email since telling the family she was sick two days earlier. She knew there would be word from all of them, some conciliatory, others a little more demanding, but since none of it would change her mind, she hadn't bothered checking. Nor had she bothered plugging in her phone to charge it. In fact, the longer she went without it, the more freed up she felt. Why did she have to be at that thing's beck and call twenty-four-seven?

But now she was curious about Alice Masters. Was she on her mailing list already? And what was Cal being so cryptic about?

She checked her hands again to make certain she wasn't going to leave paint smears on her keyboard and sat down. Email first. Get it out of the way. Then she'd look for Alice's name on her mailing list.

Her eyes widened when she saw email after email from her sisters, almost all of them with attachments. What was going on? Without really considering what was wrong, she opened the most recent one from Juliette.

Baby pictures. Image after image of a tiny round face with a thin thatch of dark curls on top, wide gray eyes slightly tilted up at the corners. A petite pink mouth, ten delicate fingers, boxy feet with button toes. Pictures of the boys gathered around Charise, Reuben holding her on his lap, Judah's arm too tight around her neck. Pictures of Granny G nuzzling the baby's neck. A darling image of Grandpa in his easy chair, holding Charise in his big, gnarled hands, the two of them staring eye-to-eye at each other. The look on the old man's face was beatific, and more than Phoebe could bear to see. She clicked out of the email without reading Juliette's words and waited for her lungs to fill.

Before she closed out of her inbox to go check her newsletter subscriber list for Alice Masters, a name caught her eye. Her hand froze. Trevor Zander?

No. No, she was not ready for whatever he had to say. From what Juliette and Gia said about him, it didn't seem likely that he'd changed one iota from the man who'd all but run her out of church all those years earlier. Granted, he didn't look the same anymore, but as she knew quite well, looks could deceive.

Phoebe opened her newsletter list and did a search for Cal's wife. Sure enough, there she was. She'd been on Phoebe's mailing list since the very beginning, since shortly after she launched her website. In fact, it would have been right around the time she'd had her first showing at Expressions Studios in the Midtown Galleria downtown, a section of the old train station that had been converted into a variety of shops and restaurants. Phoebe had picked up several names from that event and although she couldn't picture the woman's face, it seemed like Alice Masters might just be one of her oldest fans. And the fact that she had *Cerulean* hanging on her wall helped ground Phoebe a little.

She put on some Julien Dore, sashaying slowly back to the easel as the smooth boy-next-door voice crooned in French from the speakers mounted on the wall above her workstation. He begged her to tell him about summer, about her long absences, about the emptiness that destroys. The French words wrapped around her, comforting her even as they made her suffer.

TWENTY-EIGHT

It had been a good week. Trevor wrapped the navy towel around his waist and stepped out of the shower. He laughed at his reflection in the mirror. "You need a haircut, dude." He scrubbed his fingers through his curls, then grabbed another towel out of the cupboard to use for shaving. He wanted to look his best tonight.

It had been a good week; he insisted again. And musically, it had. He'd written four new songs, and all four of them were finished, already mastered, album ready. They'd come to him so quickly and already so well-formed in his mind that the editing and mastering process had been a cakewalk.

It had been a good week spiritually, too. He'd prayed and fasted Tuesday and Wednesday, and even though he hadn't stopped praying, he'd felt no change in the direction the Holy Spirit seemed to be leading him. And when he'd spoken again with Vic and Juliette on Wednesday night, they'd prayed with him again, and both confirmed that they believed he would be doing the right thing to go to Phoebe to ask forgiveness first, and then go from there as the Lord led him.

It had been a good week... except where Phoebe Gustafson was concerned.

Trevor had called her that night. The call went straight to voice mail, so he'd left a message. "Phoebe, this is Trevor Zander. We met at the gas station a little over a week ago. I carried your gas back to your car for you. Then I followed you to your sister's—well, I didn't follow you. I was going there, too, but we didn't know we were both going to the same place, so it seemed like I was following you. You probably thought I was stalking you. But I wasn't; just clearing that up. I was following you by accident but going the same direction as you were on purpose.... I don't even remember why I'm explaining all this to you. Ignore all that. Here's the reason I called: I'd like to get together with you. I have something I'd like to talk about with you, and I promise to be more coherent. Would you give me a call when you get a chance?"

He'd hung up and thrown his phone on his bed, utterly disgusted with himself. He wouldn't call him back if he were her.

He wasn't surprised when she didn't. He tried again Thursday afternoon, and this time when it went straight to voice mail again, he was prepared. He stated his name, the day and time he was calling, and asked if she'd like to go out for coffee later that evening. When she hadn't returned his call by eight PM, he stopped checking his phone to see if it was actually working.

Apparently, since he got redirected to her message box every time, her phone was off, or she'd lost it. So, he emailed her that night before he went to bed, in essence, reiterating his phone messages to her, but asking her about getting together Friday night for dinner.

He'd watched his inbox all day, but nothing had come back from Phoebe, nor had she returned any of his phone calls.

That afternoon, after he'd saved the final version of a song called *A Falling Out with You*, and closed up his studio for the day, he rang up Juliette for advice. "I know I'm probably being pushy about this, but I have a strong sense of urgency in my heart, Jules. I can honestly say it's no longer about me getting relief from the burden of my guilt and shame—God freed me up from that long ago—but I really sense that Phoebe needs to hear me say I'm sorry and to ask her forgiveness."

"I do think you'd be wonderful together, even if you only end up as friends—I've thought of little else since you told me, Trevor—but I think you'll need to tread really carefully right now." Juliette sounded weary over the phone, or worried perhaps. "But you should know that she's in one of her moods. She's not talking to anyone right now, so don't be discouraged if she doesn't respond the way you're hoping."

"One of her moods? What does that mean?" Had he set her off? Had she remembered who he was and withdrawn again the way she'd done almost fourteen years ago?

"It's hard to explain. She does this every once in a while." Trevor could hear a tapping sound in the background; he must have caught her still at work. "She's typically so easygoing and cheerful—if a bit in your face—but I think half the time it's not how she genuinely feels." Juliette stopped typing and breathed out a long sigh. "I have a feeling it might be pretty exhausting, so she shuts down and goes off the radar for a few days."

"Off the radar?" Trevor grimaced; he was turning into her echo.

"Yeah. No phone. No email. Sometimes when she does this, she won't even answer her door, even though we know she's home."

Now it was Trevor's turn to be concerned. He picked up a rubber stress ball he used to exercise his hands and squeezed it several times. He'd gone through a season in his life when he'd behaved similarly, right after his encounter with Phoebe, when he'd been so awash with shame and guilt. He'd continued to work at the church as though nothing had changed, as though the world was still at his beck and call, when all the while, under his beach boy smile and waffle weave polo shirts, he felt like the walking dead. On his days off, he'd close himself up in his apartment, not seeing or talking to anyone, sleeping longer and longer hours. He stopped reading his Bible when he was alone, stopped praying, stopped talking to God altogether. And it was during that year, as his mind became less and less occupied by things of God and more and more occupied by matters of self-loathing and self-indulgence, that Trevor opened the door to the swirling vortex of pornography.

Until one day, he'd fallen on his face before God. He stopped asking God to help him find Jo so he could make things right. He stopped asking God to help him not visit the porn sites anymore. He stopped asking God to fix everything back to the way it was.

Instead, he asked God to forgive him for being so self-centered, for playing God, and for representing Christ so falsely. And he asked for wisdom and the courage he'd need to do what he knew was right, and then he went to the leaders of the church where he worked, explained what had been going on and repented of his sin. Against the church's recommendation, he'd resigned his position as youth intern, but he had accepted a referral to counsel with a couple from another church.

"The problem with resigning right now is that you will also lose all accountability," the pastor had explained when he insisted Trevor at least get counseling. "We understand if you want to step back or even away from this job and church, but we implore you to plug in somewhere else."

Trevor had, indeed, plugged in somewhere else. He'd met with Tom and Michelle Peterson, who'd introduced him to Victor Jarrett as an accountability partner, and the two of them had become like brothers.

"How long does the whole off the radar thing usually last?" Trevor asked Juliette, his concern circling back to Phoebe again.

He thought he could hear the frown in Juliette's voice. "Actually, it's been longer than normal for her. And at such a weird time, too. No one has seen her since the hospital room early Sunday morning right after Tim got there. She group-emailed the whole family on Wednesday to say she was sick and didn't want to spread germs, but we all know it's a cover. Phoebe doesn't get sick." A moment later she added, "Maybe sick at heart...." The sadness in her voice was too heavy, and the words drifted into silence.

"What's going on?" Trevor asked, but as much as he might want to deny it, he thought he already knew. Whatever had happened to Phoebe's baby, Phoebe no longer had the child. Maybe being around a newborn was more than she wanted to endure.

When Juliette didn't respond, Trevor asked, "Would she open the door for me?" He'd called twice and emailed, too, letting her know he wanted to see her. He knew it would be pushing things with her, but if what Juliette was saying was true, and if what he thought was going on was correct, he may be the only person Phoebe could talk to. He might be the only person in her life who knew about her own baby.

"I don't know, Trevor." Juliette sounded doubtful, but she spoke slowly, as though carefully considering. "We're really worried about her, but Granny G has insisted that we not force her right now. She claims she doesn't understand the why of it, but Granny G says my dad used to have to take alone time to process things and she thought perhaps Phoebe was doing the same. She likes to say, 'Birth and death always gives us pause to think.'" Juliette released a puff of breath into the phone. "It's been more than a pause, that's for sure. She hasn't even seen the baby yet."

That last statement was all the confirmation he needed. "Do me a favor, will you? Are you heading over to Vic's when you leave the office?"

"I'm closing up as we speak. He's meeting me at my place. My neighbor, Mrs. Cork—Mr. Bobo's mom—is having us over for dinner."

"Yes. I've met her at church when she comes with you, right? Does she know Phoebe?"

"She does. And she thinks Phoebe is divine. Her word." Juliette chuckled, easing Trevor's mind a little.

"Perfect. Here's my favor. Would you three cover Phoebe and me in prayer tonight? I'm going to clean up and head over there. Something you said has me believing she may need to hear from me sooner than later. I have to at least try."

Juliette hesitated. He couldn't hear anything on the other end of the line, so he continued. "I won't force anything on her, don't worry."

"You know what, Trevor? I trust you. I trust that you've prayed about this, and I trust you when you say you believe you are doing the right thing. I trust you with my sister." She sighed again—the conversation was rife with sighs. "I just don't trust her with you."

"She already promised my virtue was safe with her." He grinned, recalling the way Phoebe's eyes flashed when she teased him.

"I'm not worried about your virtue, either," she said, although he thought she might be smiling. "I'm worried about your heart. So, I'm going to agree to pray for you and Phoebe tonight. Perhaps not for what you want to see come of this plan of yours, but that God will protect both of you."

"I understand. But it's a plan I believe in, Juliette. I have to try."

"It's a plan I believe is risky. For both of you." But she agreed he should try, nonetheless.

Now here he was, preparing for the possibility of a night out with a woman who hadn't even agreed to speak to him. And suddenly, it seemed like the stupidest plan in the world.

His phone beeped with a text message alert. He snatched it up off the counter; it was only from Vic.

Praying for you, man. "Be strong and courageous and act; do not fear nor be dismayed, for the Lord God, my God, is with you. He will not fail you nor forsake you until all the work for the service of the house of the Lord is finished." (1 Chronicles 28:20) Remember: This began in the house of God where you began your service to him. He will see you through until it's finished.

Trevor took a deep, steadying breath and filled his palm with shaving cream. He still had time to make it a good week in every way.

TWENTY-NINE

Phoebe had set aside her paintbrushes almost an hour ago and now worked with the pads of her fingers, the edges of her palms, the ridges of her knuckles, drawing the cobalt and indigo hues together, blending and smearing, the lines curving into broad, sweeping strokes that haloed the bronze and honey flesh tones of the woman on her canvas. A blood red sash draped casually across the woman's high, small breasts, wrapping all the way around her so the end fluttered gracefully over her groin and thighs in a rather sensual attempt at modesty. Phoebe had painted the woman's face turned away, as though unaware she was being studied, and the long fingers of one hand splayed across the feminine plane of her flat abdomen.

This one, the first in the series, already had a name. *Scarlet.*

She couldn't stop thinking about Alice Masters, wondering why *Cerulean* had touched her so. She'd entered an astronomical amount on the painting in the silent auction, a bid no one else even came close to, and Phoebe had just assumed the buyer was some wealthy and eclectic art collector or an equally wealthy donor who needed a charity to contribute to and liked the painting well enough to take it as a reward for their generosity. To learn that it was the wife of a small-town grocer who had probably sacrificed at least a little to come up with the funds sat uncomfortably with her... and yet, it seemed fitting somehow, too, and had her thinking that the woman who now had a painting of Phoebe's sacrifice had surely known sacrifice of her own.

Would Cal's wife see—and understand—the passion and pain behind this new series, this extension of that first painting? Had Cal recognized the connection? Had he seen the similarity in the women posing on each canvas—the postures, the lowered eyes, the contours of the face, the neck and shoulders, the presence and wonder of nature in each depiction of a woman in various stages of pregnancy?

Now Beatrice Martin's smoky voice crooned in French about dark nights and secrets hidden in the past, and carrying on, and waiting... waiting... without breaking.

Phoebe stood back and evaluated the painting—the heavy-handed technique she'd used presented a subtle undercurrent of discomfort and unease so in opposition to the graceful movement of the female form on the canvas. It wasn't complete; when the oils had set up a little more, she'd come back in with a fine-tipped brush and add defining lines and understated contouring.

Someone knocked on her door, startling her. She glanced down at her paint-spattered attire and then decided she didn't care. "*Tant pis!*" she muttered her frustration in French. "I'm an artist and this is how I do art." She headed for the door, wiping her hands on a paint rag as she went. "You'll just have to deal with it," she declared to whoever was on the front porch. At least she was no longer crying. The finger-painting had soaked her anguish up right through her fingertips.

Another knock, this one a little more insistent.

"Coming!" she called out over the loud music, not happy about being disturbed while the muse still lingered. "Give me a second!" She marveled at how much paint she'd gotten on her hands, on the long, once-white smock she wore to protect her clothes. A streak of sienna was smeared across the top of her right foot.

She yanked open the door... and froze.

Trevor Zander. Looking for all the world like he'd just showered and shaved and was ready to preach a Sunday sermon to a world of sinners.

She slammed the door so quickly that she almost caught the hem of her smock in it. The air rang with the sudden and intense silence, and then her heart started up again, her pulse pounding like a kettledrum between her ears. Why, oh why, hadn't she looked through the peephole first?

Her hands flew to her hair, smoothing it away from her face, but it was too late. He'd already seen her looking like something the cat dragged in. Thank goodness she'd changed out of her pajamas today... although her sleepwear would class her up considerably compared to what she wore under the paint-splattered smock. Old gray leggings with frayed hems and an over-sized Mid-U tee shirt Juliette had left behind after a sleepover a couple years ago. Her hair was piled in a loose knot on top of her head, the stray curls that insisted on falling around her face held at bay by a red paisley bandana wrapped biker-style around her head. No makeup, no jewelry, no shoes, and slouchy socks to boot. *Nice.*

What in the name of all that was good and holy was Trevor Zander doing here? On her doorstep? Had one of her sisters sent him to check on her? But why would they do that? Why not just come themselves? She couldn't begin to imagine his reason for being outside her front door.

She waited, wondering if he'd just go away.

Nope.

"Phoebe?" he called out. "Look. I'm sorry to just show up like this, but I tried calling. I emailed, too. I didn't know how else to get a hold of you." He cleared his throat; she heard the rumble of it even through the heavy door. He sounded nervous—and well he should be! "I really want to get together with you, and I was hoping—well, I was hoping at the very least that you'd be home tonight so we could connect."

What was he going on about? Phoebe frowned and shook her head, completely vexed at his presence, his presumption, and most of all, his faultless appearance in the face of her disarray. She couldn't think of what to say to him. She was at a complete loss for words.

"Phoebe?"

She would not open the door to him, that was for sure. But she couldn't just pretend she didn't know he was out there. On the other hand, if she simply ignored him, he'd get the message and leave, wouldn't he?

"I know this is not the way to go about doing this, but I—well, it's kind of urgent that we talk." His voice had dropped, but it came through clearer. He must have stepped closer; maybe he was even trying to speak through the peephole. The image of him crouched down with his mouth to the tiny opening had her covering her mouth to hold back a snort of laughter.

Hadn't he seen the way she looked? Wasn't it more than evident that she was in no condition to receive company? To talk? And what woman in her right mind would open the door to a practical stranger who stood on her doorstep begging to be let in? *Like the big bad wolf.*

There was silence for several moments, but she was too afraid to open her peephole cover and look out. What if he was standing right on the other side of the door, peering in? She fought down a giggle of hysteria.

"You're right, Trevor," she finally said, pleased that her voice came out steady and firm. "This is not the way to go about doing this. Please go away. I'm not comfortable with you lurking outside my front door."

The silence thickened.

"Trevor?" Had he gone after all?

"I'm sorry. You're right. It is kinda creepy." She heard him chuckle, but it didn't sound sinister or unsettling. "But I'm not leaving. Now that I'm here and I know you're there, I don't want to waste the opportunity to talk. You're a hard person to get a hold of, Phoebe Gustafson."

He wasn't going to leave? Should she call the police?

Maybe she should spray him with pepper spray through the peephole.

Maybe that was overkill.

"Please listen. Just for a minute, okay?" He was speaking quietly now, almost as though he hoped she was just on the other side of the door listening. "I... uh, well...." He cleared his throat and tried again. She had to step closer to catch his next words. "I remember you."

Phoebe's rambling thoughts came to an abrupt halt.

"Please, Phoebe. We need to talk."

No, no, no, no. She didn't want to talk to him right now. Not about that day in the church. And especially not about Lily.

Lily. He knew about Lily. Or at least he'd known she was pregnant. He might be the only one other than those involved in the program.

There was no way on earth, in heaven, or in hell that she was going to talk to him. She had no intention of acknowledging anything he could—and most likely would—use against her, even if only to her family. Her voice shook as she said, yet again, "You need to leave, Trevor. I'm not interested in talking to you."

"Phoebe, I need to apologize. I need to—"

"I don't care what you need, Trevor Zander," she cried out, cutting him off, her voice raised in anguish she could no longer contain. "What about what I needed all those years ago, huh? What about what I need today?" She suddenly yanked open the door and glared at him, no longer caring what kind of image she presented. "How dare you come to my home after all these years and tell me what *you* need? You have not changed one bit, have you? You are still a pompous, arrogant—"

This time, he cut her off.

Instead of being intimidated by her ferocity, instead of stepping back a pace, Trevor lurched forward so suddenly she could have sworn he caught himself by surprise, too. He cupped her face in both his hands and bent forward so he was only inches away. "Stop," he ground out, his mouth so close she could feel his breath on her lips. "Please stop. I'm not that man anymore. I'm not. If you'll just give me a few minutes. Hear me out, please."

So stunned by his unexpected actions, she went still for a few brief—and oh, so heavenly—moments, before reaching up between them and shoving him away. Her cheeks burned where his palms had been, and she swore she could still feel the pressure of his fingertips behind her ears and curved around the base of her skull.

"What are you doing?" she screeched. She sounded nothing like her usual calm, collected self. "You can't just manhandle me like that!"

Trevor raised both hands in surrender. "Sorry. I'm sorry," he muttered, then laced his fingers together over the top of his head. "Phoebe, I'm sorry. I have been so desperate to talk to you all week. Since I remembered." He shot her a wry but remorseful lip curl. "And clearly, I'm not the only one who has remembered."

When Phoebe only continued glaring at him, he took a small step back. "Phoebe, I was wrong. I was wrong in every way that day. It wouldn't have mattered if I'd said the sky is blue and the grass is green; I still would have been wrong."

Phoebe bit her bottom lip so hard she tasted blood. He was too much, too intense, too assertive. She didn't know how to keep a hold on the reins with him. He was still standing too close—she breathed in the delicious man smell he emitted, like her Italian Roast coffee layered with chocolate and something spicy—and his eyes were too blue, too bright. Too much.

She realized she was holding her breath and let it out slowly so he wouldn't know. "Well, as you can see, this isn't a good time for me."

"I can't even imagine," he murmured, and his words intoned that he was acknowledging far more than the fact that he'd interrupted her work.

"No, you can't," she declared, not willing to give him any rope. *Go hang yourself,* she wanted to shout at him, but even as she thought the words, she could feel the angry bubble in her chest losing air. And behind it, another one formed, this one filled with vulnerability and relief at the very thought of being able to talk to someone who already knew a big part of her darkest secret.

Could she trust him? Did she want to trust him? Did she dare?

THIRTY

She stood there like some modern-day Medusa, her gray eyes smoldering with anger and indignation. He could imagine the loose strands of hair that curled and swayed around her face, coming to life and striking at him. But instead of turning him to stone, her snapping glare had sparked in him an insane urge to reach for her, to haul her up against him, to comfort her, to soothe her... and to kiss her until she had no words left to hurl at him.

Kiss her until she had no breath in her lungs that wasn't mingled with his.

Kiss her until she forgot the pain that he'd caused her, until she wanted nothing more than to be kissed some more.

Why, oh why, had he touched her? His palms tingled, his fingers twitched, and he was having trouble keeping his eyes focused on hers, because they kept wandering to her lips of their own accord. Like an addict, he'd gotten too close to what he was missing, and now he fixated on getting one more taste. One hundred more tastes. And a thousand more.

She smelled like turpentine and oil-based paint with some kind of citrus over the top, a surprisingly enticing aroma emanating off a woman. It reminded him of his childhood when his mother handed him the aerosol can of lemon scented furniture cleaner and ordered him to dust and polish all the wood surfaces.

Phoebe's face without makeup was startlingly pale, her skin almost translucent. In the fading light of day, he thought he might be able to make out the lines and angles of the bones beneath her flesh. The baggy white painter's coat she wore hid all her womanly curves—he didn't have any trouble imagining them anyway—and he wanted to drink in her features until he could picture nothing else in his mind. Fragile, delicate, vulnerable, she reminded him of a wounded animal as she stared out at him from eyes haunted by their shared memories....

A cooling flood of remorse washed through him, steadying him, reminding him. He needed to show himself a different man than she remembered, an honorable man. A man who wasn't contemptuous of things he didn't understand or relate to. A man who held out grace to others because he understood what it meant to need it so desperately.

"Phoebe, will you go to dinner with me tonight?" he asked without any more preamble, partly because he didn't know if he could pull off small talk at the moment, and partly because he didn't want to miss his chance to ask her. Under the circumstances, she could very well duck back inside and lock her door against him. He hoped she wouldn't even consider it, but he wasn't going to take any chances.

"No, Trevor." She didn't even hesitate. She waved a hand over her shoulder at the room behind her. "I'm not in any condition to go anywhere tonight. Besides, I'm in the middle of a major project."

Well, she hadn't closed the door in his face, but her answer was nearly as effective. He needed to do something with his hands; they just hung awkwardly at his sides. He didn't want to shove them in his pockets lest she think he was trying to play it cool. He wasn't. He was dead serious and even more certain that he was exactly where he needed to be. He didn't want to cross them over his chest. He knew the vibe that kind of body language put off: *Keep your distance. Back off. I'm not letting you get to me.* He wanted just the opposite, and she had definitely gotten to him.

"Then may I bring dinner here? To you?" His rules about not being in a woman's home alone with her were his personal guidelines. He had learned the hard way that life is not constructed of immovable lines and inflexible boundaries. He veered away from them when the need arose... like when he'd said yes to taking Juliette on a date, never having met her. But tonight, spurred by desperation, he was veering away from his guidelines for questionable reasons—even he could see that—and veering into dangerous territory.

Phoebe's eyebrows—slim, dark, and sharply arched, even without makeup—rose in what he could only construe as disdain. "I thought God didn't allow you to go inside women's houses."

Ah. Twisting his words and using them against him. The oldest deflection in the book. He flexed his hands at his sides, resisting the urge to crack his knuckles. "I go inside women's houses all the time," he corrected her, making sure to keep his smile warm. "Are you referring to my own rule about not being alone with a woman inside her home—or my home, for that matter?"

Phoebe rolled her eyes, but he saw the flush creep up her neck. So, she'd done it intentionally; just as he'd thought.

"Yes, I do have a few rules about how I live and act. They are not hard lines drawn in the sand, but guidelines I've given myself to follow. This is one of them. And just so you know, it has a lot more to do with my own personal strengths and weaknesses than with any demands God might make of me."

"Oh," she drawled, her voice cool and throaty. She sounded more like the Phoebe who talked to him in his head, but he didn't like the sarcastic serration behind her voice. "You mean to tell me, Trevor Zander, Youth-Pastor-Turned-Christian-Rock-Star-Extraordinaire, that you have weaknesses? Do your groupies know this? Or is this maybe some ridiculous attempt to convince me that you and I have something in common?" She leaned back against the door frame and crossed her arms, her body language sending him her message loud and clear: *Keep your distance. Back off. I'm not letting you get to me.*

But she was still there. The electric blue door still stood open behind her, its vibrant tone contrasting with the starkness of her black hair, porcelain skin, and white smock. And the dreamy songbird still lilted French caresses in the air around them.

But I am getting to you, he thought. How he wanted to reach for her hand, uncurl her long fingers from their grip around her upper arm, to lace his own through hers. To assure her that he meant her no harm, that he was there to defend her against the likes of the man he'd once been.

"You're asking me a lot of questions. Will you let me answer them over dinner?"

She shook her head but didn't say anything.

"Anything you want. I'll even cook for you, if you'd prefer. I make killer eggs Benedict; you need to taste my homemade hollandaise sauce." He forgot to keep his hands in check and reached out to touch her shoulder. She flinched, but instead of responding immediately, he let his fingers drift slowly down the outside of her arm until he touched the back of her hand. Then he stepped back, far enough away that he couldn't touch her even if he tried. He saw her grip tighten around her arm, as though she might be resisting the urge to reach for him, too. The notion made him smile. "Of course, I'm always good for a burger from Five Guys or In-N-Out."

"I'm in the middle of a project," she repeated, but the corners of her mouth lifted, and her gaze dropped even as she continued shaking her head.

"I can wait."

"It could be hours. My schedule is dictated by my muse."

"I can wait."

"I don't want to talk to you."

"You don't have to talk. I'll talk."

"I don't want to hear what you have to say," she finally admitted, still not looking up at him.

"Come on." He shoved his hands in his pockets. He knew he was way too touchy feely, especially for a guy, but until this moment, he'd never realized how much he depended on physical contact to communicate. "Don't you think there might be a reason you and I have reconnected after all these years?"

"A reason? Like what?" She angled her face so she could look at him from the corner of her eyes, her brows lifted again. "So you could make peace with yourself? See with your own eyes that you didn't destroy me? That your verbal crucifixion—" the word came out almost like a snarl "—didn't actually kill me?" She spread her arms wide and then turned to offer him her profile, smoothing the smock over her petite form, her flat abdomen. "Look. Problem solved. I figured it out on my own."

"Phoebe," he whispered. Her words were intended to harm him, but he sensed they also harmed her. His own pain he could bear, but when she lifted her chin and met his gaze, he saw right through her defiance.

"Phoebe, I'm sorry." He took a step toward her, but when she backed up, he stopped. "Please forgive me. I was wrong, and I hurt you. I can't take it back, no matter how badly I wish I could. I can't change what that man did to you, though God knows I'd do just about anything if I could. And I can't change the fact that I made you believe you had to figure things out on your own back then. No one should have to go through what you went through alone." He paused and cleared his throat, pushing back the surge of anger that had risen when he thought about someone assaulting Phoebe. "But I can change things from here on out. You don't have to carry this alone anymore. I'm here. And I'm sorry for—"

"Please," she interrupted him, holding up a paint-smeared hand. She closed her eyes and leaned her temple against the door frame, everything about her deflating right in front of him. "Stop apologizing, please. You didn't mortally wound me, Trevor. I was a wreck long before I found my way into the back row of that little church."

"I hurt you," he insisted.

"Not intentionally," she corrected, meeting his gaze, her eyes now bright with unshed tears. "Not like him."

"I still hurt you. And I still want your forgiveness." He hated seeing her pain. He would give anything to take it from her and carry it for her like he'd done her gas can. She'd insisted she could carry it herself, and she could have. He knew that now better than ever. But she didn't have to... because he'd been there to carry it for her, to walk the road beside her, to follow her home and see her safely into the care of those who loved her. He wanted to do that for her now. For days and weeks and years to come. "That's all that really matters. It's all I ask."

The muscles in her jaw tightened, her lips pressed together, and she swallowed hard as she dropped her gaze again. "What about dinner?"

Her question caught him by surprise. He wasn't sure how to answer her. "Dinner?"

"You said all you're asking for is my forgiveness. But you've also asked me to have dinner with you."

He couldn't help it. A laugh burst out of him. "You're right, Phoebe Josephine Gustafson. Forgiveness and dinner. Those *two* things are all I ask." He moved closer again and tugged on one of her curls. He needed that tactile connection to her. "Please."

She straightened her shoulders and nodded slowly. "If you want to go pick up burgers—I want a Double-Double, Animal-Style, with cheese, no onions, extra pickles, two orders of fries—yes, two for me since you're buying—a strawberry shake, and a Dr. Pepper, easy ice. I'm not repeating that, so I hope you were listening. And don't worry. I'll be more—" She gestured at her outfit. "—presentable when you get back."

It was his turn to lift an eyebrow in challenge.

"What?" An impish grin teased her lips. "You think I can't make myself presentable in fifteen minutes?"

"That's not it at all," he countered. "As far as I'm concerned, you're perfectly presentable the way you are. Paint and all." He took her hand and turned her arm so he could follow a smear of scarlet that swirled over the pale skin. His thumb rested against the underside of her wrist, and he wondered if it was his pulse or hers that he felt. "I'm just wondering where you're going to put all that food. Do you have a hollow leg or something?"

"Actually, I haven't eaten a real meal since pizza Wednesday night. I'm starving." She reached for the handle of her door.

"Wait," he said, stopping her before she disappeared inside. "You'll be here when I get back, right? You're not just tricking me into leaving so you can escape out the back window?"

Phoebe rolled her eyes. "It's my house. If I don't want to see you, I just won't answer the door."

"You'll answer the door, then, right?" His head told him he was being silly, but his heart begged for reassurance.

"I answer the door to just about anyone who comes bearing food."

THIRTY-ONE

Phoebe leaned against the back of the door for just a moment, commanding her heart to stop its chaotic tap dance against her ribcage. What on earth had she just agreed to?

"My stomach made me do it," she murmured to herself as she gathered up her brushes and palettes and headed out to the sink in her garage where she cleaned all her art tools. Back inside, she turned the easel so that the painting faced the wall. She didn't mind him seeing it, but she thought it might make him uncomfortable.

Upstairs, she took a quick shower, tugged on a clean pair of black leggings and donned a short black baby-doll dress with cherry sprigs all over it. She rolled a red scarf into a two-inch wide band and tied it around her head, then she pulled her hair loose from its knot and let it cascade down over her shoulders and back. She fluffed it a few times with her fingers, but it didn't require a whole lot to look the way she liked it. Phoebe had her mother to thank for that—Simone had passed on her glorious hair to all her girls, even Gia, whose curls were copper instead of black.

She kept her makeup minimal, too—he'd already seen her bare face. A sweep of eyeliner that extended just past the curve of her upper lid, a few layers of mascara to define her naturally long lashes, a little face powder and blush, and a touch of clear lip gloss. She still looked washed out to her mind's eye, but she intended to be as comfortable as possible while still making an effort to look nice.

"Just in time," she quipped as she scurried back down the stairs, not bothering to put on shoes. She'd given herself a mini pedicure and painted her toenails a perfect shade of candy apple red last night and her feet were clean and soft. She'd put on socks if the night brought a chill. The

California sunshine was doggedly hanging on, so although it was well into fall, the days were still warm and the nights, perfect sleeping weather.

The doorknocker sounded again. "I'm coming!" she called out, but this time she did slide back the hatch on her peephole. "It's you," she said, and pulled open the door.

"Were you expecting someone else?" Trevor asked as he came inside with his cardboard tray of food, the aroma of all-beef patties and fresh-cut fries wafting in behind him. She ducked her head to hide her smile when she read the look of sheer relief on his face. He really had been afraid she'd not let him in.

"No one else," she said. "But the last time I opened my door without checking first, I wasn't quite prepared for what I found on my front stoop. I didn't want to make that mistake again."

Trevor shot her a bemused look, but his grin made her toes want to curl. *Ouah!* The man was lovely to look at. His close shave didn't make him look younger like it did to so many men, but instead, served to outline the full cut of his jaw, the square chin, the only thing symmetrical on his face. His lips were well-defined, but not too full, and a dimple on his left cheek made one side sit slightly higher than the other. When he smiled, it was the quintessential crooked grin of every fictional hero. His eyes weren't quite level, but that might have been due to the scar that started just above his right eyelid and cut through his brow, giving it a slightly disjointed appearance. He actually had a notch in the bridge of his nose, too, as though he'd taken a hockey stick in the face, but it only added character to his features. And the way his hair kept falling forward on one side.... No, certainly not male-model handsome, but Phoebe would put his face on the cover of a romance novel any day.

His was the kind of face she would love to paint. The kind she'd love to photograph. She pictured him in a garage, his bike mounted on a lift beside him, a myriad of tools spread haphazardly on a workbench in the background. He'd have at least a day's scruff, maybe more, and she'd smear grease along the rasp of his jaw. A gray tee shirt like the one he'd had on at the gas station, sprayed liberally so that it clung to the contours of his lithe body, but maybe with a vintage biker logo emblazoned across the chest. He'd be armed with the tools of the trade: an impact wrench in one hand, a tire in the other. His clear, blue eyes would peer straight into the camera as though he'd been interrupted in the middle of a job. He wouldn't smile. No, his mouth would stay relaxed, neutral, caught right before he'd figured out how he was going to react to the disruption. Her eyes lingered on his mouth a little too long, and she felt her skin warm when he flashed her a knowing smile.

"I'd like to photograph you," she said, figuring the truth was the best recourse. It would explain away her prolonged scrutiny...almost....

"Really?" He actually sounded intrigued, which surprised her. "Why?"

Was he fishing for compliments? Well, she wasn't shy. She'd give him a few. "You're kind of a conundrum in my eyes. You're not a big guy, but you have this big personality that makes you almost larger than life—it can be a little overwhelming, I'll have you know." She led him to her little table and gathered up the few things that were there so he could set the food down; a water glass, a series of sketches, a few soft-leaded pencils.

"So I've been told," Trevor stated good naturedly.

Phoebe continued, coming back to the table with a couple of paper plates and a stack of extra napkins. "Your build and coloring are totally boy-next-door, but the way your face is put together? Let's just say you have remarkably sensual features, Trevor. When you smile, instead of tilting up the way most people's do, your eyes curve down, giving you an almost lazy, devil-may-care look about you. Very attractive, especially to the ladies."

She went back to the fridge and pulled two water bottles out. Trevor had purchased shakes and sodas for both of them, so it wasn't that they really needed more to drink, but Phoebe needed to keep busy. Telling a man what made him attractive was something she did on a regular basis in her line of work, but Trevor wasn't here for a job.

And she still hadn't decided whether she could trust him. She wasn't ready to jump into some deep, emotional conversation with him yet, either, just to figure out whether he'd really changed like he said he had. But it was nice to have company after so many days of just herself and the folks who came bearing sustenance.

Trevor stood behind a chair, indicating she be seated first, and then he joined her on the other side of the table. He still had that lopsided grin on his face, clearly enjoying her talk him up. He didn't seem vain about it; it was more like he was fascinated by how she saw him.

"Thank you," she said, once he was seated. Phoebe wasn't surprised by his gentlemanly manners—she hated hearing people say that chivalry was dead; she simply didn't believe it—but she appreciated him all the more for it. "For bringing dinner. I really am hungry." She unscrewed the cap on her water bottle and took a long sip of it first. It made her feel a little better about the frighteningly unhealthy meal she was about to indulge in. "And for forcing yourself on me. I appreciate the company."

He blanched noticeably, his smile gone, and belatedly, she realized her tasteless choice in words. "I shouldn't have said it that way." She reached across the table to touch his arm. "I was just teasing, and it came out wrong. I mean it. I'm glad you stayed. I didn't think I wanted company, but now that you're here, I'm glad."

He nodded and then turned his arm so he could take her hand, reaching across the table for her other one. "Will you say a quick prayer with me?"

He didn't wait for her response—she should have expected this, too, but he'd caught her by surprise—and just bowed his head, and in a few words, thanked God for the food and asked him to cover them in wisdom and grace. When he lifted his head, he was smiling again. He squeezed her hands and let go. "Thanks for answering your door tonight."

They unwrapped their burgers in hushed anticipation and made meaningless small talk over the meal. It was delicious, every bite. When Phoebe realized that she wouldn't be able to eat the second order of fries herself, she slid it to the middle of the table, and they shared it. When they both reached for the same potato strip, she laughed out loud. "Which one do you want to be? Lady or the Tramp?"

"Well, I don't think I've ever been called Lady before." Trevor chuckled, letting go of his end of the fry.

"You've been called Tramp before?"

He shook his head. "Actually, haven't been called Tramp before, either, now that you mention it. But if those are my only two options, I'll go with Tramp. He was a pretty awesome dog." He picked up another fry and waved the end in her direction. "I'd say Lady suits you just fine."

As opposed to Tramp, Phoebe thought. She didn't think she was ready to ruin a pleasant evening yet, but then, would she ever be ready? The opening was there, a prime opportunity to segue into why Trevor was sitting across the table from her. She knew he wanted to talk about their brief but life-altering encounter so many years ago. He wanted to reconcile things between them, to set things right.

But Trevor Zander, Jesus freak, hadn't walked in her shoes after she'd left him standing in the church foyer, and no matter what they said tonight, no matter how good it might feel to clear the air between them, to talk to someone else about Lily—*Oh, Maman, how I wish you were here*—to share the burden of her guilt and shame and grief with someone else, it was only a temporary boon; she knew. In the end, it would still be hers to carry.

"I've been called worse." She spoke in a low, steady tone, and she was relieved that her voice didn't crack, even when her throat tightened around the words.

Trevor sat back, the paper basket of fries forgotten between them. She stared at his chest, counting the times it rose and fell, wondering which of them would speak next. But he simply waited for her to continue.

"With good reason, too," she admitted, all at once driven by the need to tell him the worst about her, to get it out where he could see it, judge it—judge *her*—and they could move on, regardless of how the evening ended. "I was pretty wild back then. My poor grandparents. They had their hands so full after my mom and dad died, and I only made their job harder, pushing them, challenging them to prove their unconditional love for me again and again."

Trevor remained still, his expression attentive and kind, and Phoebe saw the younger version of him sitting in the pew ahead of her in that shadowy church, listening to her tell him why she was there. The *déjà vu* made her pause so she could tamp down the fight-or-flight impulse that had her wanting to order him out of her house.

"By my sophomore year in high school, I had a reputation that I'd made for myself. I went to every party I could. I did things I wanted to forget the next day—this was before roofies were so prevalent, thank goodness—but it was like an addiction, you know? I hated myself and what I was becoming, but I couldn't stop, either." She studied her hands, no longer able to look him in the eye. "I hated myself, but I just wanted to be loved. I missed my mother terribly—both my parents, but my mom, especially. She seemed to recognize this darker side of me, my tendency toward living on the edge, and she met me there, time and time again when she was still alive, bringing me back from the brink *before* I did anything really stupid. But after she was gone, no one stopped me from going over. It was like a free-fall—the exhilaration and the rush that ended with a crash-landing that broke me again and again. Because I kept going back for more. Loving the rush, hating the crash."

Trevor shifted in his seat, but Phoebe kept her head down, desperate to finish now that she'd begun.

"No one came for me. No one ever showed up when I really needed someone to hold on to me. My sisters were dealing with grief in their own ways, even Gia, who was too young to really understand that Maman and Papa weren't ever coming back. We three older girls shared the guest room; we even shared the queen-size guest bed the first few months—our choice—but somehow, we all ended up dealing with our grief alone. I really believe that the only reason we're still connected is because of the G-FOURce." She glanced up at him briefly and noted the slight cock of his head, the question in his eyes. "Our sisters' secret club. We're the Gustafson Four. Grandpa always says we're a force to be reckoned with. Hence, G-FOURce."

"Ah. Yes. I remember now." She thought she heard a smile in his voice.

"Don't get me wrong. My grandparents were steadfastly there for me, for all of us, but I always *felt* like they were only there for me after I'd picked up all my shattered pieces, reassembled them into something they kinda-sorta recognized, and limped home. They didn't know how broken I was, and I never held their inability to see it against them." She frowned at her own words, realizing they weren't quite true. "At least not until that night," she amended, remembering Grandpa embracing Renata, comforting the wounded—albeit whole—sister, while she, Phoebe, stood on legs trembling so badly she was afraid to take a step lest she crumple to the floor.... She, Phoebe, the one who'd been bent and battered, who'd fallen and crash-landed one too many times.

All the girl's sisters and all the girl's friends couldn't put Phoebe back together again.

"I do understand some of what you're saying, Phoebe." Trevor's voice broke into her maddening thoughts. "I just want you to know that. I do get it—the rush and crash, the self-loathing after the free-fall. The promises made to myself again and again... broken promises every time. That part, I get." He rested his forearms on the table and leaned forward a little, but he clasped his hands together in front of him instead of trying to touch her.

She didn't know if she completely believed him—how could he possibly know?—and she was glad he didn't reach for her.

"The summer before my junior year, I decided I'd had enough. Many of my partying friends had graduated, so in a way, it was a perfect opportunity to start fresh. And I tried. I got onto the yearbook staff and poured myself into photography and design for that—that's the year I really discovered my love for photography. I didn't go out on the weekends, and I avoided the party crowd as much as I could. But Homecoming...." Her voice trailed off. She pushed aside her half-gone shake and took a long swig from her water bottle. She hadn't talked this much in ages, and for the last week, she'd hardly said more than the few words exchanged with the people who came to her door.

"I took pictures all night. I stayed as busy as I could all night long, but in the end, I just wanted to go. So I promised myself I wouldn't drink or do anything else that might alter my reasoning." Her voice cracked and she cleared her throat harshly, forcing the next words out of her like she was purging. "I'd just dance and have fun, right? Get it out of my system. And then I'd go home to bed at a decent hour and sleep in peace. No crash-landing. No regrets."

THIRTY-TWO

A SINGLE TEAR.

She shed one rebel tear the whole time she spoke.

Trevor watched the emotions play out across her face like actors on a stage. He saw sorrow, regret, anger, fear. He recognized hatred there—hatred of self, of others, of God. He watched a battle wage between love and resentment, with trust and bitterness as their seconds. He witnessed the obliteration of hope as she told him about her two-mile walk home in the dark, about the scene that played out in her grandparents' living room where she'd been assaulted and abandoned yet again, this time by those she loved.

"By Thanksgiving I suspected there was a baby. By Christmas, I knew. On New Year's Day, I left the house while everyone else slept in, and I found a drugstore around the corner. I stood in line with my pregnancy test along with other people picking up their morning after fixes—aspirin, black coffee, another bottle of cheap liquor. I wasn't alone in my particular misery; the woman right in front of me had a packet of morning-after emergency contraceptive in her hand," Phoebe said dryly.

Trevor needed a break. He needed to stand up and pace. He needed to growl and hit something. But he stayed glued to his chair, prepared to listen until she was finished talking.

"I tiptoed in the back slider, hoping I could slip down the hall to the bathroom without being seen, half afraid Granny G would be awake and whipping up breakfast already. But the house was almost eerily quiet. Everyone was still sleeping soundly, peacefully, completely unaware that I'd been gone."

Her mouth lifted in what he assumed was meant to be a smile, but it only made the pressure in his chest more intense.

"I knew, Trevor. I already knew. I had no doubt, whatsoever, that I was pregnant." She shook her head, hard. "But when I saw that stupid pink plus sign, it was like reliving it all over again. I crawled into the bathtub, curled up in a ball, and cried like a baby."

And that's when the tear betrayed her.

"No one came, though. No one heard me. No one knew." She didn't even bother wiping it away, but let it trail down her cheek to the curve of her jaw where it hung there, on the edge, before free-falling. "No one knows," she whispered. "Still."

"I know," he whispered back. "I hear you. And I'm not going anywhere."

Phoebe's shoulders were hunched up nearly to her ears, her palms pressed together on the table in front of her, her fingers laced so tightly her nail beds were white.

Trevor knew better than to touch her. She'd carried this burden herself for almost half her life, and he understood that she might need a little time to really digest the idea that she no longer had to go it alone.

How wise was it that he was the one she was pouring out her soul to? He wasn't sure he had an answer for that, but he'd called Vic while he was out getting food. He knew he'd have to answer to his friend and Phoebe's sister if he didn't toe the line.

"I need to move," Phoebe said suddenly. "I can't sit here anymore." She pushed back her chair before he could get around the table to help her. "Do you dance?" she asked.

Trevor stared at her a moment, his mind trying to catch up with her sudden change of direction. "Do I—do I dance?"

"Yes. Dance. You know, boogie? Do the hustle? Bump and grind? Maybe the Charleston?" She lifted both hands and crossed one foot back and forth over the other. "Tango?"

Still bemused, he held up his hand to stop her. "I'm a musician. I have moves. But... why?" He pushed her empty chair closer to the table and began gathering up their food wrappers and other assorted trash and shoving them into an empty food bag.

"Don't do that." She took the paper bag from him and tossed it on the table, then grabbed his hand, pulling him toward her computer. She moved her mouse to click on the speaker icon that had been muted, and *Coeur de Pirate* filled the air with a song. Trevor didn't understand a word she sang, but Beatrice's voice seemed imbued with the emotions of the story Phoebe had just told him.

"Put your arms around me and dance with me," Phoebe murmured, her voice almost as husky as the singer's. "It's the last song on the album. Hold me up for one song, Trevor. That's all I ask."

So he did. Trevor took her in his arms and cradled her against him while they swayed together, barely moving their feet. Drifting. She slipped her arms beneath his and around his waist and rested her cheek on his shoulder. He wasn't a big guy, just as she'd pointed out, but the way she leaned into him, the way her body seemed to melt in the circle of his embrace, how her tension seemed to drain out of her as they drifted around the room together... everything about the moment made him feel like a giant of a man.

Hold me up, she'd asked.

He'd hold her up forever if she'd let him.

As the song came to a lullaby end, and as their movements stilled, Trevor loosened his hold on Phoebe. But she didn't let go of him. She didn't lift her head; she didn't unwrap her arms from around his waist.

They stood there, the room filling with potent silence, and Trevor lowered his head to rest his cheek against her forehead. He could feel the warmth of her breath through the knit fabric of his shirt, the brush of her eyelashes against his neck.

Phoebe began to tremble, her shoulders curving forward, every muscle in her body tensing up against him as the dam broke loose and she began to weep. She clung to him, turning her face into his chest, her hands gripping the back of his shirt like it was her lifeline, sobbing almost soundlessly as she greedily took the comfort he offered.

Trevor bolstered himself against the onslaught of her emotions, glad to be her rock, her safe place, the one she clung to, and held her up until she was ready to hold herself up again. Even when she straightened and stepped back, he didn't release her hands.

"I'm sorry," she whispered. "Your shirt." She waved a hand at his chest.

"Don't be sorry," he insisted. "It's just a shirt."

"I need to wash my face," Phoebe said, and then pulled her hands free and headed for the stairs at the other end of the room. "I'll be right back. If you need the bathroom, there's one just down that short hall." She pointed him in the right direction.

Trevor finished cleaning up after their meal while he waited for Phoebe to return, then walked around the huge room. It seemed to be divided into four vague quadrants, each one a space with a dedicated use. The kitchenette, with its bistro-like dining area, and the cluster of mismatched furniture demarcating the living room took up the front half of the room. Then there was what looked like a photography studio, complete with background options, lighting banks, and umbrella reflectors. A door leading off the quadrant stood open, and he peeked inside, marveling at the mass of costumes and fabrics, and the vanity loaded with more makeup than he'd ever seen in one place before.

The last section of the room was clearly her art studio. From the looks of it, Phoebe's preferred creative outlet was painting. Stacks of canvases leaned against the walls, some in oils, others in acrylics, and several watercolors, too. There were canvases with rough sketches penciled on in scratching bold lines, others stood empty, stark with anticipation. There was a canvas mounted on an easel facing the wall. Just as Trevor took a step toward it, curious to know what it was that hid its face from him, Phoebe came down the stairs and stopped him.

"She's not finished yet. Wait, okay?" It wasn't a demand, but a request, so he didn't argue, even though he really wanted to see it just the way it was. He was curious about her creative process, about the way she saw things, her interpretation of her own artistic gifting.

If he hadn't borne witness to it, Trevor wouldn't have even known she'd been crying only a short while ago. He watched her descend the rest of the stairs and cross the room toward him, her feet making hardly any noise on the floor, the sight of her red-tipped toes making him smile. She seemed almost childlike in her youthful dress and sparse makeup, her bare feet, and he liked her this way. Brave and vulnerable at the same time, he recognized the girl she'd been in the woman coming toward him.

How had he not known her the moment he laid eyes on her?

"Do you want to hear the rest of my sordid tale now? Or are you ready to call it a night?" She smiled sweetly at him, letting him know in her own way that it was up to him, but he thought she might prefer to get it all out tonight. She seemed to have recovered her composure, so there didn't seem to be any reason for him to make her put it off any longer.

"Do you have coffee? If not, I can go get some. I noticed a coffee shop about a mile down the road."

"Oh no. I have coffee. I have the best coffee, you'll see." She reached for his hand and pulled him toward the stairs. "Do you want to come upstairs and see my loft suite?"

"Whoa!" He stopped in his tracks, making her stop short, too. "Remember my rule? I'm already playing with fire here." He nodded his head toward the loft. "I don't think *that* is a good idea."

She rolled her eyes. "I'm not going to throw you on my bed and ravage you, Trevor. I just wanted to show you the rest of the house. I designed this restoration, and the loft is the icing on the cake. I just thought you'd like to see it."

"As much as I actually *would* like to see it, I think I'd better pass."

"Really?" She narrowed her eyes at him as though still not sure whether he was serious or not. "You can trust me, Trevor. Remember what I said? Your virtue is safe with me." She tugged on his arm again.

"Maybe," he retorted, covering her hand with his free one and not budging. "But yours might be in jeopardy with me."

"Oh, come on. I trust you." She pulled harder.

"Well, you shouldn't. I don't even trust myself!" He laughed to take the edge off his words, but he stood his ground. She stopped, too, her arm still twined through his. He was glad she didn't pull away; he liked having her close. But no, he would not go up to her bedroom, with or without her. As blasé as Phoebe was about inviting a man—*him*—up to her bedroom to show off the architecture, he still couldn't treat the action lightly. Did she not realize what a man—*he*—might imagine, might hope for, might expect from a woman who led him to her room?

It wasn't that he couldn't control himself. It wasn't that he didn't trust himself. Or her, for that matter. It wasn't that he thought of nothing by sex and underwear. No, it was simply that he didn't want to have to put himself in the position of having to test his boundaries even more than he already was. It was that simple.

"Well, the coffee press is upstairs, so if you're not coming up with me, you'll just have to wait. Down here." She glanced up at him from the corner of her eyes. "All alone," she teased. Then she winked. "I'll be right back. Don't go anywhere."

He pointed to a coffeemaker on the counter near her kitchen sink. "Can't we just make coffee in that?"

She stopped on the bottom stair and shook her head, quirking her mouth up in an expression that told him he was being quite ridiculous. "This is your first cup of coffee in my home, Trevor. I'm going to serve you the real thing. Don't worry. You'll be glad you waited."

She disappeared up into the loft, but he could hear her rummaging around, opening and closing cupboards and drawers. "Don't you be looking at my painting!" she hollered.

He chuckled—he'd been considering doing just that. "I can't look at it knowing it's not finished?" He looked up to see her standing at the rail above him.

"No." She shook her head. "Be patient. You can wait until she's finished, just like everyone else."

"Does that mean you'll be having me back again?" The question escaped unchecked, but now that it was out there, he really, really wanted her to say 'yes.'

She grinned down at him. "I'm thinking about it." Then she twirled away and out of sight.

A roller coaster. He was on a roller coaster named Phoebe Gustafson. One minute she spoke of the details of her assault as though reciting a recipe, the next she wanted to dance. One moment she clung to him, weeping inconsolably, the next minute she was trying to drag him upstairs to her bedroom.

He was going to have his work cut out for him if he wanted to keep up with her.

And he did. Boy-oh-boy, did he ever.

Trevor made another circuit of the room, studying more closely the eclectic art that adorned her walls. It didn't take him long to realize that most of it wasn't actually Phoebe's, but a collection as vibrant and textured and counterintuitive as she was.

He was standing in front of an antique mirror in a colorful mosaic frame when Phoebe came back downstairs. He watched her approach in the slightly warped glass; in each hand she held a steaming mug. He took the one she offered him, his eyes never leaving her reflection as she stepped to his side.

She stood so close their elbows brushed, but neither of them moved apart.

"It's beautiful, isn't it?" Phoebe murmured.

Trevor agreed, but he thought the woman beside him was even more beautiful than the mosaic tiles that framed their reflections. He liked the way they looked, standing together, like they belonged to each other. Her ethereal beauty complemented his slightly rough-and-tumble image, and although he stood a couple of inches under six feet, he still was at least half a foot taller than she was without her shoes. He wondered what she saw when she looked at them.

Their eyes met in the mirror, and she smiled and took a sip of her coffee. He followed suit and then sighed with satisfaction. "Wow."

"Worth the wait?" she asked, clearly enjoying the sight of his pleasure.

"Worth the wait," he agreed. "This is amazing. Thank you."

"I know. And you're welcome." She turned to look up at him. "Shall we sit?" she asked, slipping her arm through his again and steering him toward a diminutive sofa so soft and squishy he couldn't help but think of Goldilocks fighting her way out of the too-soft cushions of Mama Bear's chair.

They sat side by side, and although there wasn't a whole lot of room between them, she drew her legs up under her and turned so she was facing him. She rested one arm on the back of the couch and poked his shoulder. "So you ready to hear about Lily Grace Rogers?"

THIRTY-THREE

IN THE SANCTUARY OF her loft room, with the smoky aroma of her favorite coffee swirling around her, she'd been certain she could do this. And now, sitting on her favorite sofa—the soft one that made her think of clouds and sweet dreams—her cup held close to her face, she breathed in the heady scent again, trying to bolster her courage.

"I'm ready to hear about Lily if you're ready to tell me about her," he answered. Then he smiled at her with that lopsided mouth of his, and she closed her eyes so she wouldn't be distracted by it, by him.

But closing her eyes was worse—she needed to see his face as she told him her story.

Trevor sipped his coffee as he listened, his attention never wandering, his gaze remaining fixed on her as she talked. Occasionally, he'd murmur something consoling, or reach out to offer the comfort of his touch. In some ways, his attentiveness to her made it easier to unload, to open up the locked places in her heart and air them out. But his very nearness, the way his fingers brushed her arm, the tears that overflowed from his eyes as she told him about the last time that she'd seen her daughter.... She'd promised herself she wouldn't cry—hadn't she cried herself out in his arms already? But his sympathy, his readiness to grieve with her without offering platitudes or empty words had her feeling vulnerable, but in a safe place.

And when the tears came again, this time slowly, falling gently like a summer night rain, he drew her up against his side. She curled into him, resting her head on his shoulder, and described her abysmal attempt to return to life as a normal teenager.

"The thing is, Trevor, I know if you asked Theresa and Jeff, and maybe even Lily, if I did the right thing, they'd all vehemently give a thumbs-up to my decision. But now? Now, I don't really know if it was the right thing to do. Even after all this time, I still wonder what might have happened had I not gone away that summer. What if I'd told my grandparents? I know they would have helped me. They would have loved Lily. All these years... well, they'd be so different, you know?" Phoebe sniffed.

Trevor nodded slowly, giving her all the time she needed. Could he possibly understand what it meant to finally, *finally*, be able to unburden this secret of hers? She liked the way it felt curled into his side, leaning on him, counting on him to keep holding her up in every sense.

"But then I remember the circumstances under which she was conceived, and I know how it would have felt to Renata, who probably wouldn't have believed the truth of what happened. I remind myself to think about what another court case for my grandparents would have done to them, to have to sit there and hear about my assault and my role in it, because believe me, Brad would surely have made me out to be a willing participant, not a victim. Which meant they would have had to listen to the sordid details of my lifestyle back then, and even though I know that they loved me unconditionally—I think I knew back then, too, but I was so afraid no one would believe me. This all would have hurt them so terribly and I just couldn't do that to them. To any of us. Our family was already all so shattered, you know?"

Trevor reached around her for a box of tissue from the coffee table and offered it to her. She turned slightly so that her back was to him, blew her nose, but didn't pull away. Instead, she drew his arm tighter around her and leaned her cheek against his biceps.

"She turned thirteen on July 10th." It came out a whisper, but she knew he'd heard her.

"Happy belated birthday, Lily Grace Rogers," he said.

Phoebe smiled to herself, pleased he'd made the effort to remember her daughter's full name.

"Do you want to know what I did to celebrate? We Gustafson Girls all went with Renata to her ultrasound appointment and watched Baby Charise perform her gymnastics routine in utero." Phoebe's breath caught, but she swallowed the lump in her throat that was trying to choke her. "It just about killed me, Trevor. And I've kinda been in a bad way ever since."

"So when Renata called you to come help her...." His voice trailed off as he acknowledged the agonizing position in which she'd found herself.

"Yep. But I shoved my little bleeding nub of a heart back in its locked chamber, and I went to help her. And it all came back to me like I'd given birth just yesterday: the breathing, the counting, the different stages. Even the things that helped to ease my discomfort and pain—it was all right there at my fingertips."

"The mind is an amazing thing, isn't it?"

"Mm-hm," she agreed. She toyed with the rolled hem of her dress, smoothing it across her thighs, pleating it, then smoothing it again and again. "There were a few times when Renata looked at me with this odd expression... and I knew she was wondering how I knew what to do, what to expect. It scared me, Trevor. Not just because I didn't want to tell her—I don't know that I'll ever have the courage to do so—but because I felt like the two births were merging together in my mind, and I didn't want my grief and regret over Lily to cast shadows on the miracle that I was witnessing in Charise's birth."

Trevor lifted his free hand and smoothed her hair away from her face, a touch meant to comfort rather than caress. Oh, how glad she was that he had insisted on coming to see her today, that he'd insisted on staying. That he'd broken his own rules to be here with her tonight.

"It happened anyway," she whispered. "And when they laid that tiny ba—baby girl... on Ren's sto—stomach..." She swallowed hard, not sure how much longer she could keep it together, but she had to get the words out or they'd eat her alive from the inside. "When they han—handed her to T—Tim." Stupid tears. Stupid, stupid tears. When would the reservoir run dry so she could get on with her life? "All I saw was the nurse handing my—my baby girl—to someone else." She pulled another tissue from the box she'd tucked against her side and pressed it to her eyes. "I kept it together long enough to congratulate them, and then I—I ran." A wrenching sob surged up from inside her. "I *always* run." The words came out jagged and rasping, grating over the sharp edges in her throat. "I'm so... *tired*... of running."

Trevor said nothing. Once again, just as he'd done earlier when the music had ended and she'd come undone, he simply held her. His kindness, his patience as he listened without giving her advice or trying to fix this irreparable broken part of her, his gentleness as he stroked her arm in a comforting gesture, the peace he seemed to embody; all those things about him that made him... well, who he was now. Phoebe knew he was a changed man.

And she was still that frightened, wounded girl, ready to run, ready to fly, ready to abandon, rather than be abandoned.

But Trevor, unlike her parents, unlike her high school friends, unlike the other men who had come in and out of her life—primarily because she made sure to leave them before they could leave her—unlike the Rogers who had stopped writing, stopped sending pictures of Lily after the first few years, unlike all of them, Trevor had come back. And refused to leave.

Was it only because he needed to exonerate himself? Or had he come back for her, for this? To help ease her burden by sharing it, by standing with her? Was it too much to hope for in a man she barely knew?

And yet—and the thought stunned her momentarily—the man who held her, whose eyes told her he saw both her outward beauty and her internal scars, the man who had come back for her and was *still here* even knowing the things about her that he did....

Trevor knew more about her than anyone else in her life.

"Trevor?" She didn't turn toward him.

"Hm?"

"I forgive you."

She felt his chest rise and fall behind her in a deep, cleansing breath, his arm tightened around her in response. "I'm glad. Thank you." He hesitated for a moment and then said, "Phoebe?"

"Hm?"

"What will it take for you to forgive yourself?"

THIRTY-FOUR

HE SENSED HER WITHDRAWAL almost the moment the words left his mouth. Even before she straightened up and slid out from under his arm, he knew it.

Too soon. Too fragile. Too prone to run, by her own admission.

Trevor wanted to suck the question back inside, swipe it from the air where it hovered between them. And yet, as he'd listened to her story—similar to so many he'd heard from women who listened to his music, to his songs about loving unconditionally, who heard him tell the story about the prophet Hosea and his recalcitrant bride, Gomer, from women who had suffered at the hands of others as well as themselves, who had wrestled with the shackles of unforgiveness in their lives—he knew it was the key that would unlock her chains.

But he also knew that without God, forgiveness of herself may never come. Until she believed that God *wanted* her brokenness, that he wanted her to come to him the way she was now—without her masks, without her running shoes, with the tears of her pain marking the exquisite beauty made in the Creator's image—she would never see herself the way God did. God saw her through the eyes of unconditional love, and he wanted to dress her in radiant white, to see her lit up from the inside. His bride.

God's only request? Acknowledge her need for him and accept his gift of sacrificial and unerring love. The changed life would follow the changed heart; Trevor knew that for a fact. She didn't need to get cleaned up or fix the broken places first. Those things were God's specialties.

Would she listen? Or would she misunderstand and see him as judging her again? Would she believe—God forbid—that he'd lured her into confessing her deepest and darkest secrets to him so that he could use them against her, to try to coerce her into saying yes to God?

I'm here. Include me.

The unspoken words interrupted his frantic thoughts, and he paused, focusing on them.

I'm here. Include me.

Trevor didn't hesitate. He knew God would speak through him. "Phoebe, I didn't just come here to ask for and hopefully receive your forgiveness, although I can't begin to tell you how grateful I am that you've given it to me." He reached for her hand, and she let him take it, even though she had pushed herself back into the corner of their shared couch, putting almost a foot of space between them. He wanted to touch her, to stay connected to her physically, in the hope she'd stay connected to him emotionally and spiritually. "Please hear me out, okay?"

If he hadn't been looking at her, he would have missed the tiny nod.

"I've known Gia for several years now. Not well—she's my cousin Ricky's friend, and he's quite a bit younger than I am. We didn't spend much time together until he was a teenager, but then he and Gia would come hang out at my place now and then. She always talked about you and Renata and Juliette, about your grandparents all the time, about how tight your family was, even though you'd lost your parents years before." He shook his head as he began to realize just how many ways God had been molding and guiding and leading them to this point in time. "I don't know why I didn't connect her story with yours—looking back, she once told me how your parents died, and how you'd all gone to live with your grandparents. I just didn't make the connection."

"Typical man," she teased from behind the waterfall of her hair. She'd swept it all forward over one shoulder, and with her head down, he couldn't see much more than her downcast eyes and the profile of her cheekbone and nose. The posture reminded him of the girl who'd sat in the pew hiding behind her hair then, too.

"But God laid it on my heart to pray for you and your sisters. I didn't know exactly why, or even what to pray, but every time your family came to mind, I prayed for you. Phoebe, I've been intentionally praying for the

Gustafson Girls for more than five years now. For each of you by name. For you. Because God put you on my heart."

He stopped and waited for a reaction from her before going on. He watched a tear slide down her cheek, but she let it fall. That was enough of a response for him to continue.

"When Gia talked me into taking Juliette out, and she ended up opening her heart to the love of Christ that night, I truly believed she was the reason I'd been praying for you."

"Trevor." She did look up then, her eyes wide and luminous. "That night changed her life. I saw it happen. I see it every day. A *joie de vivre*—this inner happiness. It's like she's come alive." She squeezed his hand, her grip surprisingly strong. But then, she was an artist who worked with her hands. "Thank you for bending your rules for her. You might have saved her life."

He shook his head, humbled by her statement, but he knew he'd only been a vessel. "What's that saying? You can lead a horse to water, but you can't make him drink?" He chuckled. "Don't quote me on that—I'm *not* calling your sister a horse. I only mean that I know God had a plan for that night, and that he wanted to use me. I said yes, that was all."

"Maybe so, but because you said yes, my sister said yes, and that's made all the difference."

Oh, how he wished she could hear herself. How he wished she could see that she could have the same thing, the same joy in her life. All she had to do was say yes. But he held his tongue, sensing that it wasn't going to be quite so simple as that with Phoebe.

"Well, I've learned the hard way that I'm not very wise when I try to take over for God. I have yet to go wrong when I do things his way instead of my own."

Phoebe took a deep breath and let it out slowly, lowering her head again as she did. Her curls fluttered prettily as she ducked behind her hair again. "I wish I could be so confident in him. God and I don't really have a good track record."

"And I know my part in that hasn't helped."

"Actually, Trevor, that's not true. Not anymore." She didn't look at him, but she turned her hand in his so that their fingers laced together, a gesture of trust on her part. He was pretty sure his heart skipped a beat. "Seeing the way Juliette has blossomed, hearing Gia talk about you, meeting you the other day... and now tonight? Everything about you makes me curious about God." She said the last words in a whisper, as though admitting a weakness. "But my own experience with him? It isn't like yours, or like Juliette's or Gia's, or even Renata's." She shook her head, her voice tight. "I don't think I can trust him. I still don't know if I can wholly trust you, Trevor. That said, if you let me down, it might just wreck me all over again, but I'll pick up the pieces like I always do, and chalk it up as par for the course."

Her words just about killed him. "I'm not going anywhere."

"I know." Her tone belied her words; she clearly still had her doubts. "But if I let myself trust God, and he lets me down? I will surely die." Another tear fell. "I don't think I could come back from that."

"I understand," Trevor said, and he did. He had lived under the same fear, but his had manifested in the opposite way. He'd become a legalistic, by the book, hard line religious fanatic, afraid of letting God down, afraid of losing favor with him, afraid of God turning his back on him. Yet, when he'd fallen off the edge, when he'd crash-landed and lay there in a messy pile of brokenness, he'd learned just how unconditional God's love was, and just how freeing it was.

"After you walked out of church that morning and left me standing there with all my religious formalwear torn to shreds, I could almost see God storming off behind you, completely and utterly disgusted with me." He grinned at the look of surprise on her face. "Yeah, you pegged me that day. Crucified me," he said, using her word. "And I knew I deserved it, even back then. It took me several minutes to catch my breath, but when I charged out of there like a bat out of hell—" He broke off and laughed. "That's probably not the best idiom to use when referring to leaving church, is it?"

"Probably not," she agreed. And there was her smile again.

"I take that back. I charged out of there like a man on a mission—better?"

"Much."

"But you were already gone." He shifted in his seat so that he was turned toward her, now serious, wanting her to hear him. "I looked for you,

Phoebe. Every Sunday, I got to church early, I stayed late, hoping to see you come in. I asked about you—carefully; I figured you most likely still hadn't told anyone—but no one knew anyone named Josephine. And I didn't know your last name."

"Josephine is my middle name."

"I know. Juliette told me."

Phoebe's head snapped up, and her eyes widened. "Juliette knows?" She tried to pull her hand from his grasp, but he held on.

"Juliette knows we met in that church, but she doesn't know all the circumstances about why you were there. I didn't tell her that." She tugged on her hand again, but he still didn't let her go. "Please don't pull away from me, Phoebe. Hear me out, okay? They know I'm here tonight. I'm bending my rules to be here, and I need the accountability. Who better to hold me accountable than a man who loves me like a brother and a woman who loves you as her sister? They know you came to that church needing a shoulder, and they know that I chased you away with my condemnation. They are praying for us, maybe even now. They have been all week—I went to them Monday night."

"She's known since Monday night?" Phoebe's voice cracked. "And she didn't say anything to me?"

"You... haven't made it easy for anyone to talk to you these last few days." He said it gently, softly, not wanting her to misunderstand and presume he was chastising her. "She was already worried something was wrong when you didn't go to the hospital with the rest of us."

"*You* went to the hospital with the family? I thought you only met Renata at Juliette's the other day." She stared at him like he'd just grown gills.

"Ricky and I had been invited to Sunday dinner at your grandparents. That was canceled, but Gia asked if we wanted to meet them at the hospital instead. So yes, we were there." Then he added, "I had hoped you'd be there."

"So you've seen her?" He felt her hand tremble just the slightest bit in his. He knew Phoebe was asking about baby Charise, not Renata.

"I have." He didn't add that he'd held her and sung to her and fallen just a little in love with the baby girl.

"Is she—is she—"

"She's perfect," he assured her. "I think she has your eyes."

"That's what Renata said."

He waited for a few minutes, letting her process the idea that Juliette knew as much as she did. He hadn't meant to withhold the information.

"I'm sorry," she finally said. "I interrupted you. What were you saying?"

He squeezed her hand and went back to his story. "I kinda went off the deep end after that. I kept asking God to bring you back so I could make things right... for myself. So I could get back in with him. Regain my good standing, you know? But when things didn't go the way that I thought they should, I spiraled out of control." He didn't tell her everything—this wasn't really about him, anyway—but enough so she'd understand that he hadn't just skipped church a few times. He told her how the pastor had handled the mess, how he'd been challenged to get help and not go deeper inside himself, and he described the freedom he'd gained when he came clean with his weakness and addictions and presented himself to God as a broken man.

"When I asked God what to do about you, how I could fix that terrible wrong, he basically told me to let him handle it, and that my part was to pray. So I did." He shook his head and chuckled as he thought back on all the years he'd prayed. "And let me tell you, woman, sometimes I'd be right in the middle of a conversation or in the thick of writing a song, or out riding, or sitting in church, and your name would pop into my head, interrupting whatever I was doing. I'd pray for you, anyway. Countless times I'd wake up from a sound sleep with the urgent need to pray for you. So I'd grumble and complain a little, but then I'd do it, anyway." He dipped his head, trying to get her to look at him. "Phoebe Josephine Gustafson, I have been praying for you, asking God to bring you back into my life, to give me a second chance with you, since the day you left that church. My motives weren't always pure, at least not at the beginning, but they changed as I did." He reached over and took her other hand, folding both of hers inside his. "I have been praying for this moment for almost half my life, *believing* that it would happen. Maybe not in my timing, that's for sure, but don't you see?"

She was staring at their clasped hands, her lower lip between her teeth.

"You have been a part of my life all this time. This isn't an accident or coincidence. He has been steering us to this time and place, chipping away the things in me that sent you running, turning me into a whole new man so that I can sit here with you now as the man you need me to be."

She lifted her eyes to his, startled, full of questions. He belatedly realized his statement had been a little more forthright than she was perhaps ready to hear. It didn't matter, though. Whether they were destined to be lovers—*please, God, please*—or just friends, he wanted to be the man she needed him to be, the man God had made him to be. He couldn't take back the words anyway, so he kept on, pouring as much conviction as he could into his voice without sounding like a freak. She probably already thought he was crazy, anyway; hadn't Juliette said as much earlier in the week? If Juliette thought he was, then certainly Phoebe did, too.

"I believe he's been working this whole time to bring us together. First introducing me to Gia, the last of your sisters I'd connect to you. She doesn't look a thing like any of you, so even though her story should have made my antennas perk up, it didn't. *But* her presence in my life had me praying for the Phoebe version of you—all along, I've been praying for the Jo version of you." He laughed at how silly it sounded when he said it out loud, but in his heart, it was like he'd stumbled upon the exact combination needed to free them from their past. He could almost see the inner workings of a lock as the tumblers inside all shifted into alignment, each one a piece of the plan that God had put in motion all those years ago. "That opened the door for me to get to know Juliette and then to have my best friend—Vic is like a brother to me, Phoebe—"

"You've said that many times," she teased.

"I have, haven't I? But it's true. And to see him with your sister? Talk about *joie de vivre*! He, too, has come alive. And with the two of them getting married, it was inevitable you and I were going to meet eventually." He tipped his head back and closed his eyes. "Am I crazy? Are you seeing this, too? Or is it just me?" He looked at her again, willing her to agree.

"It does seem pretty providential," she said with great care.

"You forgiving me, Phoebe, is a first step toward God; I know it is. The fact that you can see the difference in Juliette, and that it makes you consider, even for a moment, that God might be... an option? Another small step toward him. Trusting me in spite of everything I've done to you? Another one, because I'm here by his doing, by his plan. I'm still a broken man, Phoebe. Without God, I'm not trustworthy. Without God, I would have done more than bend my rules tonight. I wouldn't even have them for starters, but even if I had, I would have taken you up on your offer to go upstairs with you, and I would have taken every advantage you would have allowed me."

Stop, man, before you go too far.

"I have been waiting for you for all this time, and I know God has been, too." He squeezed her hands, imploring her with his eyes. "Maybe it's time to trust him again. To give him the same chance you're giving me. Maybe it's time to say 'yes' to God, too, Phoebe."

THIRTY-FIVE

SHE WANTED TO SAY 'yes.' She wanted to give in to the pull of his words, his conviction, his evidence stirred in her, but it was all so much so quickly. As Trevor pointed out how he believed God had steered and guided them and paved the way for them to meet again and clear out the ugliness between them, she, too, was looking back at her own life and seeing mile markers along the way to this day as well.

The connections they shared were undeniable. She'd truly believed that day she'd stormed from the church that she'd never see the guy again, but over the last several years, he'd become friends with her sisters and would soon be practically family when Vic married Juliette. She pretty much had no choice *but* to forgive him—they'd be bound together by marriage, and Phoebe would do nothing to stand in the way of her sister's happiness with Vic. But she wanted to forgive Trevor. She saw the change in him, saw that it was genuine, and saw that he, like Juliette, gave all the credit to God.

She'd known all along that Gia believed in God and lived fully in that belief. She never shoved it down Phoebe's throat—not the way Renata used to do all the time—nor did she ever come across as anything other than exactly who she was.

And Phoebe knew that her parents—her beloved Maman and Papa—would give anything to know that she was committed to Christ. They, like Gia, had been devout believers with huge hearts.

She saw the change in Renata, too, and although her sister hadn't come right out and said so, the softer side of her had come out of her brokenness when she lost her husband. Renata had birthed four boys before Charise and would never have asked Phoebe to be there in John's place for any of them. Yet, because of the changes in Renata, her heart had been softened toward Phoebe right before Charise was born, and Phoebe had been the sister Renata had called to share in the joy of the birth of her baby girl. That sounded suspiciously like the kind of thing God might orchestrate, according to Trevor's logic.

Trevor. He'd come back into her life at this moment when she so desperately needed someone to talk to, someone to pull her out of the pit of misery she was wallowing in. Of all people, she never would have chosen him, but he was the perfect person for the job, when all was said and done. He already knew what had happened in her life. He already knew the worst of her story—maybe not the tragic ending, but he already knew the tragic course she'd set on. And yet, here he was, sitting beside her, holding her hands, telling her that God had brought them together, that he had become the man she needed him to be, *touching* her the way she longed to be touched, with something more than lust or power or manipulation... with kindness instead, with tenderness, with *love*—

She jerked her hands out of his grasp and stood so quickly she got a little lightheaded and had to brace herself on the armrest behind her.

"Whoa. You okay?" Trevor asked, getting to his feet beside her. He reached for her, but she dodged his touch and headed toward the table.

"Yeah, I just need a drink. You want yours?" Her voice was too bright, too cheery. "Or maybe more coffee?" She hoped he'd choose coffee. Then she could escape for a minute to try to wrap her head around the insane thoughts spinning out of control in her mind.

"Water is fine." He followed close behind, and she could hear the concern in his voice. She moved around to the far side of the table to keep it between them; she wouldn't be able to think if he touched her again.

She needed a break. She needed fresh air, or at least air that she wasn't sharing with Trevor. She took a long swig of water, making a concerted effort to tamp down the panic rising up in her.

He picked up his water, but he didn't take a drink. He just stood there, watching her, waiting for her to explain her odd behavior.

"You know, Trevor, you've given me a lot to think about," she began. "I'm glad we talked. Thank you." She accidentally dropped the bottle cap and when he came around the table to pick it up for her, she practically leapt back so he wouldn't brush against her. She tried not to even touch his fingers when she took the little white lid out of his, and she stopped looking at him when she saw the hurt in his eyes.

"Thank you," she said, sidling a few steps away from him. Out of reach.

"Phoebe, don't." So many emotions flooded those two words. The way he said her name made her want to fling herself into his arms and never let go.

"I—I think you'd better go," she murmured. "I need—I need—" She broke off, not knowing what she needed. "I need you to go, please. I need—I can't think with you here. With you touching me. You make my head spin."

In two steps, he was around the table, his hands sliding up her arms to her shoulders, drawing her slowly, carefully, closer, until he rested his forehead against hers. He closed his eyes and said, "I'll leave. I will. But don't run, okay? Don't leave me. I don't want to wait another decade to find you again, but I will." He drew back the tiniest bit so he could look at her, then his hands moved up the column of her neck, his fingers threading into her hair. His palms cupped her jaw and lifted her face, one thumb smoothing over the curve of her bottom lip.

And then he lowered his mouth to hers. It was only a kiss. But in that brief touching of his lips to hers, she sensed his hope, his fear, and his promise to her. *I'm not going anywhere.*

She wanted to promise him the same thing, but she couldn't find the words. And when he stepped back and made his way to the front door, she wanted nothing more than to beg him to come back, to kiss her again, to hold her close. *Dance with me,* her heart cried out. *Stay with me,* her body echoed. "Pray for me," she whispered, surprising herself.

He paused, his hand on the doorknob. "I'll never stop." He stepped out into the night and pulled the door closed behind him.

Phoebe stood rooted to the spot, her legs trembling beneath her, her blood pounding in her veins. *Go after him! Go after him! Stop him!* But she didn't move. She couldn't move. This was about more than Trevor and his unnerving certainty about them. This was about more than her mixed emotions toward him.

This was about more than her resistance to see Baby Charise. About more than her longing to see Lily, about more than the ache in her heart for her mother.

This was bigger, broader, all of those things combined and more.

"God? Can you hear me?" She sounded like a child to her ears. "I don't want to run anymore. But I don't know how to stay. I don't know how to stop. I'm so—I'm so afraid."

The spacious room reverberated with silence, but as Phoebe waited and listened, it seemed to fill with something—or Someone—*more.* With a sense of *deja vu*, Phoebe remembered the way this felt; like she was standing on holy ground. It was exactly how she'd felt when she first entered that church the day after Mother's Day. What had Trevor said? Like she could almost hear God breathing beside her.

"Are you there?" she asked into the hushed stillness. "Will you show me that you're who you say you are?" She knew it wasn't that simple. God wouldn't flip on the television to interrupt a newscast like she'd seen in the movies. He wouldn't spell out his name in the stars. Nor would he turn a jug of water into wine. Then again, after the week she'd just endured, that sounded like the worst sign ever.

But she'd just spent the last several hours with a man who claimed God spoke to him in some way. Over and over, Trevor said God told him to do or say something, to obey or act. If God could communicate with Trevor on a regular basis, to the point that the man seemed to do nothing without first getting God's approval, why wouldn't he make himself real to her in some small way? She wanted so desperately to believe in him, to trust him, but she also wanted so desperately to know that she could, that he was who he said he was, and that he would be there for her.

She heard Trevor's voice in her head: *I'm not going anywhere.*

"I need you to promise me the same thing," she whispered to God.

THIRTY-SIX

Phoebe filled a huge glass with tap water and added ice for good measure. She didn't like the way the city water tasted, but it was fine if it was cold. She turned off the lights downstairs—it was later than she'd thought—and headed upstairs to get ready for bed. She didn't have the energy to do anything else; she felt completely drained and undone.

Tucked away in her cloud bed, she smiled at the white gauzy canopy overhead and imagined what Trevor's reaction might have been to her bedroom. "What was I thinking inviting him up here? Poor guy." And that was the case; she hadn't thought about him and his feelings at that point. She'd just wanted to distract him. And any other man would have jumped at the chance. At least the ones she surrounded herself with.

But Trevor Zander was different from the men she usually spent time with. She'd known that at the gas station when he'd left his bike behind to help her, when he'd done so, expecting nothing in return from her. Not a phone number, not an email, not a date. He hadn't dropped any inappropriate comments about her appearance or accidentally brushed up against her or made a joke about her *owing* him. She'd seen the look in his eyes—she had no doubt he'd been attracted to her—and had wondered what she'd done to make him not act the way most men would. But knowing now the kind of man he was, his behavior toward her made perfect sense.

Phoebe had known he was different when he'd claimed his relationship to her sister based on their shared belief, calling Juliette his sister in Christ. Even before she'd met him, she'd known he was different from Juliette's recounting of their date, and she'd known he was different when he showed up on her doorstep asking her forgiveness for something he'd done a lifetime ago.

No, she wasn't surprised that Trevor had said 'no' to a visit to her loft, and she wasn't surprised that he'd done so without making her feel trashy or stupid. Or rejected.

Instead, he made her feel valuable. Cherished. Pursued... in the best way; chosen, like he wanted to be with her, and her alone. What woman didn't want to be pursued that way?

He hadn't come right out and said he was pursuing her... had he? She rolled onto her side and tucked her pillow more firmly under her head, remembering how it had felt to rest her cheek against Trevor's chest when they danced.

She tried to recall all the things he'd said tonight. She'd done most of the talking, but his words, though fewer by far, carried a whole lot of weight, meaning.

"You have been a part of my life all this time," he'd said. "This isn't an accident or coincidence. God has been steering us to this time and place, chipping away the things in me that sent you running, changing me so that I could sit here with you now as the man you need me to be."

Maybe he hadn't said he was pursuing her in so many words, but Phoebe didn't know a person alive who wouldn't melt at hearing those words spoken over them.

Did he love her? How could he? They'd only known each other for a few weeks, and even that couldn't really count since they hadn't spent any time together until tonight.

But, oh, the time they'd spent together! She felt like she knew more about Trevor—about his character, his passions, what drove him—than she knew about anyone else in her life, with the exception, perhaps, of her sisters. And as well as they knew her, Trevor knew things about her that they didn't. And he'd known them for more than a decade. He'd also known her through the eyes of Gia, and Juliette, and maybe even Vic, just as she'd learned of Trevor through them as well.

In other words, they hadn't really been strangers when they met almost two weeks ago at the gas station.

And Trevor had been talking to God about her since the day she'd stormed out of the church. All this time, someone had been praying for her, praying her through her darkest nights, her deepest wounds.

"Oh God," she whispered, a sudden realization taking her breath away. "Is that why I could never go through with it?" Were Trevor's prayers what stood between her and death all those times she'd tried to take her own life? Something had stopped her every time. Something—or Someone—had pulled her back from the edge again and again. "Just like Maman used to do."

Phoebe wiped at the tears that had gathered once more in her eyes and were now spilling over. "Thank you." Was that God's answer to her prayer already? Was this revelation his way of showing her he'd been with her this whole time? She wasn't sure, but for tonight, it was enough.

And Trevor had kissed her. Softly, sweetly, tenderly, but that was no chaste peck from a man who was simply glad to have cleared the air between them. And he'd asked her not to run, not to leave him.

And he'd *kissed* her! Phoebe touched her fingertips to her lips, remembering, savoring.

• • • • • • • • • •

SHE AWOKE SUDDENLY, SITTING up in bed like she'd been shot. Her bleary eyes darted around the room and then landed on her clock. Almost two in the afternoon? She hadn't slept in that late since high school!

But oh, how lovely it felt to have gotten a good night's sleep, especially after such a rough week. And after the emotional unleashing last night. Granted, she wasn't quite ready to leave home and face the world—more precisely, to face Renata and Baby Charise. But she'd made her peace with Trevor Zander, even if the evening had ended a little rough, and she was beginning to make her peace with God, one small step at a time, just like Trevor had said.

Oh yes. She smiled and hugged herself. And Trevor Zander, Juliette's Jesus freak, rock and roll biker, had *kissed* her.

A knock sounded on the door, insistent, as though it wasn't the first time the person had done so. Maybe that was what had awakened her.

She wasn't expecting anyone. What if it was Trevor? She scrambled out of bed and slipped her arms into her white chenille robe, a vintage style she loved with its ridges and floral patterns. She dashed into the bathroom and groaned when she saw her reflection. Her eyes were still puffy from all the crying she'd done last night, and there was a crease that ran from jaw to hairline on the left side of her face.

"But, hey. At least my hair looks good," Phoebe said dryly. "Thanks, Maman." Besides, maybe it was one of her sisters, finally coming to check on her. Knowing Granny G, she'd sent Gia over with food.

She tightened the sash around her waist and hurried downstairs. "I'm coming!"

It wasn't Trevor banging on her door. Nor was it Gia or Juliette. It wasn't even Granny G herself, who would've been Phoebe's next guess.

"Rennie? What on earth—what are you doing here?" Phoebe stared in shock at her sister, who stood patiently on the doorstep, a bundled-up baby in one arm and an overstuffed diaper bag slung over her shoulder. Ren's minivan was parked in the driveway beside Xena. "You drove here yourself? Should you—it's not too soon?"

Tim was right about his wife. Renata did look radiant. Exhausted, a little frumpy, but glowing with happiness. Even the shadows under eyes were lovely, giving her a fragile, otherworldly appearance.

"My milk just let down." Renata grimaced and gave Phoebe a deadpan look. "Are you going to invite me in?"

Still stunned, but no longer immobilized, Phoebe lurched forward to take the huge baby bag. "Here. Let me help you."

"No, I got that. You take Charise." Renata levered her arm toward Phoebe, practically forcing the baby on her.

For one heart-stopping moment, Phoebe froze again, but when Ren's eyebrow rose in that perfectly Renata way of hers, Phoebe flipped her long hair back over her shoulder and took the tiny girl in her arms. She stepped back so her sister could sweep past her, and then pushed the door closed behind her.

Phoebe stood there, staring down into the little round face—all that could be seen of the bundled-up baby—the bump of a chin beneath pouting miniature lips, a nose that tipped up at the end like Renata's, and eyelids so thin they might have been made of moonbeams. Charise's features twitched and fluttered as she stirred, and then stretched, arching into the crook of Phoebe's arm, one little fist poking out of the top of the blanket, long fingers uncurling like a delicate pink orchid in bloom. Phoebe watched, mesmerized, as Charise's tiny mouth puckered into a rather French *moue*, and then her eyes popped open, one at a time.

"Hello, little one," Phoebe cooed. "It's all right. Yes, it's all right. It's me, your Auntie Phoebe." Her voice came out high and a bit strangled, but it was all she could do not to burst into tears. She'd just fallen instantly and madly in love with the precious little darling.

"I need to use the bathroom and then I'll feed her. You okay to keep her for a few more minutes?" Renata spoke quietly from several feet away, where she'd unloaded her things onto a library table against one wall. "Here's a Binky if you get desperate." She held out a pacifier and a cloth diaper. "You might need that, too; she's a dribbler."

Phoebe took the proffered items, and with great effort, lifted her gaze from the baby's face to Renata's. "Can I unwrap her?"

"Of course. I'll warn you; she might freak out a little. She really likes being a burrito baby. Poor thing," Renata added as she pushed open the bathroom door. "The boys have started calling her Little Burro. They think it's a cute nickname for burrito."

"What? No!" Phoebe called out to the closed door. Charise startled a little in her arms. "Sorry, baby girl. I didn't mean to scare you."

She crossed the room, babbling away at the baby, making for the couch she'd shared with Trevor the night before. It was close to an open window, and the sun streamed through, warming the spot nicely. "You're not a little burro, are you? No, you're not. You're a precious baby girl, yes, you are." Phoebe lifted her up close so she could nuzzle her face into the baby's neck and breathe in the almost edible newborn scent. "Mmmm," she sighed. "I could just eat you up, Charise Olivia. You're a yummy little Olive, that's what you are. My little round Olive baby."

Knowing she only had a few minutes until Renata returned, Phoebe began to gently unwind the baby's blanket. Her miniature arms flailed in surprise at being suddenly loosed, and when her legs were freed from the confines as well, Charise drew them up a little and squirmed in protest.

Phoebe sang a silly French lullaby Maman used to sing and laid the little girl in her lap so she could ruck up the soft yellow sleep gown. She reached inside it and pulled Charise's arms out of the long sleeves and then slipped the whole thing off over her head. The baby wore a pale pink onesie beneath the gown, and although Charise had been born almost two weeks early only a week ago, she was already showing signs of a healthy eater. Her solid little belly filled out the knit bodysuit, the hard knot of her umbilical cord dark under the fabric. Her squishy thighs were already forming rolls, and she sported a darling triple chin. Phoebe ran her fingertips along the velvety skin of the inside of Charise's arms, wrapped her hands around calves so small they fit perfectly in her palms, and pulled fuzzy socks off each foot, grinning like a lovesick puppy as Charise spread and flexed her pea-sized toes.

Oh, the ache in her heart as her eyes devoured the infant in her lap. This was what she'd missed, what she'd handed off to someone else. She gathered the baby up close to her chest, tucking her inside the lapels of her soft robe, and lowered her head to breathe her in. Charise seemed perfectly content to be snuggled tightly while her auntie wept quietly.

"She's been anxious to see you," Renata murmured as she lowered herself gingerly onto an overstuffed chair close by. She said nothing about the tears dribbling down Phoebe's face.

Phoebe didn't respond. She didn't think Ren expected her to. Her throat was tight with emotion—love and need and grief, all tangled together in her chest, making it hard to catch her breath.

"I heard you singing *Au clair de la Lune*," Renata said. "I'm sure Maman is smiling in heaven right now."

Phoebe nodded, not sure her voice would work. The words, the sounds so unique to that language, the lilting phrases... when she sang in French, she could almost hear Maman sing with her.

"Oh, this is lovely," Renata sighed as she sank back into the chair. "The arms are the perfect height for nursing. Is she ready to eat?"

Phoebe was loathed to give up the baby just yet, but as Renata spoke, Charise began to squirm again, emitting small mewling sounds and bobbing her face against Phoebe's neck. "I think so." She stood and took her to Renata, along with the blanket she'd peeled off the infant, and then returned to her place on the loveseat, wiping away the last of her tears with her sleeve.

She watched unabashedly as Renata unbuttoned the front of her shirt, unclipped the cup of her nursing bra, and lifted Charise to her breast. "Oh!" she ground out as the baby began to suckle. "Still a little tender when she first latches on, but it's better than it was a few days ago—yikes. I'm telling you, the first week or two? Between wonky sleep schedules and the uterus flushing out and the milk coming in and the tender places where there aren't usually tender places? It's a wonder that women keep having babies."

With her free hand, Renata deftly tucked the blanket around the baby, and then sat back, an expression bordering on euphoria smoothing the lines around her eyes. She lifted Charise's fist from where it rested against her full breast and pressed a kiss to the curled fingers. "But then, moments like this happen. The world slows, time becomes irrelevant, and all that matters is the beating of her heart in tandem with mine. It's really only an echo of what we shared when I carried her inside of me—in my heart, I know that—but I'll take the echo any day if it means I can hold her like this, carry her in my arms rather than in my womb." She sighed contentedly. "It's moments like this that make it all worthwhile."

Phoebe marveled at how easy Ren made it all look, but deep down, she was certain that she, too, would have been a good mother, had she been given the chance. She looked away, lest the longing in her heart give away too much.

"So." It wasn't a question, but a segue. Renata spoke quietly, a nursing mother unwilling to disturb the infant in her arms, but firm and demanding all the same. When Phoebe didn't offer any response, Renata expounded. "I came to you because you wouldn't come to me. Why?"

Phoebe shot a sideways glance at her sister, her emotions at war. Her arms felt empty, and her breasts ached, as though her own child had just been placed in another woman's arms all over again. But this baby wasn't hers and the woman was Renata, demanding and presumptuous as always.

She shrugged, her defenses rising, because she was Phoebe, shocking and provocative as always. "I got stone cold drunk on Sunday, stayed that way through Monday, and slept it off Tuesday and Wednesday. I really wasn't in any condition to drive." She didn't explain the last two days; she had no excuse to give.

Renata's expression didn't change. Her eyebrow—not so perfectly shaped today—didn't even arch. She didn't say a word, didn't react in any measurable way at all. In fact, if Phoebe didn't know better, she'd think Renata hadn't heard a word she'd said.

Finally, feeling a little ashamed over her childish—albeit truthful—response, she murmured, "Sorry I haven't been by to visit." She folded Charise's sleeper into a neat square and then tucked the socks into each other just to keep her hands busy.

"I'm not going to lie, Phoebe. I've been really worried. Everyone has been trying for days to reach you. In any other circumstance, I would just assume you're pulling a Phoebe, but—" She broke off, her brow furrowed slightly. "I've wracked my brain, trying to figure out what I said or did to upset you or make you feel like I didn't want you around." Renata shifted in the seat, repositioning Charise so the arm of the chair supported her weight. "Phoebe, you were my hero, my rescuer. What would I have done without you?"

"You didn't do or say anything," Phoebe murmured, not looking at her sister. She shook her head, wanting—and yet so afraid—to tell her everything that had surfaced in the last few days. Could she trust Renata with that kind of ammunition? "I guess I just pulled a really big Phoebe this time."

"Would you mind getting me a glass of water? I always forget to get it before I start, and nursing makes me so thirsty. I think it's probably more a power of suggestion than that I'm actually thirsty, but the thought of her draining me of fluids gives me this intense urge to drink." Renata rolled her eyes and added, "I'm a freak. I know."

Nonplussed at her sister's shift in topics, Phoebe rose and fetched a water bottle from the fridge. But when she handed it to Renata, her sister wrapped her fingers around hers on the bottle and didn't let go.

"You gonna tell me what's going on or am I going to have to make you hold Charise again?" She smiled up at her. "Because everyone knows you can't keep secrets when you're looking into the eyes of a baby. She's a little truth fairy—she'll charm the truth right out of you."

THIRTY-SEVEN

PHOEBE DIDN'T REALLY ANSWER her, but Renata released her anyway. When she sat back down, though, Phoebe said, "I'll talk when you give me back Charise."

"Fair enough. You have about ten or fifteen minutes to figure out what you want to tell me." Renata closed her eyes, and for a moment, Phoebe wondered if she meant to take a ten- or fifteen-minute nap. But no. "And while we wait, I'll talk."

"Fair enough," Phoebe said, echoing her sister. Although she wasn't sure she wanted to hear whatever Renata had to say.

"I love you, Phoebe Josephine Gustafson. I'm sorry I haven't been a good big sister to you. I haven't been for a very long time, and I've been so blind to my failure there. I haven't been a good sister to Juliette or Gia, either, but to you, I've been especially cruel. I don't know when or why it started; I remember being upset at you even when you were tiny. Maybe because you made me a middle child? I don't know. But then in high school? And that stupid Homecoming and Brad what's-his-jerk-face? It was like I was just looking for something to pin all my pent-up anger on, and you were always in the way of it. I'm so sorry, little sister." She opened her eyes and rested her head against the seat back, peering at Phoebe through lowered lids. "I've been thinking about this for several months, now. When you and Juliette came up to the cabin and stayed with me, it was like something slid away from my eyes, and I saw what kind of person I'd become. What kind of person I'd been for so long. I didn't really know how to be any different, but I really wanted to try."

Phoebe tucked her legs up under her. She hadn't expected this when Renata said she would talk. She swallowed hard; she wasn't going to cry.

"But then John—well, John." Renata sighed. Two tears ran from the corners of her eyes. "I miss him so badly," she murmured, her voice catching just a little. "Tim and the boys do, too, and they're all being so brave. But I was his wife, you know? He was my husband, the father of my children." She lowered her gaze to Charise's face and brushed the back of a knuckle along the curve of the baby's cheek. "I love Tim so much, Phoebe. I do. But sometimes I'm scared I won't ever be able to love him as much as I loved—*still* love—John. It makes me feel like a failure, like I'm cheating Tim out of what he might find with someone else."

Phoebe's heart fluttered in her chest as Renata spilled her secrets while peering down into the eyes of her baby girl. "He loves you so much, Ren. I don't think you should ever love him the same as you did John, but that doesn't mean you don't love him as much."

"I know. You're right." Renata smiled softly, like she was making peace with herself over her confession. "It always seemed to me that John was my soul mate, you know? Like we were predestined to be together. I knew it almost immediately. By the time our first date was over, I knew I would love him, if I didn't already. I knew I *wanted* to love him that first night, that he was the kind of man I wanted to become one with. The kind of man who would stand by me no matter what. He was that transparent, even when I wasn't, and I knew he was the man I wanted to marry." She chuckled softly and Charise's mouth popped off her breast in surprise; her little eyes widened, and her arm flailed.

"I know that's hard to believe," Renata said as she lifted Charise to her shoulder and thumped her gently on the back. "I mean, it's not like you can disprove it, right? But it's true. I'm a believer. Love at first sight happens." A surprisingly loud belch escaped the baby, and both women made appreciative and encouraging sounds.

"At least it happened to me," Renata added as she switched Charise to her other side.

"It's not hard to believe," Phoebe contradicted. "I know it happens. When you handed me Charise, I thought my heart was going to burst with all the love that poured out of it for her. And isn't that what happens to most parents when they're handed their babies for the first time?" Phoebe would never forget the look on Theresa and Jeff's faces when Lily was placed in their arms the first time. "Love at first sight, right?"

Renata nodded. "Absolutely."

"Who determines the time frame for qualifying love? I mean, if it can happen that way with a baby, why on earth wouldn't we be capable of loving another adult at first sight?" Was she trying to convince Renata? Or herself? Her heart bumped against her rib cage.

"Amen, sister," Ren agreed wholeheartedly. "And that's not only true about adults, you know. The boys are madly in love with Charise already. Even Judah. I'm still hesitant to turn my back on Charise with him in the room, but he doesn't hug her around the neck anymore." She grimaced and repositioned Charise. "But do you remember when Maman brought Gia home from the hospital? How we couldn't get enough of her?"

Oh yes, she remembered. Gia had come into the world with tiny red curls in a dandelion puff all over her head, no eyebrows, and lashes so pale they looked dipped in frost. "Love at first sight."

"Sisters. They're the best. You three are the best sisters a sister could ask for, Phoebe." Renata had segued smoothly back to the beginning of the conversation. "I'm so glad you were there for me last week. I couldn't have asked for a better partner. In fact, don't tell Tim this, but I'm so glad you were with me in those earlier stages of labor. He still hasn't recovered from seeing the birth. He keeps apologizing for the fact that I had to go through it instead of him." She giggled softly. "He's such a man's man, you know? He can't bear to see me in any kind of discomfort, and I can only imagine how hard it would have been for him to go through the laboring part."

Phoebe smiled at the thought of big and brawny Tim coming undone over Renata's labor. He loved her sister to a fault, and although Phoebe had at one time thought it unfair for Renata to have found someone so soon after John's death—someone who loved John almost as much as Renata did—she knew just by watching him that he'd carried a torch for her sister for a long time. The fact that Renata hadn't known said a truckload about Tim's honor. Phoebe was happy for them both, that Tim had been there for Ren, and the other way around, too.

"But you surprised me, Phoebe," Renata continued after a long pause.

Phoebe straightened; a tiny red warning light flickered on in the back of her mind.

"Do you watch birthing videos? I mean, you were right there with me the whole time. It was like you knew what to expect and you knew what to do to help me through each stage. You didn't panic, you didn't scramble, you didn't even freak out when I sprayed your shoes with amniotic fluid."

"It was gross. I'm pretty sure you did it on purpose." Phoebe wrinkled her nose at the memory. She'd thrown the shoes away as soon as she got home. "And I did freak out, remember? I said a very bad word."

"Ah yes. I do remember. Fine, then. I take that last bit back." Renata grinned at her and straightened in the chair, lifting Charise to her shoulder again to burp her. The baby's eyes were half-closed, and her mouth hung open, a pearly trickle of milk at each corner.

"She looks half drunk," Phoebe said with a sardonic grimace. "I should know. I looked like that earlier this week."

"You want to do this? Get a burp out of her while I put myself back together?" Renata held the baby out, and Phoebe rose to get her. Renata didn't let go, though. "Are you sure? Remember she's the truth fairy."

Phoebe nodded. "Yes, I'm sure." If Renata could open up to her so honestly after all that had been between them, why couldn't she do the same? And if Renata hated her after she learned all that had happened, then at least Phoebe would know not to trust her sister ever again. But surely—*surely!*—the change in Ren was genuine. Surely, she couldn't still hold that terrible night—what Ren believed had happened that terrible night—against Phoebe after all this time.

It didn't take long for Charise to release a couple ridiculously cute belches and a rather dainty little toot, sounds that made Phoebe giggle. She turned on the couch so she leaned against the armrest and brought her feet up onto the cushion so she could prop the baby against her upraised knees. That way, she could watch Charise sleep while she talked; she wouldn't have to see Renata's reaction at all.

"I did know what to expect," she began. "But I surprised myself, too. I didn't think I'd remember after all these years, but it must be like riding a bicycle. You just remember."

The silence that followed that statement was thick enough to taste. Then suddenly, there was a flurry of movement, and Renata was up out of her chair and sitting on the sofa beside her before Phoebe realized what she was doing.

"Phoebe." Her voice held no judgment, no condemnation, only genuine concern. Renata didn't touch Phoebe, not directly, but instead, placed a hand on Charise's water-balloon belly and left it there, as though the little girl was the bridge that connected them. "Tell me."

And so she did.

THIRTY-EIGHT

While they waited for Vic and Juliette to arrive, Gia and Ricky played Super Mario in the living room, and Trevor stood in his kitchen alone, hands planted on the counter as he watched mahogany liquid run through the drip coffee maker into the carafe. He breathed in, his nostrils flaring as the scent wafted through the air. It wasn't nearly as aromatic and rich as Phoebe's Italian Roast from her coffee press, but it made him long for her just the same. Would she even deign to drink his Yuban medium roast? He hoped he'd get a chance to find out.

He was exhausted. Right now, he didn't care what coffee he drank, as long as it had enough caffeine in it to get his blood pumping and his muscles moving. He'd been unable to sleep much of the night, so he'd prayed for Phoebe's rest, for peace for her, and he asked God to reveal himself to her in ways she couldn't deny were of him. "Not just once, God, but over and over again. Show her who you are. Beyond a shadow of a doubt."

He also readily admitted that he had a vested interest in Phoebe learning to trust in God. He loved her—yes, *loved* her. It was as though the years of praying for her and getting to know her vicariously through her sisters had instilled a ready-made capacity in him to love her without reservation. And after last night, after walking through the shadowy valley with her, he knew he wanted to walk with her through every high and low in her life from that moment on. He'd marry her tomorrow if he could... but unless she chose to give her life to Christ, his hands were tied. He had seen the struggle of many marriages when spouses didn't agree spiritually. When one served God and the other didn't, it was like mixing oil and water. They could both share the same bucket, but they'd never truly be one, especially in the things that counted for eternity.

He'd finally drifted off in the early predawn hours, but was awake again before eight o'clock, and after tossing and turning for a while longer, he gave up trying to go back to sleep and got up.

He'd spent the morning working in his studio and praying for Phoebe. He hoped she'd call him today, hoped she hadn't awakened this morning full of regrets over talking to him, spending the evening with him... kissing him.

That kiss. He'd resisted kissing her all night, even during moments when it seemed she wanted him to move in closer, to put his mouth on hers. When she'd asked him to leave, his heart had plummeted to the toes of his shoes. But when she said it was because she couldn't think straight when he touched her, that he made her head spin, he'd been so relieved, that he'd given in to the desire. Gently, with great care and respect, but with as much emotion as he could pour into less than five seconds of mouth-to-mouth contact. He hoped she'd read the promise in that kiss, his commitment to be there for her, in whatever capacity he could, no matter what. He hoped she'd sensed the passion she stirred up in him, his longing for her. But more than that, he hoped she'd realized how much he hoped *for* her, believed in her, and wanted the best for her...which meant her saying yes to God.

He snorted with derision and pushed away from the counter. "You're such a hopeless romantic," he muttered. "No one could possibly read all that into one small kiss." He opened the fridge and took out the carton of half-and-half, knowing Ricky and Gia would require it for their coffees. "Shoulda kissed her for real," he grumbled. "Full on, mouths open, hauled her up against you and kissed her like a hungry man. Then there'd be no guesswork involved."

"What was that, cuz?" Ricky called from the other room.

"Nothing!" He hadn't realized he'd spoken loud enough to be heard above the zippy electronic music of the game they played.

Nope. He'd kissed her as sweetly as he could manage, and then, against the urgent wishes of his body and heart, he'd released her and had left her home just as she'd asked. And since then, he'd not stopped praying for her, just as he'd promised.

He didn't just pray for Phoebe though, but also for Lily, for her sisters, and for her grandparents. He knew this ordeal she'd suffered through and carried alone all these years would not be fully laid to rest until she shared her grief with the family she loved, the family who loved her.

And he prayed for his part in her life, no matter what it turned out to be.

When Vic and Juliette finally arrived, they exchanged questioning glances with him, careful not to say anything in front of Ricky and Gia. He nodded as reassuringly as possible without saying anything back, but he gestured that he'd talk to them later. Then he shooed everyone into the kitchen for coffee.

They all followed Trevor into the small studio and stood close together against the back wall to listen. He'd explained his concept for the album to them all, but before he started the first song, he said, "I've chosen an album name. *Full Disclosure.*" He didn't need to explain to them exactly how he'd come up with it, but the term spoke for itself regarding the tendency for people to hide behind illusions and disguises. For Christians, especially, to hide their brokenness behind their perfect facades.

When the music finally ended, his eyes were on Juliette's face. "I know some of it is still a little rough, but give me your thoughts. The most important thing is the message here. The instrumentation, of course, must be dead on, but as a backdrop for the lyrics. More so than usual. I want people—church people—to really hear it."

Gia was practically jumping up and down. She threw her arms around Ricky and declared, "Oh my gosh, it's fantastic. Your cousin is brilliant!"

Ricky, clearly enjoying the girl's embrace, grinned like a dog getting an itch scratched. He nodded in agreement, though, and had the decency to say, "Wow, Cuz. That's pretty deep stuff. Favorite song? Rock of Ages. The base line is intense, and that alone would make it a hot number. But the lyrics? You make God sound epic."

Juliette's expression, although bright-eyed and glowing with approval and genuine appreciation, wasn't the one he should have been watching. He saw Vic swipe a hand across his cheek, and then again, and Trevor turned toward his friend.

To Trevor's astonishment, there were tears trickling from the corners of the tall man's eyes. Vic didn't make a sound—in fact, he seemed to be barely breathing—but whatever was going on inside his head and heart was clearly deeply affecting him. In all the years they'd known each other, Trevor couldn't ever remember Victor Jarrett shedding a single tear. The man was a rock. A pillar. Even a glacier at times.

Trevor reached over and placed a hand on his shoulder, gripping the taut muscles that gave evidence to the turmoil inside his friend. Juliette, too, stepped closer, sliding an arm around her fiancé's waist.

Gia whispered something to Ricky, and the two of them slipped out of the room. Trevor acknowledged their sensitivity with a quick nod as they angled past him.

No one spoke for a few moments, but silence was not an uncommon state around Vic. He didn't talk unless he had something to say, and he didn't require that anyone else fill in the blank spaces, either. Trevor was certain Juliette knew that about the man she loved, and when she rested her head against Vic's chest and closed her eyes, he couldn't help but thank God, once again, for bringing the perfect woman into his friend's life. She wasn't demanding answers or panicking about what might be wrong. No, she was simply offering her man comfort with her quiet presence.

Victor finally took a deep breath and let it out slowly before saying, "I think you nailed it, Taz." His voice caught on the old nickname. "That last song, *Broken Man?* It's as though you put my life to music. I'm that guy; the one who looks everywhere but here." He pressed a fist into his sternum.

Trevor nodded, but didn't speak, giving Victor the time he needed to put his thoughts and emotions into words.

"I'm the guy who works like a maniac to set things right in the world... but this—*this*—" He thumped his chest with his knuckles. "This is where it needs to start. Every day, I need to start with me. If I'm not willing to work on me, then who am I to try to get anyone else to change?"

Juliette still leaned against Victor, her eyes open now, studying their shoes, but Trevor knew she was listening to every word. She kept silent, though, letting the guys have the air space.

"I think I just forget. I forget that my salvation isn't my own doing. I forget that when I make rules and regiments and criteria and scales, that

I turn God into a—" he paused, seemingly at a loss for words. "I don't know. Into a preservation device, I suppose. If I can live up to the rules and regiments and criteria, then God will preserve me. But what am I preserving? A black heart?"

"Like a hyperbaric chamber," Juliette murmured.

"What?" Victor asked, leaning away from her a little so he could look down at her face.

"A hyperbaric chamber? One of those things Michael Jackson used, you know? I know what you mean, Vic. It's like we're trying to preserve this... this person we've worked so hard to become—with all our terrible plastic surgery and failed attempts to be perfect—as though what we bring to God is even worth preserving at all."

Victor chuckled and hugged her tightly. "Exactly. Me and M.J. in our hyperbaric chambers."

Trevor nodded and grinned, happy for his friend. Juliette's transparency, her unabashed willingness to say what was on her heart, was so refreshing and endearing, and he found himself once again thinking of Phoebe. He didn't begrudge Victor Juliette, not by any means, but it was moments like these when his own empty arms mocked him, and his heart ached.

"You nailed it," Vic said again. "You're going to stir up a hornet's nest with this. This album is going to shed a whole lot of light into the dark corners of the church body everywhere, and I have a feeling there will be some who won't care for that kind of exposure. You know I'll be praying for you—I have a feeling you'll need it."

"I will too," Juliette chimed in.

Trevor nodded again. "I appreciate your prayers. And thanks for the feedback. I needed to hear you say these things today, Vic."

Victor turned to look over his shoulder toward the door that led into Trevor's living room. "Ricky? Gia? Come on back."

The teenagers returned, Ricky leading the way, his hands shoved into the back pocket of his skinny jeans. "Everything okay?" he asked, his tone casual, but his eyes wide with concern. Gia stood behind him with a similar expression. They'd obviously been talking about what might be going on.

"All is well," Victor assured them. He didn't expound, and Trevor thought that might be just fine with Ricky. He figured Gia could talk to

Juliette later if she wanted more information. "Just thought you might want to join us as we pray for your cousin and this new project," Vic said.

They all bowed their heads together, overwhelming Trevor with their requests for God's blessing and protection, and for their friendship made richer because of their shared beliefs.

Just as Victor closed the impromptu prayer, Juliette's phone started vibrating in her back pocket.

"It's Ren," she reported, sliding open the screen to read her text. She looked up at the sound of a water drop; Gia had just received a text, too. "She's at Phoebe's place—what is she doing there?—and she's calling for an Emergency G-FOURce."

Gia held her phone up and nodded in affirmation. "Yep."

"Sorry, guys," Juliette said, looking back and forth between the men. "This doesn't happen very often, and if Ren and Phoebe say it's an emergency G-FOURce, then that's because there's an emergency."

Her phone buzzed again, and Gia's echoed it with another water drop. "A sleepover? At Phoebe's?"

"That's what mine says, too." Gia looked just as stunned as Juliette, but Trevor wasn't surprised. In fact, if he were to guess, he might think that one of his prayers was in the process of being answered. An emergency G-FOURce after the evening Phoebe had shared with him could only mean one of two things. Phoebe was either calling for his blood, or she was going to tell her sisters about Lily.

"Looks like you three will have to fend for yourselves tonight. Will you be okay?" Juliette asked, always looking out for everyone.

"We'll be fine," Victor assured her.

"We'll have a boys-only sleepover," Ricky quipped. "We'll have extreme meat pizzas and all-bacon burgers."

"Go," Trevor said. "And tell Phoebe I'm still praying."

THIRTY-NINE

By the time Juliette and Gia arrived at Phoebe's door, she and Renata had sorted through all the sordid details of that awful night fourteen years ago, and the difficult journey they'd walked since. Renata had grieved with her, for all of it, everything from the loss of their parents to the loss of Phoebe's childhood, to the ongoing pain of losing Lily, brought so acutely to the surface by the birth of Charise.

When Renata suggested she tell the rest of the family, Phoebe had balked, not sure she could do it all again anytime soon, if at all. She didn't want to see Grandpa's or Granny G's faces. But Ren had insisted they not wait, at least to tell the other two sisters. "We can tell the grandparents later. When you're ready," she'd said.

Phoebe hadn't missed the *we* her sister used, and it warmed her heart and made her brave.

"But we're a team, Phoebe," Renata continued. "We're the G-FOURce. The Gustafson Four. You shouldn't have had to go through this alone; that's what the G-FOURce is all about. When we stay quiet, we only cheat each other out of opportunities to do what we do best. We stand together. We love each other unconditionally. We hold each other up and come to each other's rescue. Like all of you have for me these last nine months, especially. Like we did for Juliette... although that kind of backfired, didn't it?" They both chuckled at how disastrous the Monday ManDates intervention plan had turned out to be. "Like we'll most certainly have to do for Gia one day whenever that girl discovers her teenage rebellious streak."

"She's only got two more years and then she won't be able to use the teenager thing as an excuse anymore."

"Wow, Phoebe. Can you believe it? We were just talking about when she came home from the hospital, and suddenly, Gia is an eighteen-year-old *adult*! I can hardly wrap my head around that one," Renata declared.

And so, over Granny G's yummy tuna noodle casserole—she'd insisted on sending over a meal when Gia told her about the sleepover—the box of pastries from Mona's Market—Juliette's usual offering—Phoebe's Italian Roast coffee, and Renata's contribution, the truth fairy Baby Charise, Phoebe told her story. Again. For the third time in less than twenty-four hours.

And this time, with the weight of it all spread equally on all four sets of shoulders, the burden was somehow easier to bear. In fact, Phoebe found that she could even hold her head up again. And with her head up, she could look around her, and she could see her sisters beside her, standing with her. *For* her.

She wasn't alone anymore.

• • • • • • • • •

PHOEBE HAD SLEPT SO much the night before that she lay awake, listening to her sisters slumbering on the floor around her. They'd pulled all the cushions off the couches and chairs, brought down most of Phoebe's bedding from the loft, as well as a couple of extra blankets and pillows she kept in the hall closet, and had created Pillowland on her living room floor. It was so peaceful, so reassuring—it really was like hearing God breathing, even though she knew it was her sisters—but wasn't that pretty much the same thing? Weren't her sisters God personified in her time of need? Isn't that what she'd heard Grandpa say time and again?

"We are the body of Christ. We're his hands and feet. His voice and his ears. We need to be God's representative to those around us."

If that was the case, then this night, this pile of pillows and blankets, and the love of her sisters—their willingness to drop everything and come to her side—was one more bit of evidence of who God was. One more way he was reaching out to her to show her that he loved her, that he could be trusted.

Sometime in the middle of the night, Renata got up to nurse her hungry baby girl. She sat with her back propped against a pile of pillows, Charise in the crook of her arm. Phoebe rose up on one elbow and smiled in the dim light from a night light she'd plugged in so no one would stumble around in the dark during a bathroom run.

"Hey," Renata whispered.

"Hey," Phoebe whispered back.

"Can't sleep?"

"I slept more than twelve hours last night. You woke me up when you came to see me."

Renata laughed. "That would do it."

A moment passed, and then Phoebe said, "Thank you for coming to me today. For not waiting for me to come to you."

"You're welcome." Then she added, "You'd do the same for me. You *have* done the same for me."

"Still, thank you."

"You're welcome," she said again, and Phoebe could hear the pleased smile in her sister's simple response.

A few minutes later, Charise produced a sound that let them know she'd just filled her diaper. "Of course," Renata groaned. "You couldn't wait until morning for that?"

Phoebe pushed herself up before Renata could. "Give her to me. I'll change her. You sleep."

"What's going on?" asked a sleepy Gia.

"Poopy diaper," Juliette answered from beneath another pile of blankets.

"I'm going to go change her in the bathroom. Go back to sleep," Phoebe said.

"Just change her in here," Juliette suggested, sitting up. "I need to use the toilet."

"I don't mind," Gia agreed. "Just warn me if you're going to turn on the light so I can keep my eyes closed."

"I'm turning on the light, then." Phoebe laughed, reaching for the pull string of one of the myriad decorative lamps around the living room. "I'm not about to attempt changing a poopy diaper in the dark."

By the time Juliette returned, Charise had on a clean diaper, Gia was still burrowed under her heap of blankets, but she'd created a tunnel so she could look out at her sisters without having to see the lamp, and Renata lay curled on her side, not quite asleep. "You can put her in the carrier when you're finished holding her," Ren said, waving a hand at the contraption they'd brought in from the car.

After Juliette had settled back in, Phoebe turned off the light, and the darkness settled around them again. She held Charise close to her chest so she could watch the little face in the faint light shining from the hallway.

"You need to call that man in the morning." It was Renata.

"I thought you were asleep." Phoebe whispered.

"She's right," Juliette chimed in.

"Who? Taz?' asked Gia. "If you mean Taz, then *bells*, yes! Call him."

"Love at first sight," Renata said. "I'm a believer."

Gia giggled. "I'm a believer."

"I guess I'm a believer, too, then," Juliette said. "At least Vic claims it to be true, so if you're all in agreement, then I'll go with it."

After a long pause, Phoebe echoed her sisters. "I'm a believer, too." But she didn't just mean she believed in love at first sight. Although she believed in that, too.

Something about the way she said it must have sounded odd. Juliette sat up straight and turned on the light again. Without warning anyone. "What?"

Gia and Renata both groaned. Phoebe covered Charise's open eyes.

"What did you just say?" Juliette asked, her sleepy gaze fixed on Phoebe's face.

"I'm a believer, too," she repeated. "I believe in love at first sight. And—" A quick burst of uncertainty swept through her, but she quelled it with one look down at Charise. "I believe in God. I trust him with all of this."

Juliette scrambled out from under her blankets and threw her arms around Phoebe and Charise. Gia wasn't far behind.

Renata muttered, "Can you four bring the hug-fest to me? I'm too tired to move."

So they did, giggling and tickling, complaining about bad breath and too-sharp elbows. They took turns snuggling with Charise for a few more minutes, and then Phoebe tucked the droopy-eyed baby into her carrier and crawled under the blankets herself. Maybe she'd sleep now.

"You're going to call him, right?" Renata persisted.

"Oh. My. Gosh, Rennie. Go to sleep!"

"You're going to call him, right?"

"Yes! I'm going to call him, you crazy woman."

"Good. Now I can sleep."

"Me, too," Juliette muttered.

Gia's muffled voice came from under her blankets. "Me, too."

"Me, too," Phoebe said. "I love you guys."

A peaceful stillness settled after an outburst of 'I love you, toos' from around the room.

FORTY

Early the next morning, before anyone else was awake, Phoebe tiptoed upstairs to her loft and slipped into a thick terry cloth bathrobe the color of French lavender. Each of the girls had one from Granny G: Juliette's was pink, Renata's was peach, and Gia had a blue one that matched her crystalline eyes. Her phone was still on her night table where she'd left it all week long, completely powered down. Greatly relieved to find it was still at more than 50% charged, she began tapping in a text to Trevor. It was too early to call, but this way, he'd see it as soon as he got up.

Good morning, Trevor. Phoebe here. I have some freshly ground Italian Roast ready to be brewed. I was wondering how you take your morning coffee and if you'd like to take it here with me. Call me when you wake up.

She pushed send, and then she tapped out one more text. *BTW, I said yes to God last night. I'm not going to run, Trevor. You don't have to wait anymore.*

She swiped the phone off and stood to go back downstairs when the screen lit up in her hand. She grinned at the sight of Trevor's name.

"Hi," she said, keeping her voice low so she wouldn't disturb the sleeping beauties downstairs. "Did I wake you?"

"Hi, yourself." His voice had a hint of gravel in it. "You did, but it's all good."

"I'm sorry." Phoebe felt awful. "It's so early. I should have waited to text you."

"Don't be sorry," he assured her. "I can't think of a better way to wake up."

Phoebe smiled and sat back down on her bed, leaning her back against the padded headboard. She wished she'd brought her comforter back upstairs with her, but the last she'd seen it, Gia had rolled herself up in it like a piggy in a blanket. *Mon cochon, my wee piglet.* It didn't matter that Gia was now the tallest of the Gustafson Girls—she towered over Phoebe and Renata and had finally passed Juliette up a year ago—she would always be their little sister.

She pulled the lapels of her robe closed and tucked her feet underneath her. "So how does coffee sound? Maybe in an hour?" She hadn't anticipated he'd be awake and ready any time soon. She might have to kick her sisters out in order to have him over.

"Actually, I will have to wait a little longer. Remember? I can't be alone in your house with you." He chuckled dryly. She liked the way his voice sounded first thing in the morning. *I could get used to that,* she thought. "Which could create a problem since I'd like to hire you to do my album cover."

"Oh, really?" The man and his rules. But she was still smiling; his response didn't surprise her at all. He was a man of strong convictions, and she was learning to appreciate him for it.

"You said you wanted to photograph me, right? Well, here's your chance. You can take as many pictures of me as you'd like if you'll say 'yes' to doing my album art."

Of course she was going to say 'yes,' but she had to play a little hard to get, didn't she? "Well, we do seem to have a dilemma then, don't we? My studio is in my house, after all. You'll have to come inside if you want me for the job." She was thrilled at the prospect of photographing him; she couldn't wait to find out what he had in mind.

"I'll come inside your house any day, Phoebe. Just not when we're alone anymore." He hesitated only a moment and then said, "Not if you're going to share your fries with me, force me to slow dance with you, and then try to lure me up to your loft bedroom with the promise of coffee ambrosia."

Phoebe laughed into the phone. "That's not quite how it went, sir!"

"Um, yes, I think that's almost exactly how it went. Oh. I forgot the part where you dragged me to your couch, snuggled with me—you *snuggled* with me, Phoebe! I mean, the nerve!—then you held my hand, told me to leave, and—"

"And you, Trevor Zander, Mr. Youth-Pastor-Rock-n-Roll-Jesus-Freak; you *kissed* me," she interrupted, glad he couldn't see the blush she knew colored her cheeks bright pink. "That was all you, buddy."

"Ah." His voice dropped a little, and she wondered if he wasn't feeling a little breathless at the memory of it, too. "Point proved; case closed. No more being alone with you in your home. Not until we're married."

Phoebe gasped and almost dropped the phone in shock. She opened her mouth to speak, but nothing came out. She had no clue how to respond.

"But I'll get that 'yes' from you another day when I can ask you properly," he continued, as though he hadn't just tossed those life-changing words out between them. "In the meantime, if you'll say 'yes' to doing the cover, I'll arrange for chaperones—my tech crew, Ricky and Gia, would likely agree to help out if we promise them food and Xbox."

She could work with that. "Then I guess I'll say 'yes' to doing your cover."

"Excellent! And in lieu of coffee at your place, how about I pick you up for breakfast in about an hour?" His voice sounded odd for a moment, and she thought she heard a creaking sound, like he was changing positions in bed. The thought of him lying in bed talking to her while she was in her own bed made her heart leap. *Good grief. Get a grip, girl.*

"You cooking?"

"Nope, but nice try. I'm not allowed alone with you in my house, either. How does The Griddle sound?"

Phoebe frowned, suddenly remembering what day it was. She glanced at the clock again. "What about church?"

"Actually, God likes to eat breakfast, too. He'll join us if that's all right with you. Seeing as he can be everywhere at one time and all...."

Phoebe giggled like a little girl and then covered her mouth with her hand. She did *not* want her sisters to wake up and come upstairs. Knowing them, they'd launch themselves onto the bed with her and make every effort to embarrass her with Trevor. She lowered her voice and said, "Then yes, The Griddle with God in an hour sounds perfect."

"I like hearing you say 'yes' to me," Trevor murmured. She was pretty sure she could hear the smile in his voice.

"I like saying 'yes' to you, Trevor."

"I'm holding you to that, Phoebe Josephine Gustafson."

"You can call me Phoebe Jo. Or just Jo." She kind of liked the idea of a new identity.

"Just Jo. I like the sound of that. I'll see you soon, Just Jo." He was definitely smiling now.

"I'll be waiting," she said.

"I like the sound of that, too."

FORTY-ONE

Alice Masters stood in the foyer of her home staring up at the stunning painting on the wall above the entryway table. In color, texture, and style, it spoke of joy and pain, of hope and fear, of everything that embodied motherhood. She loved it for all those reasons and more; she could stare at it endlessly.

She waited nervously, trying not to glance at her wristwatch again. Cal had been late coming home and was still finishing getting ready. Phoebe Gustafson was coming to dinner with her fiancé, Trevor Zander, an up-and-coming musician from their church—apparently, he was a hot commodity these days, his album climbing both the Christian music charts as well as the secular ones.

Cal hurried into the foyer, shoving his arms into a cardigan as he walked, one she'd given him just last Christmas. She was pleased that he liked it so much; it was his go-to "dressy sweater" now that the worst of the winter weather was over. With his modified crew cut that left his thick gray hair long on top, and his full mustache, the cabled sweater over a collared shirt gave him a rather dapper appeal.

"Figured I'd find you here," he said.

"You look so handsome!" She smiled appreciatively at her husband and slipped her hand through the crook of his arm as they headed back into the living room to wait.

Cal sat down beside her on the sofa and took her hand in his. "I'm praying for you, Angel."

"Thank you, Cal." She rested her cheek against his shoulder. He was a solidly built man, and his mere presence made her feel safe. Everything about him made her feel safe. "I love you."

He kissed her on the forehead—he knew her well; Alice's lipstick was her token first line of defense. When it was in place, she could be brave. It seemed silly when she really thought about it, but Cal understood.

The doorbell sounded, and he rose, then offered her his hand. "Let's go welcome our guests, shall we?"

· · · · • · • · · · ·

CAL MASTERS HAD TAKEN it upon himself to deliver Phoebe's bimonthly grocery order, and she looked forward to seeing him every couple of weeks. She thought Cal was probably very much the kind of man Papa would have been.

So on the third Friday in February, when Cal knocked on her door, she welcomed him into her home without reservation. But this time, along with the boxes of pasta, her favorite Jasmine rice, an overflowing bag of the best fresh fruits and vegetables in town, and various other food items, he brought an invitation for dinner from him and his wife. Intrigued, Phoebe looked back and forth between the cream linen card in her hand and the fatherly man who'd just unloaded three large bags of groceries onto her counter.

She'd nearly completed the four new paintings that had been inspired by Cal's mention of *Cerulean* back in November, and for some reason, perhaps because the original meant so much to Alice already, Phoebe was curious to know what she'd think of the new pieces.

"Before you give me an answer, there is something you need to know about us. About my wife," Cal said, briefly laying a hand over the top of the invitation in hers. His gaze was kind, but she could read a hint of sadness there, too.

"Sure." Her eyes scanned the card with its pretty handwriting again, as though looking for something she might have missed, and then she laid it on the counter next to her cell phone where she wouldn't forget it. "What is this about, Cal?"

Cal slid his hands into his pants pockets beneath the grocer's apron he wore. "My wife wants to meet you in person for a reason," he began. "I'm sure you've had your fair share of people demanding your time, but I'd like you to consider this invitation a bit before you refuse."

Phoebe nodded immediately, ready to reassure him that she had no qualms about it. "I enjoy meeting people who like my art, Cal. I'd love to meet your wife."

Cal nodded, as though he'd expected her to say just that. "Still, I'd like you to hear me out first. Then take some time to think about it. Pray about it, if you're a praying woman. Talk to your family first if you'd like."

Phoebe cocked her head at him, a bubble of concern growing in her belly. "What's this about?" she asked again. She crossed her arms and gripped the side seams of her shirt tightly. "You're worrying me, Cal. I'm not so sure I want to hear what you have to say."

"I'm sorry. I'm not doing a very good job of this. Let me try to explain." His bushy brows furrowed as he considered what he should say. "You may not remember Alice," Cal began. "She doesn't believe you two have ever met personally, and her name, especially now, most likely isn't familiar to you. She and I married only nine years ago. But she's been following your career it seems as long as I've known her. She's one of your biggest fans."

"I still don't... understand," Phoebe said, her heart in her throat. Cal's every word was carefully chosen, and his eyes implored Phoebe to listen, and to agree to this dinner. She felt a fissure of foreboding race up her spine.

"My wife," Cal said, and then cleared his throat and started again. "My wife was Alice Clinton before I married her."

She must have blanched noticeably—Phoebe felt the color drain from her face in a tingling rush.

Cal took her gently by the shoulders and supported her as he added, "Alice is Angela Clinton's mother. And she'd like to share her story with you."

· · · • · • · • · · ·

PHOEBE CALLED AN EMERGENCY G-FOURce meeting. The stunned silence that followed after she told them about Cal and Alice Masters was an exact representation of the shock that she'd felt at Cal's revelation to her. But as the sisters discussed the situation, the idea started to take hold, and the general consensus was that the meeting might be a good idea.

At first, Phoebe insisted all four of them go together. They deserved to meet Alice and hear her story as much as she did. But Juliette, always the peacemaker, the advocate, suggested that perhaps Alice would have a difficult time sitting across the table from all four of them while she told her story.

"There must be a good reason she wants to do it this way. Maybe she's shy. Or afraid. Maybe she feels like she already has a connection to you because of the painting, and it's a place to start, you know? It doesn't sound to me like she's trying to hide anything or trying to divide us—Cal did tell you to talk to us, right?"

"Yes, and he alluded to her feeling pretty vulnerable about all this," Phoebe acknowledged. "It's been four months since he told her he'd met me."

"You know, I remember her from court," Juliette mused, her brow furrowed as she tried to recall details from that terrible time. "She was so quiet throughout the trial. On the day the judge made his ruling, she cried. The room was really hushed—I think everyone knew that no matter what the outcome, everyone would lose that day. And in the silence, I could hear her. She was very discreet, and it was totally appropriate; I mean, her daughter was going to jail. But someone told her to get a hold of herself, or something along those lines. I think it might have been her husband, you guys. It was awful. I still clearly remember that man's mean whisper." Juliette shuddered involuntarily.

"So then it would be easy to assume that there was more trouble than just Angela in the Clinton household," Renata concluded. "And that most likely, the marriage broke up over it all. That would make sense. And it might shed some light on the real reason why Angela was drinking that day."

"That's what I'm hoping," Phoebe agreed. "I don't know what the connection is with the painting—that seems to be a pivotal piece in the picture—but according to Cal, it's in their front entryway for a reason."

"You don't think she knows about Lily, do you?" Gia asked, her eyes wide with concern.

"No, I don't think that's it." Phoebe had considered the possibility, too, but had ruled it out. No one had known about her pregnancy. "It's something else, and I think it may have something to do with Angela. I really do."

"Let's pray about it," Renata suggested, and all four girls scooted in closer to each other and held hands in a small circle.

Prayer had become as much a part of their G-FOURce meetings as the opening and closing rituals. Phoebe marveled at how much had changed in her life—in all their lives—in the last couple of years. When Juliette walked out of her ex-boyfriend's apartment on Valentine's Day almost two years ago to the day, it was as though she'd knocked loose a stone at the top of a mountain and had set off an avalanche that was still shaking their little world. None of them had gone unscathed, not even Gia, who Phoebe knew was balanced on the precipice of adulthood. Perhaps the landslide had yet to strike the girl with all its unchecked force, but surely it would. It was almost inevitable. Gia was trying to find a place in the grownup world without her mother and father to guide her.

At least she had her family to walk the rough terrain with her. Her grandparents. Her sisters. The Gustafson Girls. The G-FOURce.

"Are you sure you're okay with this?" Juliette asked, still holding Phoebe's hand, even though the prayer had ended. "You'll take Trevor, right?"

Phoebe didn't know how she would have survived last year without her sisters' love and support. Thoughts of Lily often kept her up at night, and she'd curl her body around the dull ache of a wound that would never quite heal. She'd decided to leave Lily in the hands of God—and Jeff and Theresa—for now. If the Rogers weren't reaching out to her, she needed to respect that, because it had never been part of the adoption agreement. In fact, it had been strongly discouraged by the program. But when the girl turned eighteen, Phoebe would contact Jeff and Theresa and ask them if Lily had any interest in meeting her. She hoped and prayed they'd say 'yes,' and that maybe she'd have a chance for a relationship with the girl, but she would let them decide. She would let God orchestrate things his way. It was the most difficult decision she'd ever made, but one she knew was right.

She nodded. "Now that my initial shock has worn off. Yeah. I think I'm ready for this." She squeezed her sisters' hands and then sat back into her corner of Juliette's sofa. "I'm a tough nut to crack, but I'm learning what forgiveness means. It's not about forgetting, you know? But about accepting who we are and where we are and why, and about learning how to move forward from that point."

Renata's head bobbed in time with her foot bumping against the baby carrier close by where Charise napped contentedly. "Well said, girlie."

"And in the process of forgiving myself, I'm figuring out how to accept God's unconditional love for me, which is really tough. It kinda goes against everything I've believed about him my whole life. But I'm starting to see myself the way he does, I think. Like a bride dressed in pure white. You know how my loft is—everything is white and fluffy. Like that." She rolled her eyes at how silly it sounded, but she added, "Sometimes I think God, himself, inspired me to decorate it that way, like he's been trying to tell me all along how he sees me."

Gia spoke up, leaning forward on her cushion with such eagerness. So often the girl had the most profound things to say, and the three older sisters turned to listen.

"Actually, I think that totally makes sense. Do you know that Phoebe means *pure and radiant*?"

Phoebe had known that, but the other two were delighted with the symbolism.

Gia held up her hand to quiet them and continued. "But get this. So does Lily. It means *pure*, too. And the lily flower is symbolic for purity and innocence. Don't you see?" She flashed that wide-mouthed smile at them, her eyes bright with revelation. "God has wiped the slate clean for you, Phebes. For all of us. And I really believe he put Lily's name on the Rogers' hearts because he wanted to show you how much he cares about you—about all of us—even when we're not aware of him working his plan."

The G-FOURce often included tears these days, but no one seemed to mind.

So Phoebe said 'yes' to one more thing she would never have dreamed of agreeing to even six months ago. She and Trevor were having dinner with Cal Masters and his wife Alice, Angela Clinton's mother.

And Phoebe was looking forward to it.

· · · ● · ● · ● · · ·

SOMETIMES HAVING THE PAST catch up with you isn't such a bad thing… at least not for Phoebe and Trevor. Now that their paths have crossed again—actually, they've *merged* this time!—Phoebe is ready to face some of the ghosts she's been running from.

Because for the first time in longer than she can remember, she won't be facing them alone.

She's got Trevor by her side… and her sisters have her back.

But Phoebe isn't the only Gustafson girl unearthing long-buried secrets, and Gia is having a hard time figuring who she can—and can't—trust.

Including herself.

About Gia & the Blast from the Past

When Gia comes face to face with a past that she didn't know she had, will she trust in a future she can't control?

Gia Gustafson has officially come of age… but now what? Her world seems to be standing still while everything and everyone around her is moving at lightning speed.

Her best friend, Ricky Zander, has gone rogue, her grandparents have grown old overnight, and her sisters have all found their happily ever afters.

Because life isn't confusing enough, the new guy at work is doing his best to sweep Gia off her feet, and Ricky is none too happy about it.

But when a stranger she'd recognize anywhere shows up unannounced on her doorstep, Gia isn't so sure she's ready to grow up, after all.

~ ~ ~

Keep reading for an excerpt from the fourth book in The Gustafson Girls Series,

Gia & the Blast from the Past.

From the Author

Dear Reader,

I have a special place in my heart for sisters. I grew up with a sister only eight months younger than I am. Yep, there are only eight months between us. But before you send those side-eyes at my poor parents, one of us is adopted. It was a case of...

"You can't get pregnant."

"Let's adopt."

"Yay! Your baby is ready to pick up at the adoption store!"

"Oh, and double yay... You're also pregnant! Surprise!"

"Wow! Let's keep them both."

"Sure. Why not?"

Or something like that.

In many ways, my sister and I are as close as twins, seeking security and support from each other in ways no one else can possibly provide. And in many ways, we are like oil and water... a beautiful mess. We now live in two different countries, and there is always far too much time that passes between phone calls and visits. But she is in my heart every single day, and I can't imagine my life without her in it.

I have another sister who arrived on the scene many years later, and with a beautiful adoption story of her own. She is the age of my children, so our sister relationship has a precious nature all its own. And again, I can't imagine my life without her in it.

You'll find "sisters" in most of my books: some by birth, some by adoption, and some in name only—friends who have become sisters.

If you're looking for fiction with realistic romance and redemptive story lines, I invite you to check out some of my other books and series.

You may meet your next BFF (Best Fiction Friend)! Or visit me online: **BeckyDoughty.com**.

I write heartfelt and wholesome Contemporary Romance and Women's Fiction. I write fiction because nonfiction is hard! Yes, I've tried. Let's just say I like to color outside the lines when it comes to facts. But emotions and feelings and the roller coaster ride that comes with all relationships? Oh yeah. That's where you'll find me.

Where hope lives and love prevails,
~ Becky Doughty

Let's stay in touch! Head over to BeckyDoughty.com and **sign up for my newsletter** for book and audiobook news (and deals!), and for fun subscriber-exclusive stuff.

An Excerpt: Gia & the Blast from the Past

Chapter 1

GIA STOOD IN THE hushed foyer, dressed in apple green and carrying a button bouquet of peach roses and paper-petaled Bells of Ireland. Beside her, Ricky stood tall and nervous in his dark suit with the slim fit pants that made him look rather debonair. But when he grinned down at her—to her surprise, even in her strappy heels, he still had a good couple of inches on her—she released the breath she'd been holding and slipped her hand into the crook of his proffered arm.

Just in front of them, Renata and Tim waited in silence for their cue, but Tim's large hand curled affectionately around his wife's where it rested on his forearm. The dreamy smile on Ren's face as she glanced up at her man gave away her thoughts; Gia was certain her older sister was remembering her own wedding only six months earlier.

Behind Gia and Ricky, Phoebe and Trevor whispered words too soft to catch, but Gia knew the things they said to each other were tender, and knowing Phebes, probably a little steamy, too, and full of promises of their own.

At the back of the entourage, the matron of honor and Juliette's best friend forever, Sharon Scoville, tended to the bride's every need. She straightened her train for the umpteenth time, checked that her shiny black curls cascaded exquisitely down her back beneath the sheer sweep of her veil, and that her bouquet of French Lavender, Lily of the Valley, Bells of Ireland, and the same peach-hued Sweet Juliet roses were clutched low at her waist so the intricately beaded neckline of her bodice wouldn't be obscured. And of course, Gramps, eyes glistening with tears that would soon spill over as he made his way up the aisle with his eldest granddaughter on his arm, stood in for Papa. His back was still strong, and his shoulders were still broad enough to bear the burdens and joys of each one of his Gustafson girls.

The gentle strains of *Canon in D* wafted from inside the sanctuary, making Gia smile. Her oldest sister and soon-to-be brother-in-law were two peas in a pod with their old-fashioned church wedding, complete with classic wedding songs and traditional vows. Even Trevor's special number he'd written to sing during the lighting of their oh-so-traditional Unity Candle, although heart wrenching and poignant, resonated with ageless beauty, as though surely, it had been part of a hundred million weddings before today.

Juliette and Vic. For a thousand years and a thousand more. Until the end of time. Gia knew it as certainly as she knew the sun would rise in the east and set in the west tomorrow and the next day and the day after that. They were each other's forever.

She darted a glance up at Ricky. Was he her forever? Would the two of them one day stand at opposite ends of a church aisle, waiting to be joined together before family and friends and God? Oh, how she loved him, she readily acknowledged. Every cell in her body thrummed with joyful contentment when Ricky was nearby. Her laughter came quickly, her smiles easy, her sorrows and frustrations handed into his care without hesitation, and she knew he felt the same about her. She couldn't remember her past before he was a part of it; she couldn't imagine a future without him in it.

And yet....

A wave of unexpected melancholy swept through her, and she hugged his arm to her side and leaned her head against his shoulder. She turned her face toward his chest so she could breathe in the heady scent of dark chocolate and cedar notes. It was a cologne she'd given him for his sixteenth birthday, one she knew he wore because she loved it so much.

"Are you sniffing me?" Ricky murmured into her hair. He rested his cheek against the top of her head.

"Why, yes. Yes, I am," she giggled, straightening slowly lest she leave a smudge of face powder on his charcoal lapel. "And I must say, you smell delicious. Good enough to take a bite of." She made a low throaty "meow" at him and then snorted at how ridiculous it sounded. She couldn't pull off sexy, even if she wanted to.

But Ricky gave her a slow smile, and he dipped his head toward her, dropping his voice so the others in the room couldn't hear him. "You know what? I think you'd like that. I think I might like that, too."

Gia's heart skidded to a standstill at the way he looked at her. He was teasing her, she knew, but she'd seen the shift in his eyes more and more in the last year, a growing awareness of her on a whole new level. She'd catch him staring at her from across the room, studying her mouth as she spoke, as she ate, making her just the slightest bit self-conscious, a brand-new sensation where Ricky was concerned. And it seemed the more flustered she got, the more confident he became.

Not that she minded. She kind of liked the way her skin flushed under his heated gaze. She kind of liked imagining what he was thinking when his eyes darkened and his lips parted just the slightest bit. She liked the way he couldn't seem to stop touching her—toying with the copper curls that framed her face, stroking the back of her hand when it rested close to his, pressing the length of his thigh against hers whenever they sat side by side. She liked how his fingers drifted down her spine to rest possessively on her back as he walked beside her, so different from the days when he'd unceremoniously throw an arm around her shoulders and haul her up against him.

When he hugged her these days? No longer did he hoist her off the ground in a rough, brotherly bear hug that squeezed the breath out of her. No, now he stepped into her, hips forward, and slid his hands down her arms to her waist. With his fingers spread wide, he swept his palms across her back, folding her into him, one hand cupping the base of her skull beneath the heavy fall of her hair, and tucking her face into his neck. Full body, nose to toes embraces. That's what they were these days, the kind of hug that sucked all the oxygen out of her in a completely different way. The kind that made her heart race.

Like it was now.

"Take a breath," Ricky whispered, his grin still taunting her. "We're up."

Gia made a small noise, one that almost went unnoticed... but not quite. Renata turned and peered over her shoulder at her, one perfectly arched eyebrow lifted. "Nervous?" she mouthed.

Gia nodded, pressing her lips together in a tight grin that probably looked more like a grimace. She hadn't been a minute ago, but suddenly, her palms felt damp, and her ankles and knees grew wobbly. Beethoven's triumphant *Ode to Joy* suddenly burst from the speakers, and Gia closed her eyes, praying the red splotches of embarrassment crawling up her neck and spreading over her cheeks would be attributed to the emotions of the day, and not the direction her thoughts had wandered.

"You're beautiful," Renata whispered with a reassuring smile, reaching behind her to squeeze Gia's fingers in a quick grab. "Breathtaking." She turned back around, and with one last adoring glance up at her husband, she and Tim led the Gustafson girls and their escorts down the decorated aisle to the front of the church where the handsome groom, Victor Jarrett, stood at attention, awaiting his sweet Juliette.

Gia remembered little of the ceremony except for the way Vic's eyes never strayed from Juliette's face, his expression filled with something so intense, and at the same time so vulnerable, that it almost hurt to look at him. But she couldn't look away. When she did, her eyes met Ricky's from where he stood behind his cousin, Trevor. And what she saw there scared her and thrilled her in equal measures.

But when the pastor said, "You may kiss your bride," and Vic just stood there lost in Juliette's starry eyes, Gia thought it was quite possible that the groom, himself, might not remember everything about the day either, except for the way his bride gazed back at him.

So Trevor, doing best what the Best Man does, stepped close and put a hand on Vic's shoulder. "Kiss her, you fool. Before she changes her mind."

And Vic did just that. He pulled his wife up against him and kissed her, surely and deeply, not once, not twice, but three times, claiming her publicly for all to see, accompanied by the hoots and cheers of the friends and family gathered.

When the pastor cleared his throat, causing Vic and Jules to come up for air, the guests quieted just long enough to hear the other set of greatly anticipated words: "And now I have the honor of presenting to you Mr. and Mrs. Victor and Juliette Jarrett!"

To everyone's surprise, instead of the traditional wedding recessional, the charming song, *Come to Me*, by the Goo Goo Dolls played through the speakers as Vic and Jules practically floated down the aisle. The congregation clapped and sang along as the chorus echoed the request of every star-crossed lover.

Come to me....

• • • ● • ● • • ● • •

Keep reading – or listening to – Gia's story in **Gia & the Blast from the Past: The Gustafson Girls Book 4.** It's available in print, ebook, and audiobook, and you can find it at **Becky Doughty Books** or any of your favorite online bookstores.